Waking in Sheol

WAKING IN SHEOL

THE SHEOL PROPHECIES • BOOK ONE

M. Alden Phillips

PUBLISHED BY GOLDNAUTILUS PRESS
CLAY, ALABAMA

Waking in Sheol.

Published by GoldNautilus Press
Clay, Alabama

First Edition: August 2025
Printed in the United States of America

The images and maps in these pages were conjured through generative art and shaped by shadow and light in Adobe Photoshop.
They were curated by M. Alden Phillips to reflect the journey's rhythm—each one a whisper of myth, emotion, and the geometry of awakening.

ISBN (Hardcover): 979-8-9996205-1-4
ISBN (Paperback): 979-8-9996205-0-7
ISBN (eBook): 979-8-9996205-2-1
Library of Congress Control Number: 2025916347

Contact the Author: Alden@mAldenPhillips.com

*The relationship
between commitment and doubt
is by no means
an antagonistic one.*

*Commitment is healthiest
when it is
not without doubt
but in spite of doubt.*

— ROLLO MAY

MAP OF THE KNOWN WORLD OF ELDRIKO

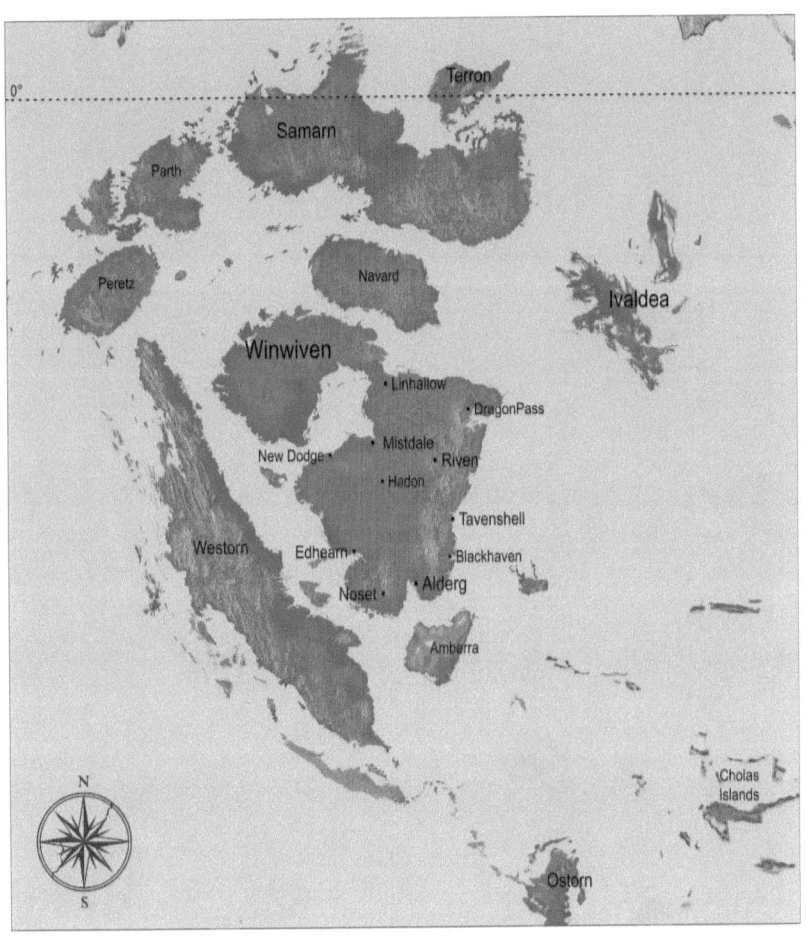

TABLE OF CONTENTS

Chapter One

The ache for home lives in all of us.

—Maya Angelou

Early sunlight filtered through the bare oak branches along the nearly frozen creek. In the stillness of the November morning, Jack heard the faint rush of the waterfall spilling over the cliff at the back of the grove—the sound that always drew deer to the acorns scattered beneath the canopy. As the sun lifted, squirrels began foraging for the coming winter.

These woods had always brought him comfort. Since childhood, the sounds of nature steadied him whenever life pressed too hard. He watched the birds and squirrels moving through the trees, their small motions stitching together a quiet rhythm. A lone turkey called from his left, its note folding into the chatter and the songs of smaller birds until the grove felt like a living symphony.

The familiar sounds helped him push old memories deeper. Wrapped in the music of the morning, the tension eased from his shoulders. He knew those memories would return eventually, but here on this part of the farm, with the hunt to focus him, he could breathe again.

A heavier rustle broke the stillness. Through the dim light, he spotted a deer easing down the game trail, grazing along the creek's edge. When it stepped free of the underbrush, he saw the shape of a magnificent buck moving toward his blind. Jack checked his bow and waited for the clear shot he knew would come.

Movement above the falls caught his eye. Another animal slipped along the water—at first a dog, he thought, until the shape resolved into a coyote stalking a rabbit. The coyote burst forward, taking its prey. The sudden motion sent the buck bolting for cover, its white tail flashing a warning.

"Damn," Jack whispered, just loud enough for the coyote to lift its head and glance toward the blind. He held still, hoping not to spook it further. The buck was gone for this hunt; he knew that much.

The coyote returned to its kill. Jack waited for it to move deeper into the woods, noticing one ear lopped over as it looked around—an old injury, maybe. But instead of leaving, the animal turned toward the blind and took a few steps in his direction.

"Great," Jack murmured.

The coyote stopped and looked toward the blind, head cocked. He shifted to his left, circling while keeping Jack's cover in sight. Only when he reached the edge of the woods did Jack slowly rise above the top of the blind. The coyote froze and stared at him.

Jack spoke softly. "There's no fooling you, is there?"

The coyote stepped back but didn't retreat. He tilted his head again, watching as Jack eased fully into view. Jack expected him to bolt, but instead the animal turned, glanced back over his shoulder, and held Jack's gaze.

2

Jack smiled. "Are we friends, then?"

The coyote paused before trotting into the thicker forest along the creek. Jack stood beside the blind, the hunt ruined by the interruption, but he found himself smiling anyway. He already looked forward to seeing the animal again.

This coyote felt like more than a predator. After the kill, he had moved with a kind of playfulness, almost dancing in the morning shadows. Jack realized the animal's presence had calmed him more deeply than the hunt usually did, settling him into a rare emotional balance.

The lop-eared coyote had a personality. Jack had faced other predators on the farm, but this one seemed skillful, balanced, even joyful. When he finally moved away, he hopped lightly, glancing back toward the blind before slipping into the woods with the ease of a phantom.

As Jack followed the well-worn path toward the homestead, he kept thinking about how he'd felt during the encounter. Even now, he could almost sense the coyote nearby. But when he looked around, there was no sign of him—only old paw prints pressed into the sandy soil.

He approached the narrows between the rock face and the cliff and focused on his footing. There was a longer, safer trail to the hunting ground, but it added fifteen minutes to the walk. Jack preferred the shorter, more dangerous path. He always slowed as he reached the tight passage, and he'd learned over time that squeezing through it brought his thoughts to a somber place.

Walking from the narrows toward the homestead, he found himself thinking again about his marriage and what he might have done differently. The only answer he ever found was

abandoning his rural roots and learning to live in the city—
something he knew he could never do.

He followed the gentle descent to the house and barn. His
father would have already finished milking the cows, and Jack
needed to hurry after taking the morning for the hunt. He
stepped through the back door into the smell of bacon and coffee,
his mother finishing the breakfast dishes in the kitchen.

f❧

"Wipe your feet," his mother called as he stepped through
the back door. Jack smiled at the familiar refrain. She had said
the same words to him and his siblings since they were toddlers,
and she still said them now, even though all her children were
grown with families of their own.

"Coffee?" she asked, already pouring a mug.

Jack sat at the kitchen table. "Thanks, Mom. Any of that
bacon left?" he said.

She set a warm plate of bacon in front of him and took the
seat across from him. "No meat today?"

He sipped the hot coffee and nibbled at the bacon. He'd
slipped out before either of his parents woke, grabbing only an
energy bar on his way to the woods. The food hit the spot.

"Not today," he said. "I saw a good buck out along Bald
Creek, but something spooked him before he got within range."

"I thought I taught you to be quiet on a hunt." Her teasing
smile made it clear she knew he wasn't the reason the deer
bolted.

4

"Mom, did you know we have a coyote in the back woods?" He nursed the mug. "I didn't think there were any around until today."

"A coyote?" Her interest sharpened. "I haven't noticed any predation, but we should keep an eye out in case he gets too close to the chickens."

Jack nodded as he finished the bacon, his thoughts drifting to how little farm life had appealed to his absent wife.

"Do you think she's ever going to come back, Mom?" His voice dropped.

She set her coffee down and met his eyes. "Would you want her to come back?"

He had never asked himself that question aloud, but he knew it was the heart of everything. He had always wanted a simple rural life—farming the land, raising a family. It was why he bought the farm next to his parents, hoping to bring his wife into the life that felt like home to him.

Jack sighed. "I don't know anymore, Mom." He stared into his mug. "I thought I did, but she never felt at home here. And if she came back, I'd have to move to the city again, and I just... I don't like that life."

His mother set her mug on the table and took his hand. "Has she even talked to you since you got back?"

He shook his head. "I don't even know where she is. Somewhere in the city, I guess."

After a long pause, she asked the question that had been haunting him. "Do you want a divorce?"

Anger rose in him—not at the question, but at hearing someone else say it aloud. "I don't want to talk about that."

Her jaw tightened at his tone, then softened. "Honey, I wasn't trying to upset you. But if that's where your thoughts are going, you should call Tom. I think he handles divorces."

Everyone in Harrison knew Tom Baker, the town's only attorney. He handled wills, contracts, and the rare divorce. Jack had never imagined needing his services for something like this. He sighed. "You're right, Mom. I just never wanted it to come to that. I hoped we could work things out, but she didn't leave a new address. She changed her phone number. That tells me she doesn't want to come back."

"Jack, do you still paint?" she asked. She hadn't mentioned his art therapy in months. He never thought of himself as a good painter, but the practice steadied him, even when the abstract pieces took darker turns.

He nodded and took another sip. "Yeah. A couple of times a week. I turned her craft room into a studio. I'm planning to add a countertop with a sink to make cleanup easier."

She smiled. "I like some of your pieces. They capture life on this farm from a different angle." She looked down at her mug. "She never understood how much painting helped you."

Silence settled over the kitchen.

His mother rose, clearing the table and rinsing their empty mugs. Without turning around, she said, "I left Tom's number on the table by the door."

Chapter Two

*In order to discover new truth, one must regard
man as God and untruth as Satan.*

—BENJAMIN FRANKLIN

The clouds looked heavier than usual for the harvest
season. Kendra wondered what that might mean for
winter, but she pushed the thought aside. One day at a time. By
late afternoon, the light had softened into the fog of evening as
she finished her chores and her duties to her uncle. She walked
the short path from the farm to the pub on the edge of the village.

She ate supper at the pub once a week to keep up with the
news of the land. Most days on the farm were spent on the work
in front of her, and she missed the hum of village life she'd grown
up with. Moving to her uncle's farm meant losing the gossip and
the stories that drifted through town, and she felt that absence
more than she expected.

As she walked, the fog thickened. Fog was part of life in
Asher, but out on the farm it settled heavier in the evenings and
early mornings. Staying on the dirt road kept her from losing her

way, though she sometimes felt uneasy walking home from the pub. Still, the news was worth the concern. Times were changing, and rumors of strangers moving closer to the village had everyone on edge.

"Kendra Hess, darlin'. Good to see you again. Is it that time of the week already?" Jakob, the pub's owner, greeted her with the warmth of an uncle. He had met her during the harvest season when she first came to the farm, and he still used her full name.

"Hi, Jakob. Yes, it is. Do you have the venison stew today?"

Jakob laughed, already ladling out her favorite meal. "Here you go, darlin'. Fresh killed this morning. And I added a little extra red wine to this batch. Tell me what you think."

Kendra blew on the spoonful and tasted it. "Mmmm. I think this is the best batch you've ever made, Jakob."

His smile widened. He refilled a mug of ale for another patron before returning to her. "Did you walk from the farm alone again?"

"It's not that bad," she said, taking another spoonful. "There were a few others coming into the village."

Jakob lowered his voice. "Darlin', you know there's talk of more strangers coming through this region every day. You need to be careful."

A loud voice rose from a nearby table. "That's right! These strangers are all over the place."

Jakob shot the big man a look. "Alaster, this is a private conversation. Mind your own business."

Alaster only grew louder. "Who knows where they came from. And they act strange, too."

Jakob rolled his eyes and muttered to Kendra, "By the gods, he's a prophet now." Then he turned back to Alaster. "I think you've had enough for tonight. Finish your mug and get back to your wife."

Alaster clung to his ale. "They come here and disrupt everything. They don't even know our customs." He lowered his voice. "There's rumor they practice the dark arts."

"That's it, Alaster. Finished or not, it's time for you to go home. Tell your wife I'll send a crock of this new stew for her to try. Now go."

Knowing he'd worn out his welcome, Alaster drained his mug and left. The pub settled back into its usual hum of conversation, friendly arguments, and the clatter of supper dishes.

Kendra looked at Jakob thoughtfully. "Do you think it's true?"

"What's that, darlin'?"

"The strangers. Do they practice the dark arts?"

Jakob smiled and took her hand. "There's always talk of magic—orderly and chaotic. I don't know if I've ever seen either kind. I've heard stories of miracles and curses, but those are just superstitions."

Kendra sat quietly for a moment. "Who are these strangers?"

"Just people, darlin', everyday people." Jakob gave her a reassuring smile. "I don't know where they come from, and I've met a few of them, but they're just like you and me."

"Is magic real?"

Jakob chuckled softly. "Now that's the question, isn't it, darlin'? Sometimes I look at the sky and think I see rays of light poking through the clouds. Is that magic, or just my eyes playing tricks? My Grandpap once told me he saw yellow light break through the clouds and stay there for five minutes. I've never seen anything like that. Was he getting old, or was he teasing me? Or was it some kind of magic?" He smiled again. "Either way, I don't think we have anything to fear from these strangers. I'll welcome them in here if they've got the coin."

"But what does that fellow have against them?"

"Alaster?" Jakob shook his head. "He fears what he doesn't understand. These strangers have been coming through for a few years now, and he took a dislike to them from the start."

"Are they dangerous? Should I worry walking to the pub?"

"They're like anyone else, darlin'. Just new to these parts. People like Alaster think the unknown ought to be feared."

Kendra thought about that for a moment. "Where do they come from?"

"I don't know. They showed up during planting. Most of them pitched in to help, and the farmers offered room and board. I think your uncle even chipped in some coin. Most moved on after planting, but a few stayed to make a home here. That was before you arrived, and I think you know a couple of them."

Kendra blinked. "I know some of the strangers? Who?"

Jakob grinned. "Last I heard, Corey and Drew still worked for your uncle."

She stared at him. She knew both farmhands well. "Yes, they still work with us. They were strangers?"

He nodded. "Before your uncle took them on, they were. Last I heard, Drew was saving to buy his own farm."

"Uncle Silas told me last week that Drew made a deal for the land up the road. He said Drew would still work with us, but he'd be setting up his own homestead." She smiled. "And it seems he's been courting one of the neighboring girls."

"There! Do you think you need to be afraid of the strangers?" Jakob laughed.

She chuckled. "No, I don't think so. Now, how about some more of that stew of yours?"

෴

The early morning fog gave way to a light mist. Kendra went about her chores, feeding the small stock and collecting eggs before helping with breakfast. Her uncle and cousins had already gone to the barn to milk the cows and tend the larger animals. By the time the morning meal was ready, the sky had brightened and the mist had lifted. Looking out the window, Kendra noticed the camp that had sprung up after dark.

"Aunt Lucy, the Fairmen are here. How many eggs do you want me to sell?"

Aunt Lucy continued clearing the breakfast plates. "Whatever's left from this morning, dear. We won't need any more today."

"Do we need anything else? You know Ander always has a delightful selection of goods." Kendra smiled, knowing her aunt rarely resisted the unique items Ander Ernaut brought with him.

Aunt Lucy wiped her hands. "Get the eggs and meet me out front. Let's see what that scoundrel has this time." She couldn't help smiling. She knew Ander was a respectable businessman dressed in Fairmen clothing, but most people in town didn't share her opinion, so she kept up the façade—and Ander played along.

Kendra went to the springhouse and gathered the chicken and goose eggs set aside over the last six days. She picked up some early garden harvest from the root cellar to trade. When she climbed out, Uncle Silas had already carried four crocks of raw milk to the yard. As Aunt Lucy walked toward the Fairmen encampment, a smiling Ander was already crossing the cart path toward the farmhouse.

"Good morn, dear lady," he called.

"Ander, you ol' horse thief, I told you to call me Lucy," she said, smiling.

"Aye, aye. Lady Lucy—I forgot," he said, though his grin made it clear he forgot nothing.

Lucy chuckled and played along. "Well, don't forget again." They would repeat this little act on his next visit, and both knew it. Lucy and Ander haggled over the goods, each pushing for the best deal, each settling on a fair exchange. Silas stood back, smiling, content to let Lucy handle what he considered the household accounts.

Kendra browsed Ander's inventory while the rest of the Fairmen tended the horses, fed caged chickens, and repaired wagons. She was nearly finished when a simple amulet caught her eye. It looked like bronze with a rounded reddish stone, nothing elaborate, but something about its design drew her in.

"Ander? What is this?" she asked, still studying it.

He saw what she held. "Ah, ye have a fine eye, little one." He leaned closer. "I came upon a deserted, burned homestead some weeks ago. Found it in the ashes beside a kitchen hatchet, mostly hidden. Overlooked when the folk moved on from their disaster. Ye can have it for five coppers."

Kendra turned it over in her hand. "Three."

Ander looked theatrically wounded. "Four, and it's yours."

She smiled, handed him the four coppers, and gently buffed the amulet on her sleeve.

Ander pocketed the coins. "Little one? Dinnae see ye at the pub last night."

Kendra sighed. Her uncle never forbade her from going, but he always seemed disappointed when she spent money in town. "Yes, Ander, I was there—just for some of Jakob's venison stew."

"He does make a hearty stew, mutton or venison." Ander never judged her trips to town.

"Ander? Did you hear that man talking about strangers around town?"

"Aye, little one. That man had a strong opinion about those he dinnae understand."

Kendra's curiosity sharpened. "Do you know who he meant?"

Ander smiled. "I know everyone on my route. The Fairmen call them Offlanders."

"Tell me about them. Are they as evil as he made them sound?"

"No, little one, they are nae. They are simple men, lost in our world."

Kendra's voice dropped. "Lost?"

Ander nodded. "Aye—lost. They are nae of our world, from what I can tell. When they first arrived, they knew nothing of the Fairmen, nor the Manos, nae even the Eratha. They are truly strangers in our land."

Kendra looked thoughtful. "Where do they come from?"

Ander's features softened. "In the century since the Fairmen first noticed them, there have been many guesses, but nae a solid answer. Some say they are devils. Others think they are angels. The Manos believe the Offlanders come here to make amends for things they did in a former life."

Kendra's mouth fell open. "From another life? How is that possible?"

Smiling, Ander met her eyes. "I dinnae know, little one. I am nae a seer. All I know is that when I treat them as I treat others, they respond in kind. Most of them seem simple, honest folk, trying to find their place on Eldriko—just like the rest of us."

Kendra struggled to imagine beings from another world. She knew the races of Asher, and she'd heard of others across the islands of Eldriko, but the idea of people from somewhere beyond all that baffled her.

"How do you know an Offlander when you see one, Ander?"

He glanced around as if sharing a secret. "They wear strange clothing."

Kendra's eyes widened. "Strange how?"

Ander smiled softly. "Some wear wool or linen but woven finer than anything our weavers can make. I've seen cloth I never knew existed on Eldriko. And the colors..."

"What colors?" she asked, leaning in.

"All the colors of the wildflowers—and more. Oh, they wear muted colors like mine, but some are shockingly bright. I've seen hues like tickseed, ragwort, bluepetal, pinkroot—even meadowfly flower. Those are the colors I've seen on some of these strangers—these Offlanders."

Kendra sat in awe. Was Ander teasing her, or was he telling the truth?

"Where have you seen them?" Her voice barely rose above the breeze.

Ander looked south. "Less than two days' walk from here, toward the hills."

Kendra followed his gaze and felt a chill. The strangers were closer than she ever imagined.

The morning light filtered through the high clouds as the fog lifted. Alaster Kempe opened the shutters of his store, letting the soft light brighten the shelves without wasting lamp oil. The windows stretched from floor to ceiling—an expense he'd insisted on. He'd spent too many hours in dim, gloomy mercantiles in his youth, and he wanted something better for his own shop.

"Da, the hens only laid eleven eggs this morning. Should I check with the Coopers to see if they have any surplus?" Donia poked her head around the doorway from the back room.

"I think we'll be fine today, Donia. We sold twenty-six yesterday, and it usually slows after a day like that. Thank you." Alaster smiled at his daughter. In another year or two, he knew the suitors would start circling. The store would eventually pass to his son, Edan, who had an eye for detail and a way with customers.

Alaster's thoughts drifted toward a future—if he lived to the old age of fifty—where he would help around the store and chase grandpups. Until then, he focused on keeping the shelves stocked and the produce bins full.

"Alaster, did you get that stove in?" A large man stepped through the door. "Caley is tired of using the fireplace to heat our cabin."

Alaster chuckled. "Good morning to you, Kieran. Yes, it came in yesterday." He couldn't help liking Kieran Weir, despite the man's neo-progressive beliefs.

Kieran's relief was obvious. "She's been hard to live with ever since you showed her that flyer about the new stoves. Can't you keep those sheets behind the counter?"

"I'm just trying to keep my customers informed about innovations," Alaster said with a grin.

"And make a profit, no doubt." Kieran laughed and clapped him on the shoulder. "Let's get it loaded. I can have it installed before the midday meal."

After loading the stove, Kieran returned for a few items on Caley's list. As he finished his purchase, a porcelain-skinned man entered the store.

"Charlie! How are you, my friend? What brings you to town?" Kieran greeted him warmly.

Charlie Endo grinned. "Doing good, Kieran, doing good. We needed seeds for the early garden, and some store soap. Astrid's tired of making lye soap herself. I guess not everything has to be made on the homestead, eh?"

Alaster moved behind the counter and waited in silence. Kieran noticed the shift in his demeanor. "Alaster, this is Charlie Endo. He has the place next to mine."

"Yes, I know." Alaster's voice was cool. "What do you want?" He stared at Charlie without warmth.

Charlie handed him a list. "These seeds, please. And a couple cakes of that lavender soap I've heard about." He glanced toward the counter. "Are those eggs fresh?"

Alaster nodded as he set the soap and seeds down. "Gathered this morning."

Charlie selected five eggs, added them to his purchase, paid, and bagged everything in a flour sack. After a final word with Kieran, he headed out.

Kieran turned to Alaster. "That was mighty cold, Alaster. What's wrong?"

Alaster straightened a shelf near the counter. "He's one of them." Everyone in town knew his opinion of the Offlanders.

"Them? You mean Offlanders?"

"You know that's what I mean. How can you treat him like he's your friend?" Alaster nearly spat the words.

Kieran sighed. "Because I am his friend. I hired him right after he came through my farm. He's a hard worker. After he met Etain, he wanted his own place, and I helped him get started."

Alaster's jaw tightened. "I'll sell to them, but they don't belong here."

Kieran shook his head. "You weren't born in this area either, Alaster. But we welcomed you when you welcomed you wanted to set up your shop. How is that different?"

"At least I'm from Asher. Only the gods know where they come from."

Kieran loaded his wagon and prepared to leave. Before stepping out, he said, "You might consider giving them a break, my friend. The Offlanders are part of our community now. Even the priest said that last week."

Alaster snorted and waved dismissively. "The priest can afford to be accepting. I'm going to keep my eye on them. I don't trust them."

"You're part of a shrinking way of thinking, my friend."

Alaster waved him off. One day, he believed Kieran would see the truth. These strangers were going to be a problem. Someday soon, the town would realize he had been right about them.

Chapter Three

Never was anything great achieved
without danger.

–Niccolo Machiavelli

The sun had yet to rise when Jack reached his parents' barn. He scooped a bucket of grain for Magic, his horse. He'd bought her to reach the more remote, rugged parts of the farm before he deployed, and in the three months they had together, they learned each other's ways. After his hospital stay, training Magic helped him heal emotionally as his body recovered.

"There you go, girl."

Magic sniffed the bucket before eating, and Jack stroked her neck.

"I'm gonna try to get that buck this morning, Magic. Just wait and see—he's a big one." He'd gotten into the habit of talking to her long before his tour of duty, and the habit stayed with him after he came home, broken in both body and spirit. Magic always listened without judgment.

"I better get going, girl. The sun will be up before long. Bye, Magic." He gave her one last stroke.

Jack picked up his bow and began the long walk to his blind by the creek. The trail always settled him, preparing him mentally and emotionally for the hunt. It wound along the lower creek, then climbed steeply to the upper woods and pastures. At the top, a short walk brought him to the only tricky part—a rock outcropping that jutted toward the creek, leaving a narrow three-foot gap between the stone and the cliff.

As he walked along the water, his thoughts drifted to the farm. He lived in the farmhouse, but it had always felt more like home to him than it ever did to Emily. The house, like the farm, was over a hundred years old. Emily had hinted often that she wanted something more modern. Jack heard the words but never listened. Maybe if he'd finished some of the renovations he promised, she would still be here.

It wasn't that he didn't plan to update the house—he just always seemed too busy with the rest of the farm. The barn needed repairs. A tractor shed still needed building.

"You idiot," he muttered. She'd complained that the kitchen was a nightmare. It hadn't been updated since the 1960s. He'd decided to start fixing it after he deposited his benefit check at the end of the month. Maybe if he made the farmhouse more livable, Emily might come home.

A prickle ran up his spine. Jack stopped and looked around. A flash of movement—the coyote. He was only a couple hundred paces from his blind, and the animal seemed determined to ruin his hunt again.

"Pssst!" Jack waved his arms, but the coyote stood its ground, watching him. He stomped the earth and waved again. The coyote didn't move, only cocked its head. Then it turned toward the blind and trotted off.

Jack sighed, worried the animal had spooked any deer in the area, but he continued toward his hunting ground.

He settled into the primitive blind and scanned the woods. Sunlight filtered through the trees, revealing the game trail angling toward the creek. Songbirds flitted through the branches. Squirrels dug through the leaves for nuts. But there was no sign of deer—no movement, no sound. Jack wondered if the coyote had scared them off again or if they simply weren't moving today.

He hoped patience would pay off. He pulled a small paperback from his pack and began to read, something he'd learned to carry to pass the time while listening for deer.

He only had the morning hours, and by late morning he put the book away and started back toward the house. It wasn't long before the coyote appeared again. This time it shadowed him. When Jack stopped, the coyote stopped. When he walked, it walked.

After the failed hunt, it felt like the animal was taunting him.

Jack stopped and sighed. "What do you want, huh?"

The coyote sat on its haunches and looked straight at him. It tilted its head, stood, and danced in place.

Jack continued along the trail, his thoughts returning to the farmhouse. A mental blueprint formed—simple renovations, nothing drastic. Enough to make the house feel new without tearing it apart. Enough, he hoped to satisfy Emily. Enough to bring her home.

He preferred not to think about the divorce papers that had arrived the day before. He knew he could make it right. He had to believe he could convince her to withdraw them.

&

The morning fog hovered over the gentle rolling hills of the southern range. Scott poked the fire, coaxing it back to life. He added oats to the cast-iron pot—the one luxury they carried on the range. The oats began to boil and thicken, ready to break their fast.

"Wake up, guys," Scott called, clanging the side of the pot as he stirred. "We need to tag this year's calves and move them to the eastern range before dark."

Ronan groaned as he stirred. "Come on, Scott... why am I always the first one up?" Scott was always awake before the rest of them. Ronan stretched and climbed out of his bedroll, trying to shake off sleep.

The smell of boiling oats drifted through the camp. Boyd pulled the blanket over his head. "Already? Where did the night go? I just got to sleep."

Sabrina and Ellis exchanged a look. Sabrina shook her head. "Are you kidding me? You kept me awake half the night with your snoring." She tossed a clump of damp dirt, hitting him squarely through the blanket.

"HEY! Why'd you do that? I'm getting up." But he didn't move until Scott yanked the blanket away.

"Boyd, get up. We've got a lot to do, and later today you'll wish you'd gotten up an hour earlier." Scott grinned at the familiar bickering. They groaned at his orders, but they worked like a family. He knew his crew outperformed any hands on this side of the shire, and they knew he was proud of them.

They ate their oats sweetened with honey, sitting close to the fire. The fog slowly lifted, revealing a high overcast sky.

Scott smiled. "Looks like a good day for tagging. I counted about twenty-five."

Sabrina swallowed her mouthful. "And about that many ready for market. We'll have to spend another night in camp before we drive them to the corral. Mr. Weir should be pleased with the size of the herd."

Ronan nodded. "Father will be pleased. This is the biggest herd since I came of age. We don't have to thin it to meet his orders."

They finished breakfast and cleaned the pot in the stream. Each packed their gear onto the mules. The herd grazed lazily as Scott moved to their left and the rest of the crew spread out in a loose arc to the right. Scott walked slowly toward the cattle, focusing on the calves. The adults kept grazing, letting him pass as he eased the calves toward the others. The young ones trotted into a temporary corral built from downed trees. Before long, all the calves were separated from the herd.

"There we have it. Good job, team. I can always count on you." Scott beamed at their efficiency.

Boyd, despite his complaining, tagged calves better than any of them—even Scott. Ellis, Sabrina, and Scott cut each untagged calf into a makeshift chute, and Boyd had the tag in place before the calf knew what happened. By midmorning, twenty-seven calves wore Kieran Weir's numbers.

Scott smiled and turned to the midday meal. "Ellis, you've got the chicory pot, don't you?"

Ellis grinned and pulled it from his mule's pack. "Right here, boss."

"Well, get a fire under it. Hot chicory is the only thing that makes these hard biscuits edible."

The others laughed. They sat along the stream, talking through the afternoon drive. They'd done this many times, but none of them minded Scott's habit of reviewing the obvious. It wasn't doubt—just his way.

"I think it's time to get this herd moving." Scott rinsed his mug and hung it from his saddle. He mounted, and the others followed.

They took their usual positions to guide the herd toward the feeding pastures near the ranch house. When Scott first became range boss, he'd used terms the others didn't understand, but Sabrina caught on immediately. He once told Ellis to "take a position at five o'clock," and Ellis stared at him like he was speaking a language from the outer islands. After Scott showed Ellis and Boyd what he meant, they moved instinctively. Only Sabrina had ridden off without hesitation.

Scott gave a quiet whistle, and the crew began to move together. Each rider worked a familiar pattern up and back. The cattle felt the gentle pressure of horse and rider and drifted in the direction Scott intended. Now and then two riders crossed paths, exchanging a few words before returning to their positions. Riding herd could feel lonely, even with your partners always in sight.

They worked across the ranch for a couple of hours until they reached the rye field where the herd would graze. The young heifers would go to market on First Day, others to auction, and a few to a local rancher needing breeders. Once the cattle settled, Scott and his crew sat down to a well-earned dinner brought out by Kieran's wife and children. They could have returned to the bunkhouse, but they preferred one last night near the pasture, talking through what worked and what didn't on the drive.

The debriefing was quick. No problems. Even the predators had behaved. They settled around the fire for a quiet night before taking two days off as their reward for a clean roundup.

Boyd and Ellis drifted into exhaustion-heavy sleep. Sabrina sat beside Scott. He knew she had something on her mind and waited for her to speak first. She stared into the fire for several long minutes.

She finally turned toward him. "Scott... how hard was it for you?"

He knew exactly what she meant. "What do you mean, Sabrina?" He wanted her to ask the question outright.

She sighed. "You know. After you came here. It's so different from home."

Scott nodded. He remembered those early days all too well—alone, disoriented, unsure of anything. "Yes. It was hard." He drew a slow breath. "It took weeks before any of this made sense. And then Kieran found me and offered me a job. I wasn't the first of our kind he hired."

Sabrina looked surprised. "I thought you were. There aren't many of us around here."

Scott shook his head. "Before us, he said maybe one a year came through near the village. Then I arrived... and two months later, there you were." He looked at her with a steady intensity that made her glance away before he asked, "Do you remember what I told you when you first got here?"

She nodded. "Yes, Scott. Keep my head down. Don't tell anyone what I am."

"Yeah. And even talking about it out here could be dangerous. Just before you arrived, a grass-roots movement started to get rid of us. And I don't mean pushing us along. Some want us eliminated."

Sabrina stared into the fire. "I thought I was safe talking to you."

Scott reached out and lightly touched her shoulder. "You are. Just be careful. If any of the natives overheard you, the best we could hope for is finding a new home." He sat quietly for a moment before adding, "Damnit, I like it here. Before the Weir farm, I never stayed anywhere. Eight weeks—that's how long I hid before Kieran took me in. Let's not screw that up, okay?"

Sabrina nodded. "Okay, boss. I like it here too."

The morning had been partly cloudy when Jack settled into his hunting blind, but by the time he headed home the sky had turned a dull, unbroken gray. He didn't remember the weather report mentioning rain, yet the air felt heavy. The temperature had dropped too—chilly at sunrise, now cold enough to bite through his coat.

Birds hopped from branch to ground in search of seeds. Squirrels dug under the oaks for acorns. Everything seemed to be preparing for a cold snap. Jack buttoned his coat and quickened his pace, knowing his dad would need help with the livestock before the front arrived.

Movement flickered to his left. The lop-eared coyote stood twenty yards away, watching him. Jack slowed.

"So, you're back, are you?" He didn't care if he startled the animal now. But the coyote didn't spook. He simply kept pace, always at the same distance. When Jack slowed, he slowed. When Jack stopped, he stopped.

Jack chuckled. "You do want to be friends, I see."

The coyote dipped his head. Jack studied him. "Where did you come from, my friend? I haven't heard of any others around here." Farmers in town were quick to kill anything they considered a predator, but Jack had seen enough senseless killing in the last year. If the coyote behaved, he'd leave him alone.

During deployment, Jack tried to share his experiences with Emily in his letters. He never gave details, but he told her how he felt on patrol. She quickly told him she only wanted positive things. So he changed his letters. They became routine, sterile—a duty rather than a connection.

The rushing sound of the cascade below the narrow path grew louder. The wind picked up, sending the birds into the thickets. As Jack approached the rock outcropping, the wind shifted sharply from right to left, making him wary of the narrow trail beside the cliff. Then, just as suddenly, it reversed.

He waited, judging the conditions. After a moment, he decided he could make it. He slung the bow loosely over his shoulder, took a steadying breath, and stepped into the three-foot gap between the rock face and the cliff.

He was halfway through when the ground began to shake. The tremor lasted only a few seconds, but it startled him. He knew there was a dormant fault line in this part of the country, though it hadn't shifted in years.

The shaking stopped as abruptly as it began. Jack braced a hand against the rock to steady himself. He exhaled, tension easing, and glanced over the edge before deciding to continue.

He took three steps.

The earth dropped out from under him.

For a heartbeat he felt weightless—a strange, impossible suspension—and then he fell.

All his regrets flashed through his mind.

"SHITTTTT!"

Chapter Four

No matter how hard the past,
you can always begin again.

—B<small>UDDHA</small>

Jack's sense of falling slowed until it felt more like floating. He tried to get his bearings, but nothing around him looked familiar. The woods, the creek, the waterfall, even the cliff—all of it dissolved into a dark fog. He felt no pull of gravity, no sense of up or down. Disoriented, he tried to remember what happened. The earth had dropped beneath him, the cliff had given way—and then nothing.

The fog thinned, and he saw others drifting nearby. When he called out, they didn't react. Their faces were indistinct, blurred by the mist. Snatches of conversation drifted through his mind—voices he knew but couldn't place. He tried to swim toward the others, but the fog resisted him, thick as wool.

Then he felt something else in the mist.

Not a body. Not a person. A presence.

It felt more like a memory than a being—familiar, distant, and somehow calling to him. The pull urged him to think left and forward. Jack hesitated, then noticed three others turning in the same direction.

Why not try?

He focused on the thought, and his position shifted. The fog around him thinned into a heavy mist. The darkness eased into a soft glow. The glow brightened, growing sharper, more intense, until it pressed against him like heat.

The light became blinding.

Jack felt himself pushed toward it—and then everything went white.

He blacked out.

💛

Jack startled awake, stunned that he could still be alive. Cold, damp earth drained the warmth from his body. The smell of rich soil filled his senses. His cheek pressed against moss, and when he groaned and rolled onto his side, pain flared through his left shoulder. His whole body ached.

He lay still, taking in his surroundings. It looked rural, but nothing resembled his farm. Birds sang in the trees. A breeze stirred the branches. Everything felt familiar, yet he couldn't attach a single memory to what he saw.

He pushed himself upright on the wet ground. He couldn't remember anything except the strange certainty that he belonged to this land somehow. To his left lay his bow. When he reached for it, his shoulder reminded him that using his left arm would be painful for a while.

Jack stood carefully, testing his legs. "Okay, the legs work. Where the hell am I?" The land looked like the pastures and woods he'd known all his life, but the hills rolled differently, as if the world had been rearranged.

Shivering in his damp clothes, he muttered, "I need a fire before I freeze." Talking to himself felt natural—muscle memory, like everything else he was doing. He found his small side pack and rummaged through it. A cord with two wooden handles surfaced, one fitted with a rounded stone, the other with an empty socket.

"Well, shit. That's useless." He dug deeper and found a familiar book of matches. "Ah. Now all I need is tinder and dry wood."

Critical memories returned in fragments.

He gathered twigs and branches from beneath an old oak, where the leaves were dry enough to use as tinder. Near the tree he found a flat rock jutting from the ground, its top covered in thick moss. Once the fire was built, he sat on the rock, letting the heat chase the chill from his clothes. He checked his pockets and found a few light snacks—not much, but enough to take the edge off his hunger.

In his back pocket he found a leather pouch. Inside there were coins and several printed cards. The largest one read *operator's license* for someone named Jack Marshall. Hunting and fishing licenses bore the same name. Another card carried a string of numbers he didn't recognize.

He stared at the name. "Are you Jack Marshall?" he asked aloud. "Huh. Maybe so." The image on the license looked like him.

A brook murmured nearby. He followed the sound until he found a quiet pool. Gripping a low branch, he leaned over and studied his reflection. "No doubt about it, boy," he sighed. "You're Jack Marshall—whoever he is."

Back at the fire, he moved to sit on the rock again, but noticed the moss had peeled back, revealing a carved mark in the limestone. A spiral. Man-made. A shiver ran through him—not from the cold. He gently replaced the moss and chose another place to sit.

Turning back to survival, he took stock. Besides the pouch and his bow, he wore clothing patterned in muted greens and browns, leaves printed across the fabric. An empty leather scabbard hung from his belt. He searched the ground where he'd woken but found no knife.

He needed shelter before dark. The evergreen thickets above the brook offered the best option. He gathered fallen pine branches for a sleeping pad. Along the water's edge he found cattail roots for food. The brook ran clear and cold; he trusted it enough to drink.

He soon realized he needed more than cattails and snack bars. Watching the pool, he noticed fish feeding. He stepped into the cool water, hands cupped beneath the surface. Patience paid off—a fish swam between his palms, and he scooped it onto the bank. A thin shard of shale made a workable knife. He gutted the fish, threaded it onto a forked stick, and propped it over the fire.

He spent most of the day preparing for a short stay. The simple meal filled him. He tossed the remains downstream and settled near the fire. The birdsong faded with the light, replaced by the steady chorus of insects.

Through the dimming dusk, a ghost-like shape moved along the edge of the woods. A coyote—the same lop-eared one, or its twin—eased into view no more than twenty paces away. It paused, looked toward Jack, then slipped into the trees.

Just as Jack began to drift into a hard-earned rest, a distant yip-howl echoed through the dark.

§♦

Kendra finally slipped away from the farm after the midday meal. She didn't mind the chores Uncle Silas assigned her, but he took her father's intentions entirely too seriously. All morning he'd gone on about the early spring festival—not just the celebration itself, but which eligible young men hoped to find a bride before planting season.

Kendra had agreed to come to her uncle's farm with the intent of finding a suitable mate, but she had no desire to rush the process. Moving from a small hamlet farm to the estate of a prosperous landholder near a larger town had been intoxicating. She found herself drawn to the town at least once a week—to shops she couldn't afford and gatherings she wasn't invited to. But the festival welcomed everyone, and she wanted to attend... just not as the future wife of a third son from a minor homestead.

After the midday meal, she usually gained enough liberty to slip into the woods for a couple of hours before evening duties. Her favorite spot was a thirty-pace stretch of bank along a small unnamed creek. The water slowed there, flirting with becoming a river before narrowing again, forming a quiet pool perfect for fishing or swimming.

She was thinking of slipping away when Uncle Silas caught up with her. One look at his face told her that her plans had evaporated like the morning fog.

"Kendra, I need you to do something for me this afternoon," he said, wiping sweat from his brow. "The boys are all busy in the barn, and I need someone to check the fence along the water. You'll take care of that for me, won't you?"

She nodded. "Yes, Uncle Silas. What do you want me to do?"

"Just check for split rails. I saw a few weathered ones last week when I rode out there. I need to know how much work it'll take to patch it up. You've got a good eye for that." He watched her expression, then raised an eyebrow. "You can take the pony, if you want."

Her eyes lit up. "Thank you, Uncle Silas. I haven't taken Misty out in weeks." Her smile gave her away.

He turned toward the barn to hide his own grin. "Don't push her too hard. We need her fresh this weekend."

Kendra grabbed a couple of apples and a wedge of goat cheese, then stopped by Uncle Silas's office for a pad and pencil. She saddled Misty, mounted, and waved as she trotted toward the pasture at the base of the big round hill.

It took half an hour to reach the fence line. She veered east, dismounted, and handed Misty an apple. "Stay close, girl." Misty followed her, grazing as Kendra inspected the rails. Most showed normal wear. Near the creek bend, she found a top rail split nearly in two with a fallen limb across it. She scribbled notes.

As she neared the western corner, she noticed a low campfire smoldering near an old oak on the far side of the fence. She tied Misty to the lower rail. "Stay here, girl. I need to check this out."

Kendra climbed over the fence and approached the fire—then froze.

A man sat on a low rock near the embers. His clothing was strange: green and brown, patterned like harvest leaves.

"Hey! What are you doing here?" she called, keeping her distance. She stood as tall as she could, trying to look larger than she felt.

He jumped, startled, then rose slowly and turned toward her. "I—I'm sorry. Am I trespassing?" He didn't move toward her, but something in his gaze held her attention.

Kendra took a cautious step closer. "You're on my uncle's farm. Now tell me—what are you doing here?"

"I don't really know." He rubbed his forehead. "I think I fell... but I'm not sure where." He looked confused, but not drunk.

"What's your name, mister...?" Her gaze sharpened as she tried to read him.

"Jack Marshall, I think." His confusion deepened.

"You think?" Her voice rose. "You don't know?"

"I found something in my pouch that says that's who I am, but I can't remember." He sat back on the rock, facing her. "If I hadn't found that, I wouldn't have a clue."

"Wait. You aren't from around here, are you?" Kendra asked, the shape of an idea forming in her mind.

"No... I don't think I am." His voice dropped to a whisper.

"My name is Kendra Hess. I live on this farm with my uncle." She hesitated. "When did you eat last?"

"I had something last night. Not much. And some water."

"Here." She tossed him an apple. "Eat that and tell me what you can remember."

Jack bit into the apple, savoring the sweet-tart flavor. "What I think I remember—after seeing I had some kind of permission to hunt, and a bow—is that I was out hunting. For what, I don't know. This land looks familiar, but not in any specific way. It could be any woods and fields... but it's nice." He smiled faintly as he looked around.

Kendra glanced at the unusual bow lying at his feet. "That's a strange bow. I've never seen anything like it."

Jack shrugged. "I don't know. It feels right to me. I know there are different styles of bows, but... this one is mine. That's all I know for sure."

Kendra nodded slowly. "You said you ate something last night. What was it?"

Jack laughed. "Not much. A couple of... something that looked like biscuits wrapped in a strange covering. And a fish. Did you know there's trout in that stream?"

"Is that what you call them?" Kendra smiled, intrigued by the fragments he remembered. "How did you eat it? Raw or roasted?"

Jack held up the sharp piece of shale. "Roasted it over the fire. It was good."

She tilted her head. "But you don't know how you got here? On our farm?"

Jack shook his head. "I don't even remember the hunt. There's evidence that's what I was doing, but the actual memory?

Nothing. I don't even know if I really know how to use that bow—but it feels familiar when I pick it up."

Kendra felt a cautious trust forming. "Will you show me how that type of bow works?" Curiosity overrode her better judgment.

Jack picked up the bow and stood. "What should I shoot at?"

Kendra pointed to a patch of soft moss along the creek. "There. It's soft enough for your arrows."

Jack nodded, nocked an arrow, drew, and released in one smooth motion. The arrow struck the center of the moss. He turned to her. "I guess I do know how to use it." He rubbed his left shoulder, wincing.

"Yes, you do." She saw fatigue in his eyes. "Listen... I might know a place where you can get out of the weather tonight. But you have to promise no mischief if I take you there. Agreed?"

Jack's eyes widened. "Oh, yes. No trouble from me—especially if it means I can sleep somewhere dry. What is this place?"

"My uncle has a line shack nearby." Kendra walked back to Misty and led her toward a gap in the fence. "It's back this way."

Jack followed beside her as she guided Misty through the woods. Before long, the small shack appeared through the trees and the lingering mist.

"There it is," Kendra said. "Uncle Silas comes out here to put deer in the larder. He doesn't like killing his cattle when the meat is walking around out here." She opened the door, lit the lamp, and hung it from the center hook. Dim light filled the one-room cabin.

Jack took in the simple space—fireplace, table, chair, single bed. Clothing hung on pegs near the door: an oiled coat, a couple of shirts, a pair of worn but clean trousers.

Kendra moved to the small counter. "Uncle Silas keeps dried beans in this box, and a pot should be..." She rummaged beneath the counter. "Yes! Here it is. You can hang it on the hook in the fireplace. I'm sorry—he doesn't leave smoked meat here, but hot beans should be a welcome change."

"Thank you," Jack said, smiling. "This is much better than sleeping under a tree in the rain."

Kendra walked to the door. "I'd better get back. But I'll come tomorrow afternoon—if you think you'll still be here. I can bring different clothing." She looked him over. "You can't go around dressed like that. They'd spot you right away."

Jack blinked. "Who would spot me?"

Kendra opened the door. "Those who don't like strangers around town." Before he could ask more, she mounted Misty. "See you tomorrow."

Jack nodded. "Yes. Thank you for everything. Until tomorrow."

Kendra reined Misty left, nudged her into a trot, and headed back toward the barn.

Jack climbed from the cot as light crept through the small windows. He searched the containers beneath the bench and found some cut grain with a nutty aroma. He cooked it over the open fire the way instinct told him to—like oatmeal. It thickened into something with the texture of Irish oats, bland but warm and filling.

Sitting by the fire, he tried to make sense of what had happened. Yesterday was clear enough, but everything before that was a blank. It felt like waking from a dream he couldn't quite remember. Some things came naturally—how to use his bow, how to build a fire—but others were puzzles. The empty scabbard on his belt, for instance. He knew it should hold a knife, yet he couldn't find one. Maybe he'd lost it wandering before he reached the stream where he met Kendra.

He remembered feeling cautious when she approached, but not afraid. She knew who she was. He needed a piece of paper in a leather pouch to tell him his own name. The thought unsettled him. He had the sense—deep, instinctive—that he was someone who usually controlled his circumstances. He needed to reclaim that feeling. Fate was something he'd heard of but never accepted.

He explored the cabin. The ground was rich, the flora varied, and deer sign marked the stream behind the shack. When he examined his arrows, he realized the broadheads were incomplete—the core was there, but the cutting blades were missing. Another mystery.

As he returned to the cabin, Kendra rode up on her horse.

"Good day, Jack." She smiled as she dismounted. "I hope you were comfortable. It isn't much, but my uncle stays out here for days when he's hunting stags."

"It was good," Jack said. "I found some cut oats to eat. I hope that was all right."

"That's fine. Uncle keeps some here, but they don't stay fresh long. Better to eat them than let them spoil." She handed him a bundle. "These should fit you. They aren't fancy, but you won't be identified as an Offlander dressed in them."

Jack paused. "You keep calling me an Offlander. What is that?"

Kendra took a breath. "Asher has many peoples. The Eratha—like me—make up most of the farmers and villagers. The Fairmen are nomads and traders. The Manos... well, they're mysterious. Reclusive. Most of what we know about them comes from stories told around campfires." She watched his face before continuing. "Offlanders are outside all of that. They appear out of nowhere, wearing strange clothing, with unusual customs. They don't fit into life on Eldriko—at least not at first."

Jack considered this. "You think I'm an Offlander."

Kendra nodded. "Honestly? Yes. But you seem like a good man, wherever you came from."

"Is that why you're helping me?"

"I never liked the stories about how Offlanders were treated. Until yesterday, I'd never met one. You're my first." She smiled. "I decided to take a chance."

Jack returned a small smile. "Thank you. Yesterday I had no idea where I was or who I was—other than a name on a card." He looked at his bow. "I know I've hunted with this, but the arrows are wrong. The heads are missing something."

Kendra thought for a moment. "On the way here, I saw a Fairmen caravan camped by the road. They might know something. They sell all kinds of goods."

Jack frowned. "How would I buy anything? I don't have anything of value to trade."

Kendra smiled. "Let me see what I can do about that. The Fairmen of this clan are friends of mine. I'm sure I can work a deal for what you need." She nodded east. "They're only about a third of a mile that way. A short walk past the hedgerow if you're ready."

Jack looked toward the hedges. "Only a third of a mile? No problem. Let's go." He took a step, then glanced back to be sure she was coming. Kendra quickly matched his long stride across the field.

They reached the hedgerow in less than a sixth of an hour. Once they pushed through the brush, the wagon camp came into view just off the dirt road bordering the farm. Kendra recognized the color scheme of the wagons and smiled. She walked straight toward the fifth wagon, knowing she'd find Ander nearby.

"Ander, you scoundrel!" she called, grinning broadly.

His head snapped up. When he saw her, he put on a mock-wounded expression. "Ye dinnae say things like that, Kendra. Someone might hear ye and believe it." He pulled her into an enthusiastic hug reserved for old friends. Then he looked past her at Jack. "And who have we here?"

Kendra lowered her voice. "Can we take a walk along the water? I'll explain everything."

Ander studied Jack, then Kendra. "Of course. Everything good?"

"Everything's fine," she said. "We just have a slight problem, and I don't want anyone else knowing my business."

The three of them walked to the river and sat on some rocks, speaking in hushed tones.

"Ander, this is Jack Marshall. I met him yesterday in the back woods past the creek." She glanced around before continuing. "He's an Offlander. You should've seen how he was dressed. He looked like a walking tree." She chuckled at the memory.

Ander looked from her to Jack. "Offlander, ye say?" He kept his gaze on Jack. "How long have ye been here?"

Jack shifted uncomfortably, but if Kendra trusted this Fairman, he could too. "I don't remember anything before yesterday."

Ander let out a low whistle. "Ye are truly lost in the woods, are ye?" He turned to Kendra. "What can I do for ye, my friend?"

Kendra exhaled in relief. "He's having trouble with his arrows."

Ander examined Jack's bow and quiver. "No doubt about it—ye are Offlander. What's the problem?"

Jack pulled an arrow and handed it to him. "The broadhead is missing the cutting blades. See?"

Ander nodded. "Were the blades iron or steel?"

"I'm sure they were—or at least had steel in them. Why?"

"That's the problem," Ander said. "When Offlanders come to Eldriko, they cannae carry iron, or anything that contains iron. Such things are left behind when ye arrive."

Jack thought for a moment. "That explains what happened to my skinning knife."

"And anything else with iron," Ander added. He examined the broadhead closely. "I dinnae think we can make blades this thin. How does the head come off the shaft?"

Jack unscrewed it and handed it over. Ander studied the craftsmanship. "We might be able to fashion a broadhead that fits this kind of fitting." He glanced at Jack. "Ye'll have to learn to aim all over again, like when ye first picked up a bow." He eyed the bow itself. "Someday ye'll have to let me get a closer look at that bow."

Then his face lit with an idea. "I'll tell ye what. I'll craft ye three dozen broadheads and secure another two dozen arrows. Ye let me study that bow while my boys do the work, and we'll call it even. How does that sound?"

Jack nodded quickly. "Yes, I accept!" His smile suggested he thought he'd gotten the better end of the deal—but Ander knew he'd just become a wealthy trader.

Chapter Five

*If you can, help others; if you cannot do that,
at least do not harm them.*

—DALAI LAMA

A laster walked down the third row of his warehouse in Hadon, searching for space to store the ore from the new mines near Marn. The Fairmen contracted to transport it would arrive in a fortnight with the first shipment. He needed clear room for the sacks before sending them on to the refinery in Edhearn.

"Donia, can you bring me the holdings journal?" he called toward the front of the warehouse.

"I've got it right here, Da," she answered—much closer than he expected. She appeared a moment later with the records in hand. "Here it is. Are you going to have enough space for those sacks?"

Alaster smiled at her tidy efficiency. "This order is just a test of the ore's quality. But if it's as good as I think, we may need to rearrange the whole warehouse."

"Is the ore that important?" Donia asked, trying to gauge his expectations.

"If I'm right, it could produce a finer grade of steel—the kind the Baron will want for his men-at-arms. And that would make me a wealthy man." Alaster allowed himself a small, satisfied smile.

"I've cleared the space by the back door, Father." Edan stepped in from the rear entrance. "What do you want me to move back there?" He'd worked with his father for three years and could nearly read his intentions, but he never assumed.

Alaster thought for a moment, then pointed out the goods he wanted shifted. Edan nodded knowingly. Alaster trusted his son to take over the business one day—Edan had an instinctive sense for order, and Donia excelled at the books. One day she would be an asset to whatever household she married into, but that was still years away.

As Donia took notes, Alaster and Edan rearranged the row, condensing and shifting goods to make room for the ore. Donia kept careful records so nothing would be lost in the shuffle. By the time they finished, the afternoon mist had begun to creep into town.

"Donia, it's getting late. You'd better get home to help your mother." He valued her help, but her mother needed her too. "I'll be home in about an hour."

Donia returned the journal to the shelf above his desk. "Da, I'm going to stop by the goods shop for some material for the dress I need for next week's dance."

48

Alaster smiled. "Don't take too long. Your mother will blame me if she thinks I kept you."

She laughed. "I won't. I already know what I want. I'll be in and out. Mother won't even know I stopped if I wasn't bringing cloth home." She gathered her yellow cape and stepped into the misty streets along the riverfront.

Alaster watched her go, then returned to the final tasks in the warehouse. Edan came from the back door. "Everything's locked up, Father. When will the ore arrive?"

"About a fortnight," Alaster said without looking up. "It's coming from Marn."

"Marn?" Edan blinked. "I didn't realize we reached that far."

Alaster paused. "I heard rumors of a rich iron ore vein up that way and checked it out last month. If it's as good as I think, it could put us at the top of the chain."

Edan grinned. "Then we'd better get this arranged. Is it a big shipment?"

"Just a test run," Alaster said. "I can't waste coin on the unknown. We'll send it to Edhearn, and once we get their report, I'll decide if it's worth our involvement." He swept the floor where they'd condensed the inventory. "Finish up here, Edan. I'm heading home. I'll see you at supper."

Alaster took his jacket and stepped into the darkening streets toward the rowhouse he'd bought years earlier. It had been a safe place to raise his family—far enough from the rough riverfront, close enough to the heart of town.

The mist thickened into showers as he walked. Through the rain, he saw a cluster of people gathered along the street, lamplight glowing gold through the haze. Their voices drifted toward him.

"It's so sad."

"How could this happen?"

"She was so young."

"Isn't she his daughter?"

Alaster pushed through the crowd—and froze.

On the ground, surrounded by a widening pool of blood, lay a small figure in a yellow cloak.

"No... no—it can't be." His voice barely escaped him. But he knew. His knees buckled, and he collapsed beside Donia, tears streaming down his face.

Then his voice returned—raw, broken, anguished.

"NOOOO!"

♫

Morning light revealed a high, overcast sky—the kind of day the Fairmen used to their advantage. Every member of the band was out: repairing wagons, restocking loads, hunting, gathering fresh food. Ander moved his bench and tools outside to work on Jack's arrowheads in the natural light. Once he determined the proper thread pattern to match Jack's arrows, the work went quickly. It took him a couple of attempts to fashion broadheads strong and light enough to satisfy him.

Jack had thought about returning to the hunting cabin, but Ander wouldn't hear of it. He set up a wall tent with a sturdy cot near his wagon, insisting he needed Jack close by to test each broadhead for accuracy. Kendra returned to her uncle's farm each evening, but she was back every morning.

By midmorning, Ander approached Jack with the three dozen arrowheads he'd promised. "Master Jack, here are those points." He handed over an oak case lined with polished, lampblack-coated broadheads.

Jack lifted one, admiring the craftsmanship. "These are beautiful, Ander." He turned it in his fingers—and nicked himself. A bead of blood welled up. "Ow. Sharp too." He grinned.

Ander beamed at the praise. "Will ye allow me two or three days to examine your bow?" His eyes were already drifting toward the strange metal limbs and unfamiliar design.

Jack handed it over. "Take your time. I'm in no hurry." Ander drew the bow experimentally, surprised by its light weight, then carried it to his workbench. He opened a sketchbook and began drawing, measuring, and asking Jack the occasional question.

As he worked, Kendra rode up and tethered her horse. She walked to Jack and nodded toward Ander. "He looks like he's in paradise."

Jack chuckled at the sight of Ander hunched over the bow like a scholar over a rare manuscript. "I just hope I get it back before the trade days he mentioned."

Kendra pulled a camp chair from Ander's wagon and sat beside Jack. "Jack," she said, "you asked yesterday why I took a chance on you. Offlanders aren't all bad."

Jack nodded. "I woke up here completely confused. You were the first person I saw. Thank you for treating me kindly."

"You made it easy, Sir Jack." She smiled. "I spoke with my uncle last night. He's cautious—he hasn't met you—but he trusts my judgment."

Jack looked startled. "I didn't mean to cause trouble with your family."

"No trouble. At least not from my uncle." She grinned. "My aunt is another matter. She doesn't think it proper for me to spend time with an Offlander when I'm supposed to be presenting myself to the local young men."

Jack laughed. "I'll try not to ruin your chances. Any promising prospects?"

Kendra gave him a sideways glance. "A few think they are. But I want more than tending chickens and milk cows and being a broodmare in some forgotten corner of Asher. Since coming here, I've learned the herbs of this region—their culinary and medicinal uses. I want to be an herbalist."

"Herbalists are the healers here?"

Kendra nodded. "In the cities they have surgeons, but they're just herbalists with fancy titles. Here, herbalists do the healing without pretense. Some learn midwifery too."

"That's admirable. Is there formal training?"

"Most herbalists learn as they go. But I want more. That means finding a Manos practitioner willing to teach me."

Jack found himself admiring her—not just for helping him, but for her ambition, her curiosity, her desire to help others. She had a spark he recognized from home, even if he couldn't remember the details.

"What about you, Jack?" she asked. "You can't live in my uncle's cabin forever."

"I grew up on a farm. I could work for your uncle until I find my place here. But first... I need to find out who I am. And how I got here."

Before she could answer, a figure emerged from the woods— a woman slightly taller than Kendra, dressed in forest green, carrying a longbow and a sword. Jack's attention fixed on her.

Kendra smiled. "That's a Manos ranger from Mistdale. She may need supplies."

Jack's interest sharpened. "Are we close to Mistdale?"

Kendra shook her head. "Not close. Ten days on foot. I wonder what she's doing this far south."

Ander noticed the ranger and joined them. "That's Asta Rhann. She's been covering this region for a year or so. She must be low on something. She usually stays in the forests."

Asta stopped several paces away. "Ander. Good to see you again."

"Greetings, Asta. How may I help ye?"

She handed him a parchment written in carbon stylus. "I have a few needs before the long trek. You still accept Manos coin?"

"Always," Ander said. He passed the list to his quartermaster. "Wrap everything in oilcloth."

Asta sat when Ander offered a seat. He asked, "What brings ye this far south? We usually see ye a couple days north of here."

Asta hesitated before answering. "Teyr Elenya, the Madam Chief of the council, sent word for me to locate a particular Offlander. New to Eldriko."

6♦

Kendra stared at Asta in surprise. "You're looking for a new Offlander? How will you know him when you find him?"

Asta met her gaze calmly. "The Offlander I seek has only been on Eldriko a few days. Teyr sensed his arrival a fortnight ago and sent word to me. I received the notice about ten days past. She gave me a few simple tests to identify him."

"What kind of test?" Kendra asked.

"I will touch his essence," Asta said. "To determine whether he carries the traits Teyr foresaw. I am to search for specific markers in his psyche."

Kendra frowned. "What markers? What do they mean?"

Asta sensed the tension rising in her. "I do not know what the markers signify. I only know how to recognize them. Teyr's understanding is her own."

"But it could be anybody," Kendra said.

Asta shook her head. "Teyr explained that this Offlander has been on Eldriko less than a fortnight and possesses traits and skill foretold in the ancient prophecy. A prophecy only she can interpret."

Kendra swallowed. "And when you find him... then what?"

Asta's expression didn't change. "I will take him to Mistdale to meet with Teyr Elenya and the council."

Kendra tried to absorb that. "Teyr foresaw him here? In this region?"

Asta uncapped her waterskin and drank. "Yes. I have been tracking his essence for five days. He is close." She looked at Ander, then at Kendra. "Is there an Offlander in the camp?"

Ander glanced at Jack, but Jack spoke first. "I'm an Offlander. At least, that's what I've been told."

Kendra slumped in her chair.

Asta turned to Jack. "How long have you been here?"

"Maybe a week," Jack said. "I've lost count."

Asta studied him for several long seconds. "Would you oppose me testing you?"

Jack's concern flickered across his face. "What does it entail?"

"I place my hands on your face," Asta said. "Then I open myself to the power and let the essence of your traits flow through my mind. It lasts a minute or two. You will feel nothing."

Jack took a slow breath. "And if I am the one you're looking for... when would we leave?"

"Immediately," Asta said, without hesitation.

Jack stiffened. "Just like that? I have no choice?"

Asta shook her head. "Not like that. Teyr said that if you possess the traits, when I touch your mind you will want to come. There will be no coercion. You will desire to learn more about yourself."

Jack considered this, then nodded. "I need to know. Go ahead."

Kendra burst out, "NO! Don't let her, Jack." She flushed, embarrassed by her outburst.

Jack turned to Asta. "If it's me, may my companion join me on the journey to Mistdale?" He glanced at Kendra, then back.

Asta followed his gaze. "She may."

Jack faced Kendra. "I need to know if there's more for me here than the obvious. And if I am who they're looking for, you could gain something too—the chance to learn whether you're a healer, not just a country herbalist."

Kendra's voice was small. "What if I'm nothing special? What if I can only make simple poultices?"

"Then you would know," Jack said gently. "But what if you're more—and you never take the step to find out? What if that desire burns in you because you are gifted, but fear keeps you from knowing? What if you become just a farm wife, living far below your potential? I'm taking a frightening step. What do I have to lose? Take it with me."

Kendra stared at him, shaken. What if he was right? What if she was meant for more—and never dared to find out?

"I would want to know," she whispered. "But my family... I need to think about that."

Asta pulled her chair closer and faced Jack. "Are you ready?"

He nodded and closed his eyes.

Asta placed her hands on either side of his face. She drew a deep breath, reached inward, and opened herself to the power. A moment later, her heart pounded as something vast and unfamiliar flowed from Jack's essence into her mind.

"Ohhh..." The sound escaped her before she could stop it. It was exactly as Teyr had described.

She broke contact abruptly and sat back. "The gods be praised. It is you."

Jack exhaled. "What did you feel?"

"The marker Teyr described," Asta said. "It is you."

Jack straightened. "Then we're going to Mistdale—with Kendra, if she wishes?"

Asta nodded. "Yes. When you are ready, we leave."

Ander jumped in. "Wait now—can ye give us a couple more days? I haven't finished examining that bow."

Jack looked to Asta. "I did promise him time."

Asta considered, then nodded. "A day or two. No more."

Ander sagged with relief.

Jack turned to Kendra. "Will you come with us?"

Kendra felt drained, overwhelmed, but she nodded. "Yes. I'll need to tell my uncle, so he won't worry." She sighed. "Who am I kidding—he'll worry no matter what. But I can't just disappear."

Chapter Six

Lay this unto your breast:
Old friends, like old swords, still are trusted best.

—JOHN WEBSTER

They were just breaking for the midday meal. Thankfully the rain and mist held off, and Scott's crew had accomplished more than he expected when they set out to clear the brush in the east field. Once cleared, the horses would have safe, rich grazing come late spring.

"Let's get it all cut, and we can try to burn it after we eat."

Scott worked alongside his crew—something most overseers never did. Others sat on stumps and barked orders. Scott pitched in, finished the work faster, and then gave his hands a little freedom afterward. He usually used that time to bring down a deer or boar, so his crew stayed well fed.

Today they ate deer jerky and beans simmered over the fire while they finished the last of the morning tasks. The banter flowed easily. Scott looked around the circle—his regulars mixed with the extra hands he'd requested for the larger job. He'd chosen them carefully. They fit in well, and they knew better than to treat Sabrina with anything but respect. Scott's crew teased her like siblings, but the gods help anyone else who tried.

As the meal wound down, Scott nodded to Ronan. "Let's get them up and at it. I want the brush to settle before we light it."

Ronan rinsed his plate in the creek. "You heard him," he called to the others. "Let's move. I want some downtime after we burn this mess."

They started the fire and watched it carefully. The temporary hands hoped to join Scott's team someday—though his regulars rarely left.

The dry brush went up fast, sending dark smoke into the overcast sky. Flames crept southward before Ronan noticed.

"Ronan, get Ellis and one of the new guys to the south before we lose control," Scott called.

Ronan waved acknowledgment and shouted to Ellis. Ellis grabbed young Sam, and together they stamped out the creeping flames. Scott smiled. Even the new hands took pride in their work when they rode with his crew.

They circled the fire, keeping fresh eyes on every side. As Scott moved south, he noticed three figures on horseback riding along the forest edge of Master Weir's range. He stopped, watching them for several minutes as they continued north.

"Ronan, saddle my horse," Scott called, still watching the strangers.

"Sure thing, boss." Ronan quickly prepared the gelding and led it over.

"Problems?" he asked.

Scott didn't look away. "Not sure. But I'm going to check."

He mounted and cantered toward the trio, who hadn't changed course since he first spotted them.

Scott pulled up about ten strides away. "Can I help you?" he called. He'd never encountered strangers on Weir land before.

They continued at a slow, steady pace. The man riding behind the two women answered without stopping. "We're just passing through."

"You're on Master Weir's land," Scott said, firm but controlled. "He's protective of what's his."

"We'll be gone by dark," the man replied. "We mean no harm." He turned slightly toward Scott as he spoke.

Scott opened his mouth to respond—then froze. A strange flicker of recognition rippled through him. He leaned forward in the saddle. "Do I know you, mister?"

The man didn't slow. "I can't see how. I'm a stranger in a strange land."

Scott's breath caught. That phrase—he hadn't heard since Earth. His old commander quoted that author constantly. And something about the man's face...

Scott stared harder. A hint of familiarity. A sense of danger and safety at once. A memory tugging at him.

He took a deep breath. "Is that you, Lieutenant?"

Jack's head snapped toward him. He stared for several seconds, disbelief dawning.

"Hello, Sergeant Boudreau," Jack said. "How the hell did you get here?"

❧

Scott's expression betrayed his shock. Jack saw the flash of recognition, followed by confusion. Scott looked good—far better than Jack expected, considering the last time he'd seen him was on a battlefield, bleeding out while the skirmish raged around them.

"Sergeant Boudreau, you look terrible," Jack said with a grin, "but it's good to see you." He dismounted and walked forward to shake Scott's hand.

Out of instinct, Scott saluted. "Sir!"

Jack chuckled. "I don't see uniform or rank here. Scott, isn't it?"

"Yes, sir—" Scott caught himself. "I mean, yes, Jack." He smiled. "It's good to see you. I thought I lost everyone I ever knew when I woke up here."

"How long have you been here?" Jack asked, patting his horse's neck.

"About a year. It's a strange place, this foggy world." Scott shook his head. "Have you noticed? Not one day of seeing the sun."

Jack nodded. "Yeah. I asked about that. They have traditions hinting the clouds covered their world eight thousand years ago. Since then—clouds, fog, rain."

"It's eerie as hell," Scott muttered.

Jack hesitated. "I couldn't remember anything before coming here. Now I'm getting shadows of memories."

Scott gave a humorless laugh. "I had too many memories when I landed here." He looked down, then back at Jack. "I remembered you kneeling over me after that grenade went off. I knew I was done, but there you were. The fight still going, and you stopped to check on me." His voice softened. "Thank you. It meant a lot—not dying alone."

Jack fell silent, moved by the memory. Before he could respond, he noticed another rider approaching. "One of yours?"

Scott turned. "My boss's son, Ronan. Solid kid. Not like most heirs of entitlement."

Ronan rode up cautiously. "Everything okay, boss?" He kept a careful distance from Jack, positioning himself well.

Scott nodded. "Everything's great. Remember when I told you about serving in the army? This is Jack—my former commander."

Ronan studied Jack, noting the lack of uniform or insignia. "Are you here to return Scott to the army? Whose army do you represent?"

Jack's expression softened. "No army. I'm not here to drag him anywhere. Until just now, I hadn't even thought about armies in this world."

Ronan relaxed. "There haven't been armies here since the Great Purge fifty years ago." A faint smile. "Glad you're not bringing that madness back."

Scott tilted his head. "Jack, what are you doing out here? And who are the women with you?"

Jack sighed. "Long story. Short version: that redhead was the first person I met after waking up here. She took me in when I was confused and a stranger. She didn't have to—but she saved me." He glanced toward Kendra with a small smile. "She introduced me to the right people. You know the Fairmen?"

Scott grinned. "Yeah. Strange folk, but good. Essential to the economy in Asher—probably all Eldriko."

Jack nodded. "I hadn't thought of it that way. I just saw talented craftsmen with a gift for shrewd bartering."

Scott laughed. "Make no mistake—there'd be no trade without them. Some city folk don't trust them, but they've never treated me unfairly. Maybe that's why they're called Fairmen."

Ronan dismounted, reassured by Scott's ease with Jack.

The two women rode back toward Jack and dismounted. The redhead hobbled her horse. "I assume we're setting camp here tonight." Her expression held mild disapproval, but she said nothing more.

Scott raised his eyebrows. "Want to share our camp? You'll get a hot meal out of it." He looked at Ronan. "We're done for the day, right?"

Ronan snorted. "My father can't figure out how you get so much done while taking so many breaks."

Scott laughed and pointed at Jack. "Ask him. He wondered the same thing when we served together."

Jack shook his head. "Don't drag me into your employment debates." Then he added to Ronan, "He got more work out of people because he pitched in."

Ronan barked a laugh. "Truth. Other bosses just shout orders. This one jumps in with everything he's got. When we match his effort, we sometimes get half a day off. Father trusts him implicitly." He grinned. "I told Father I'd only work with Scott."

Jack turned to Kendra and Asta. "What do you think? We could stop early and camp with my friend."

The two women conferred quietly. Finally, Asta stepped forward. "You trust this man?"

Jack nodded. "With my life."

Asta inclined her head. "Then we should set camp before darkness."

Scott and Ronan led them back to the creek-side camp. Scott's team watched curiously as their boss returned with three strangers, though Ronan's relaxed posture eased their concerns.

Ellis lit a fire with pine branches, sending thick smoke upward. He started a simple stew, adding extra venison and smoked meat for the guests.

Jack, Kendra, and Asta set their camp just north of Scott's crew—close enough to show trust, far enough to respect boundaries. For the women, it signaled comfort with Jack and acceptance of Scott's presence.

Soon Kendra and Asta were laughing together, the kind of easy camaraderie born from shared journeys. Jack's comfort with Scott spread through the camp, and before long, Scott's crew and Jack's companions were trading stories with growing warmth.

Jack sat around the fire with Kendra and Asta, along with Scott's crew, after they finished the stew. Kendra smiled easily, slipping into the banter with Scott's team, while Asta sat slightly apart, listening. Her experience with Erathas and Offlanders outpaced most Manos, but she still watched with quiet curiosity, absorbing everything.

Kendra asked about herbs in the high plains. Ronan asked for news from town. Jack and Scott, in low voices, drifted into memories of a world neither fully remembered nor fully escaped.

"Weren't you married, Jack?" Scott asked, sipping hot chicory.

Jack stared into the fire. "Yeah. But it didn't last."

"What happened?"

"She couldn't accept life as a military wife." He paused. "And she never really fit into life on the farm either." He took a slow drink. "When I got home, she was already gone."

"That sucks," Scott muttered. "You went back home—near your folks?"

Jack nodded. "Only home I knew. I bought the farm next to theirs. When they retired, I was set to have it all."

"That was ambitious. Aren't your folks dairy farmers?"

"Second generation." Jack's voice softened. "I hope they're okay. Since I'm here... they're on their own. They're not young anymore. Dad counted on me."

Scott nodded. "They'll adjust. Life goes on—for them, at least." A quiet chuckle escaped him.

Jack's head snapped up. "What do you mean by that? You make it sound like I died." His tone carried an edge.

"I didn't mean anything by it. Just being a realist."

Their voices rose, drawing glances from the others.

Jack lowered his voice. "Sorry. It just sounds so final." He stared at the fire. "Scott... earlier, when we met up, you said something strange. You said you appreciated that I stayed with you when you died."

Scott held his gaze for several seconds, deciding. "Jack... that's what I meant. Back on the battlefield, I did die—on Earth."

Jack blinked. "Come on, Scott. Be serious."

"I am serious. I died after that skirmish. You were there. You know I did."

Jack stared at him, stunned. "But you're here. Alive."

"Alive on Eldriko," Scott said quietly. "Dead on Earth."

Jack stammered. "How...?"

"I don't know how. But it happened." Scott set his mug down. "When I first got here, I was confused. Lost. You know what that's like."

Jack nodded slowly. "Yeah. I think I would've gone crazy if Kendra hadn't been there when I woke up."

"Exactly. For me it was a Manos named Halan. A wanderer. A kind of social researcher. He helped me understand what happened."

Jack leaned in. "What did he do?"

Scott laughed softly. "He took one look at me—bloody camos and all—and asked if I knew how I died. No lead-in. Just that. I told him I wasn't dead, and he laughed. Said, 'Of course you are dead. How else do you think you got here?' That's how I found out."

Jack stared at him for what felt like forever. "Are you saying I'm dead?" His voice was barely a whisper.

Scott took a sip of chicory. "Yeah. That's what I'm saying. Halan said our kind come here after we die—when there's something more for us to do."

"What do we have to do?"

Scott shrugged. "No idea. Halan said it's different for everyone. Sometimes obscure. I haven't figured out mine yet."

Jack sat in stunned silence. The fire crackled. The night pressed close. Everything felt too alive, too immediate, too real to be death.

"Scott," he finally whispered, "what about my parents?"

Scott looked at him for a long moment, weighing how to answer. "Jack... I know this is hard. But on Earth, life goes on. The people we leave behind mourn, and then they pick up and move forward. They miss us—you know how it is—but they still have their lives to live."

Jack's heart hammered. His breaths came shallow and quick. Words flickered through his mind—this isn't fair. But whoever said life was fair? And who said death was? It felt as if the ground had been pulled out from under him.

And then, like a blow to the chest, he remembered.

How he died.

Scott's voice cut through the rising panic. "Listen, Jack. You should talk to someone in Mistdale. It's a Manos city, only a couple days' ride. Someone there can help you understand what's happening."

"You're not going to believe this," Jack said quietly, "but one of their elders sent Asta to bring me to them. I don't know why."

Scott's mouth fell open. "They sent for you? I've never heard of them doing that."

"We need to leave in the morning," Jack said.

Asta, who had been listening, nodded. "We do. Teyr expects your prompt presence."

Scott looked north, as if he could see Mistdale through the fog. Then he looked at his crew, then back at Jack. "Could I come with you?"

Ronan stared at him. "You're thinking of leaving?"

Scott blinked, realizing his crew had heard everything. "I have questions, Ronan. Do I have a destiny here? If Jack will let me, I can find answers in Mistdale too."

Ronan stepped closer, voice steady. "I have questions too. You told me about your other world. I kept your secret—not even

Father knows. I need to know if you're coming back, or if you have a new journey waiting. If you're leaving, you'll need me at your side."

Jack turned to Asta. "Would Scott be welcome as my guest?"

Asta considered, then nodded. "As your guest, Teyr would allow it."

Jack turned back to Scott. "If that's what you want, I won't stop you." He glanced at Ronan. "When will you tell your boss? We need to move at first light."

Scott stood and called out, "Sabrina! Come here."

She rose immediately. "Yes, boss?"

"You're in charge of the crew until Master Weir says otherwise. Understand?"

She hesitated only a moment. "Yes, boss. What should I tell him?"

"Tell him I'm going to Mistdale to find answers about my fate in Asher. And tell him I couldn't stop Ronan from following me." Ronan grinned at that. "He won't believe you, but he'll understand. Ronan's been my right hand since his father assigned him to me."

Sabrina smiled, already imagining Master Weir's reaction. "Boss, he'll want to know if you're coming back. What do I tell him?"

"Tell him you don't know. Because I don't. If I can, I'll come back. I like working with you—and for him."

Chapter Seven

I accept chaos, I'm not sure whether it accepts me.

—BOB DYLAN

The gentle rolling hills of the interior slowly flattened into a coastal plain as they rode toward Mistdale. Pockets of wooded fields grew denser as the morning passed. They picked their way through old-growth forest, where the Manos had long protected the ancient trees. The high canopy filtered the light and discouraged the thick undergrowth that choked younger woods. A soft symphony of birds and insects filled the air.

They rotated positions as they traveled, speaking quietly so as not to disturb the wildlife. Only Asta kept her place at the front, guiding them with the certainty of someone who knew every bend of the land.

Jack rode beside her for a quarter hour before finally asking, "When were you last in Mistdale?" He hoped the question might open a door with the reserved ranger.

"Almost a year ago," she said, adjusting her reins slightly west as if following an unseen marker.

"A year? Do you have family there?"

"Some. A sister. And my mother still lives." Her voice softened at the mention.

Jack sensed the shift. "It'll be good to see them again, right?"

Asta glanced at him, surprised she'd revealed so much. "We see each other once a year, since Father died."

Jack hesitated, unsure if he should press further, but Asta continued—uncharacteristically.

"I used to be close to my sister and Father. Mother served on the council, so she was rarely present. A good mother, just... not there. After Father died, the council offered me a place as ranger and courier. I took it."

Jack nodded, sensing the boundary. They rode in silence for a while, and his thoughts drifted—to Earth, to the impossible truth that he was dead, to the strange new life unfolding around him.

Then something shifted.

His perception thinned, as if he were looking at the world through a painting. The forest ahead dissolved into cultivated fields sloping toward a glimmering city by the sea. He saw brush, copse of trees, and wide swaths of farmland woven into the old forest.

To the east, an older woman walked through a formal garden. Dressed in a rose-colored gown with a ranger-green apron, she carried a wide straw basket and gathered cuttings—herbs, Jack guessed, since he saw no blooms.

His perspective shifted. He was no longer riding toward her—he was moving toward her. Then his vision snapped to the right, focusing sharply on a rabbit, the rest of the world falling away.

And then he was back in the forest, riding beside Asta.

"We are less than two days from the city," Asta said, pointing left. "Tomorrow we should see the spires above the trees." She looked at him when he didn't respond. "Jack? Are you well?"

He blinked. "Hmm? Yes. I'm fine. It's just..."

"What troubles you?" For the first time, genuine concern colored her voice.

"I thought I saw something strange." He tried to piece it together. "A woman outside a city by the sea, gathering herbs. But it wasn't like normal sight. It was like looking at an old oil painting. Real, but... not."

Asta listened intently. "Anything else?"

"The scene shifted. Suddenly I was focused on a rabbit—like it was the only thing in the world. Then I was back here."

"Did it seem darker? Lighter? Like through a window?"

Jack shook his head. "Just... like a living painting."

Asta looked ahead for a long moment. "Jack, when we reach Mistdale, you should tell Teyr about your vision."

"The elder who sent you? Why would she care?"

Asta shifted in her saddle. "I think you have gained an animal spirit. You may have been seeing through its eyes."

Jack stared at her. "That's... crazy. I've read things like that in novels, but not in real life."

Asta's expression softened. "It happens. Rarely, but it happens—especially in this forest. The spirits are active here."

Jack fell back in the line as Scott moved forward. He mulled over Asta's words. At first he thought she was telling a folktale. But the more he considered it, the more he realized she had shared something deeply believed—and deeply real to her.

Even when Kendra rode beside him, their conversation stayed light. Jack's thoughts churned beneath the surface.

That night he slept fitfully, dreaming of the old woman and the coyote. At first light he woke unrested, his mind unsettled. They broke their fast and continued on.

Within a couple of hours, Jack saw the towers of a city rising above the fields.

And again—with his own eyes—he saw the older woman gathering herbs in the garden.

"Ma'am, are you sure about this?" Delon asked as he helped her with her ceremonial robes. "You already face strong opposition on the council."

Teyr Elenya watched him adjust the fabric with practiced precision. "Delon, you worry too much."

Unflustered, he continued preparing her for the council's reception—the first time in history an Offlander would be admitted to these chambers. A sizeable minority had argued fiercely against it, but Teyr had secured a narrow majority. Even so, she knew she must tread carefully.

When Delon finished, Teyr glanced in the mirror and smiled. "As always, you make sure I look the part. Thank you."

He bowed his head modestly, pride flickering in his eyes. For three decades, he had helped her hold this council together.

"Check if they're assembled," she said.

Delon opened the hidden peephole, scanned the chamber, and closed it quietly. "They are ready for you, Madam Chief."

She straightened her shoulders. Delon opened the door, and she stepped into the council chamber.

"I thank you for gathering on such short notice," she began. "Our guest arrived only this morning. With your consideration, I would like to—"

"Madam Chief," Jaren Gwath interrupted, his voice booming. "I must object to allowing an Offlander into these chambers. Tradition demands—"

Teyr stepped forward, her presence cutting him off. "Councilman Gwath, your objection is noted. And the matter has already been voted upon." Her stare froze him in place until he sank back into his seat.

A whisper drifted from the left. "Give it a rest, Jaren. You lost."

Teyr swept her gaze across the circle. "Any further objections?"

Silence. The vote stood.

She nodded to the Master of Arms. "Bring them in."

Jack entered first with Asta at his side, followed by Kendra, Scott, and Ronan. The Master of Arms halted ten paces from the council.

"Madam Chief, honored councilors—Master Jack Marshall and his companions." He stepped aside and withdrew, closing the great doors behind him.

Teyr studied Jack for a long moment. "Master Marshall, thank you for accepting our invitation."

Jack blinked. "That was an invitation?" he murmured to Asta.

A voice snapped from the side. "Show respect to the Madam Chief!"

Teyr raised a hand. "No need for that." She turned back to Jack. "Master Marshall, I apologize if my 'invitation' was not conveyed properly." Her eyes flicked toward Asta in silent reprimand.

Jack caught it. "Madam Chief, I'm sure it was my misunderstanding. Asta has been nothing but respectful." He offered Asta a small smile before facing Teyr again. "Thank you for receiving us. How may I help you?"

Teyr's expression softened. "A majority of this council believes you are here because the gods willed it. Others believe it is luck or error." Her eyes flashed toward the dissenters. "But the official stance—by narrow margin—is that you were destined to find us and destined for deeds that may restore our world to its purpose."

Jack's confusion flickered across his face. "Madam Chief... I can't say if this is fate or a mistake. But I'm not someone a god would choose. I'm just a man. Wounded more than most. Wounded... and alone."

Asta cleared her throat, this time seeking recognition.

"Ranger Rhann?" Teyr asked.

Asta stepped forward. "Madam Chief, I have traveled with Master Marshall for several days—from the Fairmen camp, along the trail, and through his dealings with Masters Boudreau and Weir. He is anything but a simple man. I have witnessed maturity, sound judgment, and leadership—even in silence.

She paused, gathering her thoughts.

"He may be wounded. You have seen his limp. We all carry scars long after battle. I cannot speak to the wounds you cannot see, but he bears them with strength. And as for being alone..." She gestured to Jack's companions. "Look at them. They refused to let him enter alone. In the short time he has been in our world, he has formed an intentional family—one that would die to protect him."

Every head nodded.

"And I, Asta Rhann," she said quietly, "count myself part of that family."

Silence fell like a stone.

Manos did not give allegiance lightly. And never quickly.

Teyr stared at Asta, stunned. In all her years, she had never seen the ranger moved by anyone's plight. Yet here she stood, declaring loyalty to an Offlander she had known mere days.

Something had shifted. Something profound.

Teyr drew a slow breath. "Thank you, Ranger Rhann."

She scanned the council. Their faces were unreadable, but the silence spoke volumes.

"If there are no comments," she said, "I ask your indulgence to speak with Master Marshall privately."

No objections.

Teyr turned to Jack. "Master Marshall, will you accompany me to my office?"

She nodded to Delon. "Join us."

Delon stepped forward. The Master of Arms opened the door, and the three disappeared inside. The door closed behind them, and the Master of Arms took his place before it—a silent warning to anyone who might consider following.

Passing through the door into Teyr's office felt like stepping from a palace into a garden. The council chamber had been all stone, ceremony, and authority. Her office, by contrast, revealed the woman beneath the title—shelves of plants, sketches of animals, soft chairs arranged near a great window overlooking the northern sea. Only the desk belonged to the Madam Chief. Everything else belonged to Teyr Elenya, the healer, the gardener, the woman who still grieved.

She gestured to the chairs. "Please, sit." She took the seat nearest her desk. "We are away from prying eyes. May I call you Jack?"

Jack understood immediately—the shift from public persona to private self. He took the chair by the window. "Thank you, Madam Chief."

Teyr shook her head. "Please. In here, call me Teyr. No need for all that formality." She reached for the teapot. "Tea?" She poured before he could answer.

Jack inhaled the aroma—rose hips, something earthy beneath. "Thank you."

She watched him relax into the moment. "We needed to escape those vultures. They're always waiting for me to stumble." She sipped her tea. "I'm sure you're wondering why I sent Asta to find you."

Jack nodded. "The thought had crossed my mind."

"The answer is not for the council to hear," she said. "And it is... personal." She straightened, gathering herself. "My tale begins over thirty years ago."

Jack leaned forward, listening.

"I was a young healer then, establishing my first herb garden. Young for a healer, I should say. I was one hundred twenty-eight."

Jack blinked. "You're over a hundred years old?"

She grinned. "One hundred sixty-three, actually. Still young for a Manos. You wouldn't know that, of course."

"I had no idea your people lived so long."

"Not all people of Eldriko. Only the Manos." She refilled their cups. "Before I continue, I have one request. May I touch your face?"

Jack held still. "I am at your service."

Teyr stood before him, placed her hands on his cheeks, fingertips resting at his temples. She closed her eyes and hummed a low, haunting melody. After a long moment, she withdrew, visibly drained.

"I knew it was you," she whispered, sinking back into her chair.

Delon glided to her side; concern etched across his face.

Jack waited, then asked softly, "Who do you think I am?"

Teyr breathed deeply. "Allow me to finish my tale first."

"Of course."

"Over thirty years ago, my mate, Jassinn Elenya, discovered a fault line between our worlds—here and Earth—inside a cavern near Mistdale. At first it was barely measurable. But over months, it grew. He found he could pass objects through, if his timing was perfect."

Jack's breath caught.

"One morning, he told me he would attempt the crossing himself." Her voice thinned. "He did not return for months. I believed him dead."

She paused, gathering strength.

"When he finally came home, he looked as if he had fought death itself. He collapsed at our door. He survived only a few weeks."

Tears welled and spilled freely. Delon rested a hand on her shoulder. She squeezed it in gratitude.

"In those final weeks," she continued, "he told me what he saw on your world. The bright ball of light in the sky. The way it marked time. The flora, the fauna. And the languages—different but somehow understood by those who crossed."

Jack nodded slowly, remembering how he had simply known the common tongue.

Teyr continued. "The crossing disoriented him. He lost the way back. It took him months to find the breach again. And during that time... he met someone."

Jack's pulse quickened.

"A young woman. A maiden. She found him one morning, and they became companions. He had lost hope of returning. He fell in love with her." Teyr's voice softened, not bitter but mournful. "Her name was Anabel Knapp."

Jack's world narrowed to a pinpoint.

"Where did he meet her?" he whispered.

"In a small farming community in the southern tier of New York state."

Jack's mouth fell open. "Anabel Knapp is my mother."

Teyr reached out, cupping his cheek with the same hand that had touched his essence. "Yes. I knew when I touched you."

Her voice trembled with certainty.

"My Jassinn is your father, Jack—your birth father."

ॐ

Jack sat in stunned silence. The world he thought he understood—even the fractured version he'd pieced together since waking on Eldriko—tilted beneath him. With one sentence, Teyr had cracked open the foundation of his identity. Beliefs he'd never questioned suddenly felt like childhood stories. His life, once linear and ordinary, now seemed shaped by forces he had never imagined.

Teyr watched him carefully. "I'm sorry to shock you, Jack. I meant to reveal your heritage gently once I confirmed it." She moved from her chair and knelt before him, the gesture intimate and maternal. "But recently I discovered a long-lost parchment that changed everything. It speaks of our history, our dangers, and a prophecy of restoration."

Jack tried to focus on her words, though his mind churned with implications he could barely grasp. "What does that have to do with me?"

Teyr rose and crossed to a bench-height table in the corner, where an ancient map lay unrolled. "Come. I want to show you."

Jack joined her. The map, yellowed with age, reminded him of the early exploration charts he'd seen in Earth museums—part science, part myth.

Teyr handed him a pair of soft gloves. "This map is three centuries old. Please use these." She donned her own. "It reflects what they believed Eldriko looked like then—a blend of knowledge and legend." She traced the edges. "These regions remain uncertain even today."

She sat and motioned for him to do the same. "Our history and myth have intertwined for millennia. What I tell you is both."

Jack listened, steadying himself.

"Ten thousand years ago, Eldriko was at peace. The gods were at peace. Chaos and order were balanced, and the land prospered. As a symbol of that harmony, the gods created a perfect gem—the Heart of Sheol." She glanced at him. "The gods dwelled in Sheol, though its location is lost to us now."

She continued, voice low. "One night, a god of structure decided chaos must be purged. While the others slept, he stole the Heart and hid it from gods and mortals alike. Since then, the world has been... diminished."

Jack frowned. "Is this more myth or history?"

Teyr smiled faintly. "Aren't they often the same? All peoples deny it, yet all stories share roots." She looked at the map. "Somewhere, the Heart of Sheol still waits to be returned."

She reached for a small pouch and withdrew an older parchment. "This is what prompted my search for you." She unrolled it carefully. "Can you read it?"

Jack looked at the words on the undated skin parchment:

> *Collodd Plant y Wlad, gan anghofio dysgeidiaeth y duwiau, Galon y Wlad. Paradwys y Wlad, wedi lleihau a gwasgu, offrymodd ei Chalon yn aberth...*

Jack stared at the unfamiliar script. "I'm sorry. I can't."

"Then I will translate." She used a feather pointer to avoid touching the skin.

She read:

> *The Children of the Land, forgetting the teachings of the gods, lost the Heart of the Land. Paradise of the Land, diminished and pressed down, offered up its Heart as a sacrifice for the Children's disobedience. The Heart, removed from its rightful nest, fell into a deep sleep, thrusting the land into a state bereft of the Light of the gods. The Children, thrust into the mist of unbelief, begged the gods to reveal the Heart to their Children, ending their foggy existence.*

Her voice softened as she continued:

> *The gods, hearing the cries of their Children, reached across time and space to find a Warrior of two worlds. A Warrior, called from a broken land, called to a broken land. A Warrior, broken in the test of battle, broken by the loss in battle, and of battles. A Warrior, giving his last full*

measure of devotion, abandoned the broken land of his creation. A Warrior, regardless of his intent, found the broken Land of his Fate. A Land of Darkness, Mist, and Fog. A Land to heal his broken spirit with the healing of the Land.

She looked up at him, then read the final stanza:

A broken Warrior, of two Lands and two Races; of two Spirits and one Fate.

A Warrior formed of an Ancient People; formed through a fledgling race.

An ordinary Warrior finding an extraordinary Fate.

A Fate of Restoration,

A Fate of Redemption,

A Fate of Healing—

For people and Land.

Teyr set the pointer down and let the silence settle, giving Jack space to absorb the prophecy's weight.

Chapter Eight

Magic is believing in yourself, if you can do that, you can make anything happen.

—JOHANN WOLFGANG VON GOETHE

Jack didn't move when Teyr stepped away from the table. He sat frozen, trying to make sense of everything she had revealed—Eldriko's history, its mythology, its prophecy, and now his own bloodline. This was a world where prophecy wasn't metaphor but lived belief, and he was suddenly standing in the center of it.

"I—um... what I mean is..." Jack struggled for words. He looked up at Teyr, wide-eyed, like a deer caught in a shooting lane. "Y-you think this means me?"

Teyr's expression softened. She understood the weight she had placed on him. "You match the descriptions laid out in the parchment."

Jack's gaze darted between the prophecy and the woman who had just become his Manos stepmother. "It can't be me. I'm a stranger in your world—a nobody."

Teyr smiled gently. "Yet you are the son of Jassinn Elenya, my husband. You carry his Manos blood and, I suspect, his power."

"Power? What kind of power?" Each new revelation dug his emotional grave deeper.

"Magic, my boy. Magic." Teyr's smile held pride and sorrow. "Jassinn wielded the magic of both scholar and warrior. It stands to reason you would share his warrior traits."

"You expect me to fulfill this prophecy?" Jack stepped back from the table, as if distance could lessen the weight of the parchment.

Teyr remained still, her concern plain. "Jack, no one can force you to do anything. I have translated the scroll faithfully. I've given you my interpretation. And I can only hope you will choose to take up this cause—to restore my world, and now yours, to its ancient glory."

Jack sank into the chair by the window, avoiding the parchment. Outside, he saw Kendra walking slowly through the garden. Even as he looked away, the prophecy pressed on his thoughts. "If I accept this task—and I mean if—where would I start?"

Teyr exhaled, relieved by the hint of acceptance. "There are other scrolls that will guide you. And I will ensure you have the proper supervision to complete the task."

Jack stiffened. "Supervision?"

"Jack, I cannot send you out without someone to guide you. It is best for everyone."

He stood abruptly, turning toward the window. "No. Absolutely not." His anger rose. "This prophecy isn't a road map. It's a set of suggestions—pointed at me, yes—but still suggestions."

"Yes, but—"

"If this prophecy is meant to lead me, then it will. If I accept the challenge." His voice carried the same command he once used on the battlefield. "I don't need supervision."

Teyr's mouth fell open. "You must have a representative of the Manos with you if there is any hope of completing the quest."

Jack paused, then spoke with measured clarity. "I understand you want someone to make sure I don't screw up. Fine. Send Asta. I trust her. And since she is your daughter, I assume you trust her as well. Agreed?"

Teyr saw the resolve in his eyes and nodded. "All right, Jack. I accept your terms. Will you promise me something?"

"What is it?"

"Two things, actually." Her voice softened. "Will you set things right for Eldriko? And... will you not get yourself killed?"

Jack laughed despite himself. "I'll do my best."

Teyr smiled in relief. "I just found my husband's long-lost son. I would like to know him when this is over."

Jack lowered his head. "This will take some getting used to. For thirty-one years, the man my mother loved—the man I did chores with—was my father. And now I learn I don't share his blood. That someone from another world was my real father."

Teyr placed a hand on his shoulder. "What is his name, Jack? The man who raised you."

His voice was barely a whisper. "Ben."

"Jack, Ben was your father in every way that matters. He raised you to be a good man—a man others trust. My Jassinn gave you flesh, but nothing more. The crossing between worlds destroyed his body. Even if he had stayed on Earth, he would not have lived to see your first natal day."

She crossed to a wardrobe and returned with a cloth-wrapped bundle. "Jassinn could not be there for you, but in his final days he wondered what might have been—if he had stayed or brought you and Anabel here. Our culture allows multiple mates; Mistdale would have accepted you both. But knowing what I know now, all three of you would have died within the year."

She laid the bundle on the table, covering the prophecy. "This is Targonith. It belonged to Jassinn. He would want you to have it."

She folded back the cloth, revealing a sword of exceptional craftsmanship, etched with ancient markings.

"His father gave it to him before dying of battle wounds. It has been in his family nearly a thousand years." She traced the engravings with reverence. "I was preparing to pass it to Asta when I found the prophecy. Supporting documents confirmed the Keeper of the Heart would be of Jassinn's line. When I touched your face, I knew."

She held the hilt toward him.

Jack met her eyes. "Are you sure?"

Teyr nodded. "It belongs to you, son. Trust it to guard you—but don't rush into battle. This blade can shift fate, but it cannot save you from foolishness."

Jack accepted the sword with reverence. "It's beautiful. But... I've never used a sword. I'm good with a bow, but blades weren't needed in my world."

Teyr smiled. "Speak with Asta. She understands edged weapons better than most men. She can teach you."

Jack looked into the eyes of the woman who was now his mother on Eldriko—and saw concern, pride, and love. She had known of him for thirty years before he ever set foot in her world. He was a living bridge to her lost husband.

"Bring my Asta back to me, Jack. And..." she paused, then grinned, "bring yourself back in one piece. Otherwise, I will have to hunt you down if you get yourself killed."

➤

Jack stepped out of the council chambers and into the courtyard. The air felt cooler here, quieter, though his mind churned with everything Teyr had revealed. Kendra sat beneath a broad-limbed tree, talking with Asta and Scott. Ronan had cornered one of the council guards and was deep in conversation. Jack felt drained—hollowed out by truth.

Now he had to tell them.

He approached the bench. "Asta, your mother would like to speak with you inside."

Asta's expression chilled instantly. "She told you?"

Scott and Kendra exchanged a glance. Jack nodded.

"Of course she did." Asta rose and disappeared back into the council house.

Kendra looked up at Jack. "What was that about?"

Jack motioned for Ronan to join them. "I have a story to tell you—and a decision I've made." He glanced toward the plains just in time to see the lop-eared coyote trotting toward the forest.

He told them everything—the prophecy, the lineage, the task ahead. When he finished, he added, "I have a week to prepare."

Four voices erupted at once—and a fifth joined as Asta returned from the chambers. The courtyard became a tangle of overlapping demands and declarations.

Jack raised both hands. "Hold on. One at a time."

Silence fell, brittle and expectant.

Scott broke it first. "If you're going on an adventure, you better believe I'm coming too."

That set off another round of voices until Jack herded them into a quieter corner of the courtyard, away from the curious Manos who had begun to gather.

"Scott," Jack said, "your decision doesn't surprise me. We've faced trouble together before." He gave him a small grin.

Asta spoke next. "I will be joining you as well. Mother... requested it." Her tone made it clear how she felt about that "request."

Kendra stepped forward. "Of course I'm coming. When do we leave?"

Jack blinked, surprised by her certainty. "A week."

Kendra exhaled in relief. "Good. I can't help with preparations beyond my own supplies, but the high healer—Jalianna Emeria—agreed to train me. I'll ask her for a quick course so I can actually be useful."

Ronan nodded once. "I go where Scott goes. If he trusts you on a journey like this, so do I."

Jack looked at each of them—these people who had chosen him before he had chosen himself. "All right. Since you're all determined to join me, let's get organized."

He opened the Manos journal Teyr had given him.

"Teyr assigned me a storage room for preparations, and she's giving Asta and me pack horses. I'll ask for more."

He turned to Scott. "Will you act as quartermaster?"

Scott nodded immediately.

"Asta," Jack continued, "you know this land. I'll rely on you to keep us from being surprised on the trail."

Asta gave a curt nod.

"Kendra, you'll be our healer. That includes herbal remedies, right?"

"Yes—mostly herbs for simple healing."

"Good. Since herbs are also used for food preservation, would you take on that duty as well?"

Kendra smiled. "I can do that."

Jack turned to Ronan. "I don't know you well, but Scott trusts you—and that's enough for me. Can you work with Asta to provide security?"

Ronan straightened. "Yes. I hope everyone has some skill with a weapon."

Jack rubbed the back of his neck. "I'm good with a bow. But..." He touched the sword at his side. "I've never used a blade like this."

"I'll teach you," Asta said quickly. "I know that sword well."

Jack nodded. "Good. Then let's begin."

He pointed toward a blue building. "The storage room is there. Let's meet every evening to review our progress." He looked at Kendra. "Can you get away from training for half an hour after dinner?"

Kendra smiled. "I can manage that."

"Then let's get to it," Jack said. "Seven days isn't much time to prepare for a journey like this."

Jack arrived at the Mistdale training grounds early the next morning, Targonith resting across his shoulder. Asta glanced up from her warm-up routine, her expression cool and assessing.

"You are late." She flowed into slow shadow-sword movements, each one precise. "Loosen up. We begin in a quarter hour."

Jack fell into familiar military stretches, letting muscle memory take over. By the time Asta finished her warm-up and faced him, he felt ready.

She pointed toward the edge of the grounds. "Is that your animal?"

Jack followed her gaze to the lop-eared coyote resting in the shade. "Seems he's adopted me." He grinned, answering the question she hadn't asked. "He comes and goes, but I feel like we've formed some kind of connection. I don't think he'll harm anyone unless they attack me." He shrugged. "I think he's decided to protect me."

Asta's expression didn't change, but something in her eyes sharpened.

"You may set your sword on the bench. You won't need it yet." She placed her own blade aside. "Stand with your weight balanced. Not forward, not back."

Jack followed her instructions. She led him through balance drills—shifting weight, grounding through the feet, moving from the hips. Twice he overextended and nearly fell, but his body remembered echoes of similar training, though he couldn't place where.

They worked for nearly an hour before she said, "Get your practice sword. We try again."

Jack retrieved his blade. Asta was already in position ten paces away, sword extended in a ready stance.

"From now on, move like your life depends on it," she said. "Because it will, once we're on the trail. Begin."

Asta's movements were fluid, effortless. Jack's were stiff, uncertain. The Manos longsword felt foreign in his hands, and the tip dipped more often than he realized.

"Watch your sword position!" Asta barked. "Tip up. Guard high."

Her corrections were sharp, relentless—but fair. Slowly, Jack found a rhythm. They practiced thrusts, parries, slashes, always in the controlled dance of shadow fighting. By midday, he was sweating and sore but no longer fumbling.

After a brief rest and food, they switched to wooden blades. Asta did not hold back.

She struck his arms, his ribs, his shoulders—not cruelly, but with the precision of someone teaching through contact. Jack learned to counter, to anticipate, to feel the opening before it appeared. When he corrected a mistake, she acknowledged it with a curt nod. When he repeated one, she corrected him without hesitation.

Late in the afternoon, she pressed him hard, driving him backward with a flurry of strikes. Jack stumbled, recovered, and—without thinking—reversed her attack with a sharp pivot and counterstrike that forced her onto her heels.

Asta froze.

"Where did you learn that, Jack?" Her voice held genuine respect.

Jack lowered his wooden blade. "It just felt like the right thing to do. Was it wrong?"

Asta shook her head, a rare smile tugging at her mouth. "No. It was exactly the right response. I'm impressed."

She took the wooden sword from him. "Do you think you're ready for live blades tomorrow?"

Jack grinned. "Same time, same place."

Asta walked off the training field with a new, quiet respect for Jack Marshall—a man who learned fast, moved on instinct, and carried the blood of a warrior he had never known.

🙢

The rain had begun long before dawn, steady and cold, but by midday it softened into a thin mist. Inside the Healer's Shed, Kendra moved between the sorting table and the small desk where the journal of medicinal herbs lay open. She cataloged the previous day's harvest, trying to impose order on the chaos.

Every so often, one of Jalianna Emeria's students hurried in from the garden and dropped another bundle of herbs onto the table—anywhere, anyhow—before rushing back outside. Kendra tried to direct them, but they ignored her suggestions, scattering leaves and stems across her carefully arranged piles.

"Can't we find some order for the harvest?" The frustration burst out before she could stop it. She tried to reorganize the latest heap, jaw tightening as her work unraveled again.

Madam Emeria entered through the half-door at the back of the shed. "Kendra, is there a problem?" She approached the table, her eyes sharp. "You seem at odds with everyone and everything."

Kendra startled. She hadn't heard the Master Healer come in. "I—I'm sorry, Madam Emeria. I'm just trying to keep these samples organized." She sighed. "Every time I get ahead, another bundle gets dumped on top."

The Master Healer examined the sorted herbs with a practiced eye. "These are in good order. You're doing adequately." She turned to Kendra. "But that is not what troubles you, is it? Tell me the real issue."

Kendra sank onto the stool. "I thought I was going to learn healing magic. All I've done today is sort herbs—herbs I already know."

Madam Emeria looked over the collection of medicinal plants on the table. "Tell me, girl—what does this one do?" She pointed to the green leaves of an herb gathered that morning.

Kendra recognized it immediately. "That one stems bleeding." Pride flickered across her face at the quick identification.

The Master Healer pointed to another pile—the same leaves but dried for a week. Kendra frowned. "Madam Emeria, that's the same plant, just dried. It stems bleeding."

"Does it?" Madam Emeria's sharp tone made Kendra's stomach drop. "Girl, you have much to learn. They are the same herb, yes—but the dried leaves do not stem blood. They strengthen it."

Kendra stared at the two samples. The difference in color was obvious, but she had never imagined the difference in function. Her confidence wavered. She realized, with a sinking feeling, how shallow her understanding truly was.

Madam Emeria continued. "And the qualities of the green leaves, the dried leaves, even the seeds—all change with the application of simple or complex spells. One common herb can treat a dozen ailments, if you know what you are doing."

Kendra lowered her head. "Yes, Madam Emeria. I'm beginning to understand. What should I do next?" Her voice was quieter now, her pride giving way to humility.

Madam Emeria smiled. "Now you will be able to learn. Spend the day sorting the herbs that are harvested or collected from the drying shed. Ask questions—even about the herbs you are sure you know. Rural midwives often misassign attributes to herbs without realizing how the state of the plant changes its nature."

Kendra nodded, recognizing the weakness in her own knowledge. She resolved to learn everything she could from the Master Healer.

Over the next two days, she worked steadily—sorting, studying, asking questions, and discovering how much she had misunderstood. By the third morning, Madam Emeria began quizzing her. To Kendra's surprise, she answered well. The Master Healer's expression softened with approval.

"Kendra," she said, "your diligence shows. You have learned much in a short time. Tomorrow, we begin the next step—the path from simple herbalist to Healer." She took Kendra's hand gently. "I can feel the essence of a true healer in you. Rest well tonight. Magic infusions drain even the strongest among us."

Chapter Nine

Knowing your own darkness is the best method
for dealing with the darknesses of other people.

—CARL JUNG

A laster had spent too many nights in the pub, and this night was no different. During the day, when customers demanded his attention, he could push his grief aside long enough to keep the store running. But once he shuttered the windows and barred the doors, the pain of his daughter's death surged back, heavy and suffocating. Rum was the only thing that dulled it.

When the pub called "last call," Alaster found himself forced to face the walk home—a home without his dear Donia. He staggered into the thick fog, managed to orient himself, and started down the street. At this hour, the town had gone quiet; only a few respectable souls still moved through the mist.

He stayed upright for a block and a half before bouncing off the front of a competitor's storefront. As he passed a narrow alley, a voice cut through the silence.

"Kempe, you are a sight."

A man stepped from the shadows, dressed plainly, keeping a polite distance from the inebriated merchant.

Alaster squinted. "Do I know you, sir?"

"We have crossed paths on occasion," the man replied, his baritone steady. "You don't seem well."

"If you know me, then you know the reason." Alaster's words came out sharp and uneven.

"I do know the reason." The stranger's voice softened. "My name is Julleg, Kempe. It hurt my heart to hear of your loss. Did they catch the bastard who did it?"

Alaster drew a breath that hitched halfway through. "They have not."

Julleg waited while Alaster steadied himself. "Kempe, I believe I can be of assistance."

Alaster focused on him, confused. "How can you help me? She is gone and buried."

Julleg stepped closer. "I know a man who will soon come into information that could ease your grief."

"Sure, he will." Alaster barked a humorless laugh. "He can't bring her back. Nobody can."

"You can never be too sure, Kempe. The knowledge this man gains may do just that."

Alaster laughed again, harsher this time. "If you believe that, you've had more rum than I have."

Julleg lowered his voice. "I know it sounds impossible. But tomorrow night, a monk will sit in the pub you just left and speak louder than he should about something called the Heart. Go there. Listen. If what he says matters to you, I will be in touch."

"How will you know if it matters to me?" Alaster tried to focus on the man's face.

Julleg smiled—a smile that made Alaster both excited and uneasy. "I will know. Remember: tomorrow night. And Kempe... stay off the bottle. You need a clear mind to hear what he says. Time is not on your side. Others are already preparing to find the prize."

With that, Julleg slipped into the fog-shrouded alley and vanished.

§♦

Kendra slept deeply that night in Mistdale. Early the next morning, her rest slipped into something deeper still. She found herself walking the streets of her birth-town, surrounded by childhood friends—no longer children now, but grown, moving through their adult lives.

Then an unfamiliar figure appeared on the main street. The young women around her stopped to stare, whispering excitedly, wondering where the stranger had come from. They pressed toward him, eager to make their interest known. Kendra looked more closely, trying to understand their fascination.

She froze.

Standing in front of the general store, surrounded by eager suitors, was Jack.

A hand shook her shoulder. Kendra jolted awake.

"Come on, Kendra. Madam Emeria already waits in the refining lab."

Kendra groaned and rolled away from the persistent student.

"Kendra, the sky will be light too soon now."

She finally pushed herself from the hard bed and dressed.

"Does she rise this early every day?"

"Yes. Now hurry." The student pulled her across the compound to the small building behind the sorting shed.

Kendra rushed through the door into the dimly lit blending lab. Madam Emeria, without looking up from the base potion she stirred, said only, "You are late. Do not let it happen again."

Kendra took her place across the bench. "Yes ma'am. I'll be prompt for future lessons."

Six bundles of herbs lay on the prep table. "I selected herbs with variable effects depending on preparation," Madam Emeria said. "These will give you a range of healing abilities as you travel with Master Jack."

She pointed to each bundle in turn.

"Willow bark—fever, inflammation, pain.
Lion-weed—digestion, skin irritation, internal
cleansing.
Flame Root—nausea and pain.
Meadow Mint—congestion.
Calm Breeze—nerves and sleep.

*Wayfarer's Leaf—wounds and bites, if not too
serious. Remember them."*

Kendra studied the herbs. Some she knew in their fresh
form, but she had assumed their effects remained constant.
Madam Emeria explained how preparation changed
everything—fresh, dried, powdered, infused—each step altering
the strength and nature of the treatment.

Kendra had never seen a lab like this. One area for
separating plants at harvest. Another for collecting seeds. Water
tables for wet preparation. A separate bar for infusions. Until
now, she had seen only a narrow gap between herbalist and
healer. Here, the difference widened.

After the infusion work, Madam Emeria ended the lesson.
"We stop here. Tomorrow, we begin the art of healing. It will be
unlike anything you have ever attempted." She left the lab
without saying another word.

True to her promise, Kendra arrived early the next morning.
She had already laid out the previous day's preparations when
Madam Emeria entered. The Master Healer arranged the
sachets, placed her hands lightly upon them, and spoke ancient
spells over each one.

Kendra saw no change, but Madam Emeria slumped slightly
as she finished. Her eyes were tired. "Label these carefully. The
spells define their effects, but there is no way to tell them apart
once mixed." She handed Kendra paper labels and ink.

Kendra marked each treatment as instructed while Madam
Emeria rested in a corner chair, drained from the work.

The next two days were spent with Kendra casting the spells
herself under the Master Healer's watchful eye. By the end of six
days, she had a satchel of treatments she had prepared with her

own hands—ready for the departure of Jack's companions in two days.

"Bartender, bring me another sloe brandy."

The young monk called from his corner table, voice already thick. He had arrived at the Temple only three weeks earlier but had quickly discovered where to find his favorite regional spirit.

Before the owner could turn, the monk added, "And leave the bottle."

The server brought the sweet, complex liquor and gathered the temple coins left on the table. Many merchants preferred the coin of the realm, but she knew the temple silver was purer. Jewelers paid extra for it, eager to melt it into fine rings and amulets.

Alaster sat on the stairs leading to the girls' rooms—not for their charms, but to escape the reminders of his daughter's death only weeks before. He avoided the expensive anise-flavored liquor, preferring simple rum for its blunt effect.

He sipped and watched the monk across the room. He wondered which order would accept a young man with such a taste for costly brandy. Most Brotherhood monks in this region wore rich brown robes. This one wore a simple gray-blue. Alaster made a mental note to ask the Temple priest when he next saw him.

The monk filled his glass again and drank freely, ranting just above the din.

"They talked about it like I wasn't there. In the open. They must not have seen me—but they are of my sect. I know the relic."

He took a long draw, anger tightening his face.

"I studied the relics," he shouted to no one in particular. "I know those parchments."

The owner approached the corner table. "Brother Amets, can you hold it down? I know they treated you poorly, but my patrons have their own troubles."

Brother Amets nodded. "I'm sorry, Jakob. I didn't mean to cause grief." He turned back to his drink, mumbling to himself.

Alaster's curiosity sharpened. He crossed the room.

"Do you mind if I join you?"

Amets looked up from his half-filled glass, nodded, and motioned to the empty chair. "How may I help you?" He had already learned that people always wanted something from monks.

Alaster sat and shook his head. "I thought you might want company." He raised his glass in salute and took a slow sip. "Sounds like you had a stressful day. Have you been posted to the Temple?"

"For the next year..." Amets drained his glass and reached for the bottle. "Some brandy. It's the deep sloe style."

Alaster declined with a gesture and signaled for more rum. "I'm not much of a brandy drinker. Thank you, though." He sipped. "Are you one of the academic monks?"

"So they tell me." Amets considered his words, then sipped instead of shouting. "There are three approaches at the Temple now. The priests focus on expanding orthodox thinking. One group of my order translates ancient texts only in ways that support the priests' goals." He glanced around the bustling room. "But a small group of us examines the sheets for more... complicated meanings."

Alaster leaned in. The mention of less orthodox parchments stirred something in him. "It sounded like you might have found something exciting."

Amets studied Alaster's face over the rim of his glass. "They found—something."

Alaster lowered his voice. "What did they find?"

Amets looked around again, then leaned closer.

"I shouldn't tell anyone this, but they confirmed the oldest parchment yet found. They say it is three millennia." His last words barely reached Alaster. "I heard there were seven sheets, but the document is incomplete. They estimate three are lost, and the rest are damaged by wear and pests."

Alaster hung on the monk's words. "What did these sheets speak of? Is it a relic?"

"You can't tell anyone—not even your whore."

Amets glanced around the room, lowering his voice. "Maybe we should retire to the drawing room."

Alaster barked a laugh. "They have one of those in a place like this?"

Amets stood, steadying himself, and led the way through a side door. "There is need for confidential business discussions, even in a brothel."

The smaller back room offered a quiet refuge from the chaos of the Great Room and the girls' quarters above. Brother Amets carried his bottle of brandy with him and sat at the central table.

"I was in a back nook reading some two-thousand-year-old sheets when I heard someone enter." Amets leaned forward. "Two of my brothers came in but didn't bother to check if they were alone. They had been discussing their morning research. They were looking for ancient documents to support the priests' push to inject the Temple deeper into everyday life—and they stumbled on the oldest parchment they had ever seen."

He took a slow sip. "The parchment spoke of an ancient relic, from the days when the gods walked the land. A relic that could change the face of the world."

Alaster's eyes widened. "Change the world how?"

"That was their debate." Amets's voice grew animated. "The younger brother spoke of restoring the land to its former glory— bountiful harvests, unquestionable miracles. Even healings of fatal ailments and resurrection of the dead."

He raised a hand. "I swear, that is exactly what he said. But the relic he spoke of has been lost to us."

"How did it become lost? Did the gods lose it?" Alaster's voice rose.

"There are myths," Amets said, "that one of the gods let his anger build after being excluded from the plans for the land." He drew a breath. "According to that myth, the god slipped into the Chamber of Blessings one night, after the others had celebrated with women and wine. He stole the relic, hid it in a leather sack, and vanished by morning—taking the Heart of Sheol with him."

Alaster frowned. He had never heard the name. "Brother Amets, what is Sheol?"

Amets chuckled. "I forgot the Temple scrubbed all mention of Sheol from the parchments. Sheol was the ancient name of Eldriko." He poured the last of the brandy. "It no longer exists. Seven thousand years ago, some disaster struck the islands of Sheol, and they slipped beneath the waves. A perpetual fog bank hides the region now—hundreds of square leagues."

"Did they say where this Heart of Sheol is located?"

Amets laughed. "Only hints and clues in the ancient tongue." He studied Alaster's expression. "You aren't thinking of searching for the relic. It's a fool's errand."

"But you said you had the parchment..."

"I said two of my brothers read the parchment in one of the archival rooms." Amets tilted his head. "Why would you want to find this relic? How would it help you?"

Alaster drew a long breath and told him of his daughter's death. "With the Heart, I could resurrect my Donia. I could bring her back."

Amets shook his head. "That's part of the myth. I don't think it ever existed."

"But," Alaster blurted, "what if it DID exist? What if you could find it? What would you gain by discovering the epic relic of ages past—the gem of the gods?"

Brother Amets Izar suddenly felt sober. What if he discovered the Heart of Sheol?

6♦

Scott laid the bags of dried beans on the shelf in the storage room and looked over their accumulating supplies. He nodded with satisfaction. As they gathered what they needed, he kept a close eye on weight and bulk, reminding Jack and Asta that they had to balance immediate needs with their ability to restock and forage on the trail. Even with the deadline looming, he felt good about their progress.

As Scott locked the storeroom, Jack and Asta were finishing their daily sword practice. Jack picked up his bow and sent five arrows into the straw targets, each one landing in the center rings. Scott smiled. Any brigand closing on their team would regret it if Jack had his bow in hand.

Then it struck him: he had been focused on food stores, but not on their defensive supplies. His military training had drilled that instinct into him. Jack was closing the gaps in his own training. Asta, as a ranger, clearly knew her weapons. Ronan faced predators and bandits often enough to be competent. But Kendra... Scott had never seen her hold a bow or a sword.

He needed to evaluate everyone's readiness.

Scott walked over to Jack. "Hey LT, looking good. You could drop a bear at fifty paces."

Jack grinned. "What did I tell you about calling me LT. We aren't in the army anymore."

Scott shrugged. "Old habits, ya' know." He handed Jack another arrow. "I was thinking—you and I are good with our weapons, and so are Asta and Ronan. But what about Kendra?"

Jack lowered his bow. "She's a healer in training, Scott."

"I know, LT. But things go sideways once weapons are drawn. She needs a basic understanding of how to protect herself."

Jack studied him, then nodded. "Do you think she needs a sword like mine?"

"That would be too much. But I've seen some of the Manos carry short swords. That will help her if someone gets close—if we train her." Scott paused. "And she needs a bow. She might not hit anything, but if attackers are dodging her arrows, they might not see ours." He grinned.

Jack considered it. "That might be best. Can you handle it? I have to meet with Teyr in an hour."

"Sure thing, LT." Scott grinned when Jack rolled his eyes. "I'll talk to Asta. She knows all the best vendors."

He found Asta behind the smith's shop, sharpening her longsword. "I love that sword of yours," he said. "Where did you find it?"

Without looking up, she grinned. "You can find them anywhere in Mistdale. Manos smiths forge the finest blades in the world."

Scott chuckled at her pride. "I need a good short sword. Who should I talk to?"

Asta paused, smirking. "Is that not too short for a man of your stature?"

"Not for me. It's for Kendra. She's armed only with a dagger. That needs to change." He glanced around. "She'll need a short bow too. Something light—under forty pounds, maybe thirty-five."

Asta wiped her blade clean and oiled it. "I know just the place. Come with me."

She led him through the market streets, turning toward a narrow building near the city armory. She entered without knocking. The shop was deeper than it looked—a sales room, a woodworking area for bows, a forge in the back, and stairs leading up to living quarters.

A gray-haired man stepped in from the rear. "Asta! It's been a long time. What can I get you? Nothing happened to that sword I sold you last year, I hope."

Asta drew the blade and handed it to him. "Good as the day you sold it, Varen."

He examined it and returned it. "Not a nick. Are you wearing it just for show?"

She smothered a laugh. "You know better, Varen Katars. I have no hesitation in killing someone who deserves it." She sheathed the sword. "My friend needs weapons. Teyr has commissioned us for a task."

Varen turned to Scott. "And this gentleman is...?"

Asta flushed. "Sorry. This is Scott Boudreau, one of the Offlanders leading the expedition."

"An Offlander. That is a surprise." Varen looked at Asta. "And Teyr authorized this band?"

"She did more than authorize it," Asta said. "She selected us. We leave in two days."

Scott pulled out his notebook. "Master Katars, I have a list. I'm not sure how I can pay for all this."

Varen waved him off. "If Teyr Elenya authorized it, I'll send the invoice to her council office. They'll pay. What do you need?"

They worked through the list. Varen didn't carry arrows but directed Scott to a nearby fletcher. Asta packed the weapons carefully before they left.

On the way to the fletcher, Scott asked, "Did he mean that— about billing the council?"

Asta grinned. "That's common in Mistdale. If the council commissions a project, they cover the costs. Mother may even give Jack a letter of credit."

The fletcher said the same thing as he filled out an invoice. Asta winked at Scott.

After they left, Scott shook his head. "I wish I knew this earlier. I owe the supply house owner three hours of weeding for what I bought this morning."

Asta laughed. "All right, Scott, I'll help you clear her garden. I should have told you sooner—the council funds essential projects." She swatted his shoulder.

Chapter Ten

There is no security on this earth; there is only opportunity.

—Douglas MacArthur

Mistdale woke early. First light caught on the bright Fairmen wagons that had slipped into town during the night, and the green filled quickly with voices. Children darted between the tents, calling to one another as if the festival had already begun. Adults moved with purpose, setting out goods and preparing for a day of bargaining with the craftsmen who traveled the roads in color and song. Whatever plans the townsfolk held for the morning dissolved the moment the caravan appeared.

Kendra rose to the sound of children urging their parents toward the fields where music was already drifting. By the time she stepped outside, the sturdy wagons had unfolded into compact shops, their canopies bright against the pale sky. She recognized the flags at once—Ander Ernaut had come.

She found Jack on the training grounds, working through a quiet sequence with his blade.

"Jack," she called. "Ander is here. He must have arrived before dawn."

Jack lowered his sword and turned. "Ander? The one who traded me those first broadheads?"

"Yes. He wanted a closer look at your bow." Her smile gave away her excitement. "I wonder if he managed to copy the design. Come on."

Jack sheathed the blade and followed her toward the trading grounds. Kendra headed straight for Ander's wagon, but he spotted them first and waved them over with both hands.

"Kendra! Jack! When did ye come in?" Ander's grin widened as he looked at Jack. "I've something to show ye. Come, come."

He hurried to the back of his wagon, rummaging through crates as he spoke. "I dinnae expect ye so soon, but I finished it. It's here somewhere." He muttered to himself, shifting bundles aside until he let out a triumphant sound. "Aha. There ye are."

He drew out a wrapped bundle with surprising care and set it on a camp table.

Kendra glanced at Jack before asking, "What is it, Ander?"

"A project that took longer than I'd hoped," Ander said, already unwrapping the cloth. "More complex than I expected, even for me." He pulled the last layer free.

A bow lay in his hands—not merely functional but crafted with reverence. The shape echoed Jack's compound bow, yet the Fairmen artistry transformed it into something finer.

Jack stared. "That's... astonishing."

The riser bore delicate engravings that looked like runes, though Jack could not read them. Ander offered the bow with both hands.

"Try her, Jack. I hope she meets the standards of your own."

Jack accepted the bow as though it might vanish. He glanced toward the training grounds. "Let's see how she shoots."

Ander gathered a handful of arrows and followed. Jack stepped to the line, nocked one, and drew. The bow settled into his grip as if it belonged there. He held for a breath, then released.

"Oh," he murmured. "That's smooth."

The arrow struck just low and right, easy enough to correct. He loosed another, and this one landed an inch off center.

"How strong is the pull?" he asked.

"Same full weight as yours—sixty pounds—but I found a way to increase the let-off another ten percent," Ander said, pride warming his voice. "Are the pulleys smooth enough?"

Jack nodded, still studying the bow. "Smoother than anything I've handled." He hesitated. "I'm almost afraid to ask, but... how much?"

Ander's grin returned. "I dinnae think I can sell her. She already has an owner."

Kendra caught the flicker of disappointment on Jack's face— and the mischief in Ander's. "And who might that be? Perhaps we can bargain with him."

"Kendra, my dear, the owner holds her now." Ander gestured to Jack. "She belongs to him."

Jack's head came up sharply. "What? I can't—"

Ander cut him off with a firm wave. "Ye can, and ye will. I'd take refusal as an insult. I've already sold two others to Manos rangers. This one is the prototype—my tribute for letting me study your Offlander bow." His expression softened. "Please, Jack. Accept it."

Jack looked down at the craftsmanship, the engravings, the care in every line. "Then I'm honored. Truly."

Kendra nodded toward the refreshment tent. "Come on. We should toast this collaboration." She was already walking. "My treat."

They found a small table in the corner and settled in. Jack spoke cautiously about his upcoming journey, keeping to the guidance Teyr had given him. Whenever he strayed too near dangerous details, Kendra nudged his leg under the table and redirected the conversation.

"The Manos want us to search for a lost artifact," she said lightly. "Something important to them."

Ander leaned in. "I've heard rumors. Someone else is hunting a Manos treasure."

Kendra and Jack both looked up, surprise flickering before they masked it.

"What kind of treasure?" Kendra asked, sipping her mead as though the question was idle.

"That I dinnae know," Ander said. "Only that a merchant down south and some mad monk have taken up the chase. I doubt they understand what they're after. They heard the word treasure and ran."

Kendra let out a slow breath, hiding her relief behind her mug. "I hope they keep to their own path. May the gods send them to Ostorn, and may a storm keep them there." She winced at her own words, murmured a quiet prayer for forgiveness, and hoped those other adventurers were not seeking the same Manos relic.

❦

The river moved gently past Mistdale, its slow current winding toward the western sea. Beyond the town walls, the plains opened into fields and scattered stands of trees, the water threading quietly between them. Scott and Asta had found a small grove about four hundred paces from the western gate, and in the late afternoons they walked there, speaking through the final preparations for their journey.

"I think we're close," Scott said, checking the small notebook he carried. "The storeroom's four-fifths full. Can you think of anything else we need to secure?"

Asta shook her head. "We have a strong stockpile already." She glanced at him. "But I want every weapon inspected before we leave. Even Jack's new bow." A faint grin touched her mouth; she knew exactly how Jack would react to that suggestion.

Scott laughed. "I'll leave that to you. I'm not foolish enough to threaten his favorite weapon." They followed the curve of the riverbank, the light softening through the trees. "Once, I had to take his rifle for a few hours to make repairs. You'd have thought I was stealing a child's toy. Lord."

Asta laughed at the image. "Do all your warriors form such attachments to their... rifles?"

"Some did," Scott said. "Most saw them as tools. But Jack's rifle saved too many in his company. It became part of him." His expression softened. "He cared for his men. When one was hurt—or killed—he took it as a wound to his own family."

Asta slowed. "Personally?"

"Yes. If you harmed someone under his command, you harmed him. And he made sure the cost was felt."

They walked on, the woods thinning toward the fields. Then Scott stopped abruptly.

A man stood only a few paces ahead—dressed in unfamiliar native clothing—and before either of them could speak, he collapsed with a cry.

"NO—!" The shout broke off as he hit the ground and went still.

Scott dropped beside him, checking pulse and breath. "He's alive." He searched for wounds and found only deep, strange bruising.

Asta knelt opposite him. "He still breathes." She touched the man's side. "Scott... have you seen bruising like this?"

Scott nodded grimly. "Back on Earth. When a fast, heavy vehicle struck someone. It often killed them."

Asta looked at him, her voice low. "Perhaps it did. On Earth, I mean." She brushed the man's clothing. "I've never seen garments like these."

"I have," Scott said. "At festivals for the indigenous peoples where I'm from. They wore traditional dress, and others came to watch and buy their crafts."

The young man groaned, eyes fluttering open. He stared at Scott, then Asta, confusion widening into fear.

"Who are you? Where am I?"

Scott helped him sit, offering a waterskin. "What do you remember?"

The man studied him for a long moment before answering. "I was at an event... I think. Then a pickup truck plowed into the crowd. I saw Beth flip over as it hit us, and then—" His brow tightened. "Am I dead?"

Scott lowered his head slightly. "You might be. What's your name? Where are you from?"

"I'm Nathan Martin, from the Finger Lakes." His voice trembled. "Who are you?"

"My name is Scott Boudreau," he said. "I came here about a year ago." Scott sat beside Nathan, arms resting loosely on his knees.

"A year?" Nathan looked between Scott and Asta, trying to anchor himself. "Where did you come from?"

Scott exhaled slowly. "You're not going to believe me. But it's the truth."

He explained what he knew—the accident, the impossible transition, the strange world they now stood in. Asta added details where Scott's knowledge thinned, her voice calm and measured. Nathan listened without interrupting, his expression shifting between disbelief and dawning fear. When Scott finally fell silent, the weight of the moment settled between them.

Nathan studied their faces. "At first, I thought you were lying. But you're too sincere for that." He hesitated. "Which leaves the possibility that you're both crazy... but that doesn't seem likely either." He looked around at the unfamiliar landscape. "Can't say I arrived on the best day of the year. When does the sun come out?"

Asta frowned and glanced at Scott. "What does he mean?"

Scott shook his head lightly. "He's talking about weather. And Nathan... this is a beautiful summer day. It doesn't get much better than this. It can get a whole lot worse."

Asta touched Scott's arm. "Enough for now."

But Nathan shook his head. "No. I need to know what's happening."

"You know the worst of it already," Scott said gently. "You died back on Earth. From what you described that truck killed more than one person." He reached into his pack and offered a piece of fruit. "Eat. It'll help with the soreness. When we get back to the city, a healer can look you over."

Nathan followed Scott's gesture toward the distant white towers. "Where... am I?"

Asta rested a hand lightly on his arm. "Near the city of Mistdale. On my world—Eldriko."

Nathan stared at them both as if they had escaped from an asylum.

Scott gave a sympathetic half-smile. "I know. I thought they were all crazy when I first got here too." He offered his hand. "Come on. Let's get you on your feet."

Nathan rose unsteadily, bracing himself.

"Careful," Scott said. "It takes a few days to get your land legs. Try a few steps. If you can't walk, I'll run back for a horse."

Nathan took a few tentative strides, then steadied. "I think I can manage. It's only... what, a quarter mile?"

"About that," Scott said. "We'll go slow."

They walked toward the city, Nathan turning his head constantly, trying to take in the strangeness of his new world. As they neared the gate, a ginger-haired pixie darted toward them.

"Kendra," Scott called, "easy. He just arrived, and he's bruised up."

Kendra slowed, but her words came in a rapid cascade. "What happened, where are you hurt, when did you get here—"

Nathan opened his mouth to answer, but she was already halfway through her next question.

Scott stepped between them. "Kendra. Slow down. He's confused enough. And yes, I already told him he's dead." He gave her a crooked grin.

She shot him a cold look. "I swear you enjoy telling people that."

Nathan blinked. "You've told others they're dead?"

Scott laughed. "You should've seen my old lieutenant's face."

Kendra shook her head and began examining Nathan with practiced efficiency. "Stand still. I won't hurt you." She checked for injuries without disturbing his clothing. "Nothing too serious for a new Offlander." She met his eyes. "But you should see my mentor for a proper scan."

Scott sighed softly. "Look, I know this is a lot. There are other Offlanders in our company. Travel with us until you decide what you want to do."

Nathan nodded slowly, then turned to Kendra. "What's an Offlander?"

❦

The oil lamp cast a dim, wavering circle across the table deep in the library archives. Beyond that small pool of light, the stacks dissolved into shadow. Alaster returned with his bull's-eye lamp, its narrow beam cutting briefly through the gloom as he retrieved the next volume Amets had requested. They had spent five days searching for any trace of the artifact Amets had mentioned when they first met.

When Alaster pulled a leather-bound tome from the shelf, a cloud of dust rose and made him sneeze.

Amets set aside the book he had been reviewing and opened the new one near its end. "This may be the one." He read in silence, pausing now and then jotting a note in his journal. After several minutes, he exhaled sharply. "Just when I think we've found something, another collapse." His lips tightened as he turned a few more pages. "No. Nothing else. They give me a hint, and then the trail vanishes." He closed the book with a soft thud. "Come. Let's take a break. It should be dinnertime at the pub."

Alaster followed him through the stacks. The monk moved with the ease of someone who had spent a lifetime in this labyrinth; Alaster knew he would be lost within minutes without him. By the time they stepped out of the Temple, darkness had settled over the city.

They took their usual table at the back of the pub and ordered the stew of the day. Alaster ate slowly, lost in thought.

"We're not making any progress," he said at last. "Did we find anything useful today?"

Amets considered as he sipped his mead. "Perhaps." He frowned looking into the mug. "No—not today. Two days ago." He nodded to himself. "Yes. There was something about a relic of power... or life. I didn't pay it much mind at the time."

Alaster's irritation flared. "Why dismiss it?"

"The text was interesting enough," Amets said, tearing a piece of bread, "but it came from the later journals of Brother Dorren Orgado. No one reads those anymore."

The pub was filling with supper patrons. An old man took the table behind them. Alaster lowered his voice. "Why? Was he a heretic?"

Amets laughed. "Nothing so dramatic. His mind failed him in his later years. Events from an hour earlier vanished, yet he could recall things from forty years past as if they'd happened that morning. His early writings are revered. His later ones... less so."

"I see," Alaster said, annoyance still in his tone. "But what caught your eye?"

"A description—or something like one—of a place where a relic was said to rest. He didn't name the relic, but he gave a location, if you can call it that." Amets leaned forward. "He wrote that it lay 'hidden in the grotto of the queen of the heir of life in the shadowy vale.' Traditionally, that refers to mythical repositories of forgotten artifacts. But some in the Nyehtor Aneglur claim such phrases point to literal places, cryptic though they are."

Alaster glanced toward the next table before returning his attention to Amets. "Who are the Nyehtor Aneglur?"

Amets took another bite of stew. "This venison is fresh today." He swallowed. "The Nyehtor Aneglur are the most orthodox of my order. They hold all obscure things as literal truth. If there is ever a dispute among us, they take one side, and most of the rest of the Brotherhood takes the other."

A gravelly voice cut into their quiet conversation. "Never held with the Nyehtor Aneglur myself—too 'holier than thou' for my taste."

The old man at the next table continued eating, apparently unaware that he had intruded.

Alaster glared. "Excuse me. Do you mind? This is a private conversation."

The man didn't look up. "Shouldn't have had it in a crowded pub then, should ya?"

Alaster's temper rose, but Amets placed a calming hand on his shoulder. "Peace, my friend. He meant no harm." He turned to the stranger. "Are you a student of the Aneglur?"

"Read a bit of their public writings." The man sipped his mead. "Like most religions—some worth keeping, some hog slop."

Amets smiled. "A common sentiment. Some of our brothers accept disagreement more easily than others. The Umari Aneglur are more flexible than the rest."

A faint smile crossed the old man's face. "Glad to hear it. Name's Fred Dietz." He raised his mug.

"Amets," the monk replied, lifting his own. "And my quick-tempered friend is Alaster."

Dietz nodded. "Sounds like you're searching for something in that Temple library. Not much help, is it?"

"No," Alaster muttered.

"What was that, sonny?" Dietz grinned, pleased to have drawn him back in.

Alaster cleared his throat. "I said the library hasn't been much help."

"Didn't think so. Libraries like that always censor what they don't approve of." Dietz shook his head. "Happened where I came from, too. Frustrating as hell."

Alaster's expression softened. "You know truth when you see it."

Dietz took another drink. "There's a place—an archive of sorts—about two days from here. And I can promise you the staff won't give ya any trouble." His grin widened, knowing he had caught Alaster's interest.

Chapter Eleven

*Live as if you were to die tomorrow. Learn as if
you were to live forever.*

—Mahatma Gandhi

A light breeze moved through the hickory stand southeast of Mistdale, setting the crowns of the trees into a gentle sway. The storms from the night before had shaken loose several branches, scattering fresh wood across the forest floor. Jack welcomed the find; hickory added a rich flavor to his smoked venison. He pulled his handcart behind him, already half-filled with what he jokingly called his wooden gold. If he worked quickly, he could smoke one last batch of jerky before leaving on his journey.

He loved mornings like this—alone, outside the city walls, surrounded by the quiet pulse of nature. Even Mistdale, pleasant as it was, could not match the peace he found in the open air. The scents met him first: loamy soil, early wildflowers, the soft decay of last year's leaves. Every fragrance carried him back to the farm on Earth. Of all the memories he had recovered, those were the ones that brought him the deepest calm.

He reached for a fallen branch when something shifted. A new scent cut through the familiar ones—sharp, foreign, wrong. His breath quickened. His heart thudded hard against his ribs. He scanned the woods for danger, but nothing moved.

Jack froze, staring into the trees he considered a second home. His vision began to change. The world around him blurred at the edges, his focus narrowing past the hickories, past the plains, past the horizon itself. A tunnel-vision sensation closed around him, and a scene formed within it: a young red-haired woman, her eyes darting in panic as three men closed in on her.

Her mouth moved, but Jack heard nothing. One of the men reached for her, and only her quick sidestep saved her from his touch. The trio taunted her, herding her toward a place she could not escape.

The vignette tightened. Jack felt himself pulled into the moment, the peaceful glade falling away. A predator's spirit surged through him—swift, focused, unyielding. He watched through eyes that were not his own as he lunged toward the tormentors with startling speed. A growl filled his ears, vibrating through his chest as he struck.

The three men broke instantly, fleeing in different directions without looking back. The woman remained rooted in place, trembling, then collapsed to the ground in sobs.

Jack saw her shaking. He felt himself—or the creature whose eyes he borrowed—move closer, stopping about ten paces away. He scanned the field for renewed danger, but the brigands had vanished into the distance.

The woman's sobs quieted. She lifted her head and looked toward him, fear still etched across her face. Jack wanted to speak comfort, but no words came.

He turned toward the woods. The body he inhabited rose—lower to the ground than his own—and trotted toward the shelter of the trees. At the edge of the forest, he looked back. The woman stood now, watching him disappear into the thicket.

Jack blinked.

He stood beneath the hickories, the branch still in his hand. The vignette faded. His breathing slowed. His heartbeat settled. The scents of the forest returned to their familiar balance. He looked toward the plains, but saw no one—no woman, no brigands, nothing.

When the visions first began, he had feared for his sanity. Over time, he learned to recognize the signs: the shift in scent, the narrowing of sight, the sense of stepping sideways into another layer of reality. The perspective was always lower—one to two feet off the ground.

He gathered the remaining hickory branches and returned to Mistdale. After storing them, he made his way to the council chambers to ask if Teyr could spare a moment. Delon Oakel appeared from the front office and ushered him inside.

"Jack, it is so good to see you." Teyr crossed from her desk and embraced him. "You must be getting excited about your impending departure. How are your preparations?"

Jack smiled politely. "We are almost ready, Madam Chief. It looks like tomorrow morning will see us on our way." He sat in the chair offered and drew a steadying breath. "Madam Chief, I meant to ask you when I first arrived. Asta wanted me to talk with you about something, and I forgot."

Teyr studied him. "If Asta suggested you ask me about something, it was not something to be forgotten. What is on your mind, Jack?"

Jack looked down at the rug beneath his feet—a woven scene of Mistdale's flora and fauna. "Since I first came to your world, I've been having daydreams, uh, visions, I guess."

Teyr leaned forward, waiting. When he hesitated, she guided him gently. "What visions do you see, Jack?"

"I'm in a real place, sometimes alone and other times in someone's company. The scene slowly takes an unnatural appearance. Once I saw only the center clear and bright while the edges had dark outlines, forcing my eye to the subject. Another time, it looked like I was in an art gallery or..." He glanced at the rug. "Like I was viewing something like this rug."

Teyr nodded. "Was your angle of vision similar to overseeing the scene, or did you see the land from a different perspective?"

"It was between one and two feet off the ground. Is that important?"

"It could be." Teyr stood and stepped closer. "Jack, do you remember our first meeting?"

"Of course, how could I forget that."

"I would like to read your aura like I did that day with your permission."

Jack nodded. "Yes, Madam Chief, you may." He closed his eyes. Her hands cupped his cheeks, and a gentle current of power flowed between them.

After several minutes, she spoke softly. "Jack, keep your eyes closed for a few minutes and just breathe deeply. When you are ready, I want you to focus on your most inner spirit, which makes you truly Jack in every sense, understand?"

Time passed—more than he expected. Finally, he whispered, "Madam Chief, I am ready."

Teyr's voice softened further. "When you open your eyes, I want you to look at my rug. Don't rush your feelings. Let them come. Look at every visible part of the rug, then tell me when you are ready."

Jack opened his eyes and studied the rug as if seeing it anew. He scanned the scenes, then leaned in, absorbing the details. At last, he looked up. "I'm ready. What now?"

Teyr smiled—a smile that did not entirely reassure him. "I have one question only. When you looked at my rug, what caught your attention the most?"

Jack looked down again, to the right of center, above a hickory tree in autumn color, to the small animal dancing at the forest's edge. "Him! I can't get him out of my mind."

Teyr nodded with a quiet sigh. "Yes. Of course that is what you are drawn to as your spirit. The Trickster. The Wise One. The Mystic."

"What does that mean?" Jack leaned back, startled and uneasy.

Teyr regarded him with layered emotion. "Your spirit is playful and skilled but directed by the Chaotic magic. Life will not come to you in an effortless way. It will lead you down difficult paths and through dangerous trails. Your companions are blessed that your spirit oversees their journeys as well as your own. But the Chaos of your inner magic overpowers their magic of Control. Take care through your quest. Great blessings come at great cost."

Jack blinked. "Maybe I shouldn't take this journey."

Teyr shook her head. "No, Jack, it is your destiny, as it is of your companions. Those who survive will find great treasure, but not necessarily in wealth or in personal growth. Take care, my son. And keep Asta close. She recognizes the hidden dangers more than you think."

§♦

The next morning began before light filtered through the high clouds. Mistdale stirred early, its inhabitants hurrying to make final purchases from the Fairmen before the caravan rolled out. The Fairmen themselves moved with their usual organized frenzy—tents collapsing, canvas rolled and stowed, wagons repacked with practiced efficiency. Even the children, normally wild with play, lent their hands to the work of departure.

From her office window, Teyr watched the controlled chaos unfold, her gaze lingering on Jack's part of the morning circus. Jack and Scott were loading bulky supplies onto the side of Ander's wagon at the Fairman's insistence. Asta organized the pack horses, with Nathan providing the muscle. Kendra sat alone at a small table, sorting and resorting her herbs into packs and saddlebags. Jalianna Emeria, Mistdale's High Healer, arrived with two pouches of freshly distilled tinctures.

Dawn crept in from the east, soft light revealing the caravan as a beehive preparing to swarm. Final crates were secured to wagon sides. Panels were closed and locked. Ander walked the length of the train, reminding older children to keep pace and lifting the youngest into their wagons beside mothers or aunts.

The men walked alongside, eyes sharp for problems before they could grow.

Teyr soon stepped outside to bid them farewell. She thanked Ander, as always, for his service and friendship. Then she turned to Jack as he joined the Fairman.

"I will admit that I have come to recognize you as the son I could not give my Jassinn." She looked westward. "Take care, Jack. The road may seem secure, but dangers abound. Even our archives are not as welcoming as one might think. Like most of the orthodox of Erathan Temples, factions exist with their own agenda. Asta can help you navigate those breakers." Her gaze softened into something somber. "May the gods guide your path. Not many know this, but all Eldriko depends on the success of your journey. Farewell, my son."

She turned to Asta and embraced her—a rare gesture. She whispered something, and Asta nodded. "I will—I promise." Asta kissed Teyr's cheek before mounting her gray horse. Teyr returned to the council chambers; she believed the roadside farewells belonged to the mothers of the realm, not the Madam Chief of the Manos.

The city shrank behind them as the caravan rolled toward the next town, three days' distance. Western Asher held fewer settlements, but the occasional hamlet offered fresh produce and a brief rest. Children spilled from wagons at each stop, running free for an hour before the road called them back.

Jack took his place along the left flank of the train, moving from front to back, watching for danger. Into his second hour, he noticed the lop-eared coyote—the one who had become a familiar shadow. The animal trotted along the southern side of Jack's patrol.

"So, you decided to come back, did you?" Jack kept his voice level. "Did you see anything interesting out there, hmm?" He smiled at himself for talking to a wild creature. "I'm not crazy, you know. It just gets a little lonely on guard duty."

The road stretched on. Jack's thoughts drifted to his companions. Scott—steady, proven in battle. Asta—a ranger whose skill revealed itself more each day. Ronan—someone he barely knew, but Scott trusted him, and that was enough. Nathan—new to Eldriko, still finding his footing.

The coyote kept pace as Jack rode his circuit. Jack's mind turned toward the one companion he hadn't yet sorted.

"What about Kendra?" he murmured, not realizing he'd spoken aloud until the coyote tilted his head and yipped.

"What? Okay, I know she is easy to look at, and she never holds back with camp chores. I admit that I like talking with her." He fell silent, lost in thought.

The coyote trotted beside him, ears flicking. Jack glanced down. "If we are going to be friends, I can't just call you coyote, can I? And Wile E. just seems wrong." He grinned. "How about Loki? Does that fit you?"

The coyote skipped a few steps before settling back into his gait.

"What do I do about Kendra, Loki?" Jack asked quietly. "She's done a lot for me, but was it just like caring for a lost kitten? I don't know." He scanned the left flank, glancing toward Kendra as she rode beside Ander's wagon, speaking with her old friend. "She is so welcoming and accepted by everyone she meets."

A light rain began to fall. Jack pulled his over-jacket close. "She always looks to help, so it makes sense she wishes to train as a healer. You know what I mean, right?" Loki looked up at him now and then, as if listening. Jack chuckled. "Of course, you can't know what I mean. You are a coyote. Boy, do I feel silly now, but you are such a good listener."

He tossed a piece of jerky to Loki, who snapped it up the moment it hit the ground.

"If you don't mind, I may talk with you about things I can't share with anyone else." Jack began humming a tune from some distant memory. Ahead, Ander steered his wagon toward a grassy clearing near the river, signaling a midday halt. As Jack turned his horse toward the wagons, Loki slipped into a nearby copse of trees.

ॐ

Each day blended into the next, as it often did for Fairmen traveling between villages. Their rhythm was steady: break camp at first light, ride until midday, rest briefly, then continue through the afternoon. Adults drove the draft teams while others watched the horizon for danger. After the midday halt, Ander signaled the caravan forward again, the road to New Dodge stretching a day and a half ahead. The wagons rolled on, and the younger Fairmen walked or played beside them, keeping pace with the easy joy of those born to the road.

A child's scream shattered the routine.

"BRIGANDS!"

Small fingers pointed toward a copse of trees to the north. Fifteen horsemen burst from the tree line, accelerating from a trot to a full gallop as they angled toward the wagons.

137

Fairmen defenders appeared instantly, bows in hand, arrows loosed in rapid succession. Asta targeted the lead rider, assuming him the commander; he toppled from the saddle. The attackers faltered for a heartbeat, searching for a new leader, then pressed on.

Ronan released an arrow but misjudged the rider's speed; it passed harmlessly behind him. More brigands fired from horseback with unsettling accuracy. Asta saw a woman to her left release an arrow—then fall, an enemy shaft buried in her breast.

Ander leapt from his wagon, drawing and releasing two arrows in swift succession, dropping another attacker. Children scrambled to the wagons, handing arrows to the adults defending them. Nathan, armed only with the Iroquois bow that had crossed over with him, targeted the closest threats. An arrow struck his left shoulder, staggering him. He seized a fallen tent pole, braced it in the earth, and met a charging brigand with a desperate thrust—the improvised lance pierced the rider's chest.

The Fairmen, seasoned by past attacks, began to turn the tide. Ander counted six brigands down, with three more wavering in their saddles. Then two Fairmen riders swept in from east and west, releasing arrows as fast as they could. Their shots had limited effect, but the sudden pressure from two new angles broke the assault.

Six unwounded brigands scattered in different directions. One took an arrow in the back and fell, his horse galloping on without him.

Jack and Scott, now riding together, pursued for only thirty paces before returning to the wagons. The Fairmen moved with practiced efficiency, assessing damage and tending to the wounded. Kendra rushed forward with her pack, triaging injuries. She passed over minor wounds and focused on those she might save. Two Fairmen lay beyond her help. With no time to grieve, she moved on.

Ander directed the drivers to form a defensive circle. Jack and Scott organized the burial detail. The Fairmen dead received a respectful ceremony; the brigands' bodies sparked a heated debate. In the end, the men agreed to drag the brigands into the woods and leave them unmarked and unspoken for.

Evening settled around the wagon circle. Adults spoke quietly while children played within the safe ring of wagons. Kendra overheard several Fairmen remark that it had been many years since brigands dared attack a caravan. The last such assault had driven the Fairmen back to their enclave in southern Asher for two months, halting trade across the continent until nobles united to drive the brigands into the eastern mountains. Their numbers had dwindled to a quarter of what they once were.

Ander set sentries with stern warnings to stay alert. The camp quieted. Kendra sat by the fire with Jack.

"Do you think they will come back?"

Jack considered the question. "I guess it depends on several things. Do they think we are really that strong or do they think it was a fluke?"

Kendra looked up. "A fluke?"

"Yeah, you know—did we get lucky in beating them?" He stared into his mug of chicory. "Maybe we did, but we won't know sitting in the dark." He stood and reached for his sword, turning toward the perimeter.

Kendra rose quickly and grabbed his arm. "You can't go out there, Jack. You have been up and on alert for eighteen hours. You need your sleep."

Jack pulled free. "I'll sleep in the saddle tomorrow." He walked into the darkness.

Chapter Twelve

And fate? No one alive has ever escaped it.

—Homer

Morning revealed a high overcast as the fog lifted from the plains. Scott rode the left flank of the wagons with heightened vigilance after the previous day's attack. It appeared the surviving brigands had decided to give the caravan a wide berth, but Scott trusted caution more than hope. The road ahead led toward another village where the Fairmen planned to trade for two days.

Half an hour earlier, he had noticed a small clump of trees about forty paces off the road. Something in the shadows had moved—nothing threatening, but enough to keep his attention fixed on it. He angled his horse closer, reins loose in his hand.

As he neared the tree line, he saw her: a woman trying to hide behind a trunk far too narrow to conceal her. He rode a few more paces, then dismounted, letting the reins drag so the horse would stay put. He walked parallel to the woods, not looking directly at her.

"It looks like you are a long way from home." His voice carried across the open field, but he kept his gaze forward, careful not to startle her.

She pulled back behind the tree. A small voice drifted out. "I-I am."

Scott turned slightly toward her. "Have you been out here long?"

She peeked around the trunk, and Scott saw what he expected—an Offlander, and a newly arrived one. "A week, I think. I don't know where 'here' is."

Scott faced her fully now. "If you're looking for food, I've got some trail rations with me." He held out a pouch of deer jerky. Seeing her hesitation, he softened his tone. "I'll tell you what, I'll set this right here and wait with my horse. You can come and get it if you want. I won't try anything. Just leave the pouch, would you?"

He set the bag on the ground, walked back to his horse, and picked up the reins. When he turned, she was already at the pouch.

"What should I call you?"

She sniffed the jerky, took a tentative bite, then devoured it. "My name's Lily," she said through a full mouth. "Who are you?"

He smiled. "Scott. I'm Scott. I'm riding cover for that caravan over there. Traders, mostly."

She glanced toward the road. "You're a trader?" She pulled another piece of jerky and finished it quickly.

Scott chuckled. "No ma'am, not me. But we are traveling with them. They're good people, and traveling in a group is safer." His expression dimmed. "We got attacked by brigands yesterday. We drove them off but lost a few good people in that attack."

Lily swallowed hard. "Is that who they were? Three rough looking guys attacked me almost a week ago. If it hadn't 'a been for a coyote racing in and scaring those three away, I might not be here now."

Scott patted his horse's neck. "You could travel with us, if you want." He smiled gently. "The women will take care of you. Fairmen women are good at making you feel like you belong."

She blinked. "There's women in those wagons?"

"Kids too," Scott laughed. "Yesterday wore them out, so they are riding in the wagons this morning. Otherwise, you would see the kids running along with the wagons."

As if summoned, a woman climbed from one of the wagons with two pre-teen children. The children immediately began a game of tag while their mother urged them to keep an eye on the fields.

Lily walked closer and tossed the pouch back to Scott. "Thank you for the jerky. I haven't had any protein for two days." She looked toward the wagons. "Will they really welcome me, or do I need an introduction?"

Scott laughed and shook his head. "Come on, I'll introduce you to the ladies down there. You'll think you just found long-lost sisters." He walked his horse a few paces ahead, giving her space to follow at her own pace.

As they neared the wagon, the Fairmen mother looked up. "What have you found there, Scott? Another one of your kind?"

"Yes, ma'am. She's as lost as Jack and I were on our first day."

Scott left Lily in the capable hands of the Fairmen mother and rode up to Ander's wagon.

"I found an Offlander named Lily up in those woods to the south. She is hungry and scared. She finished off my bag of jerky."

Ander laughed. "If she ate your jerky, I know she was desperate." He shook his head when Scott snorted. "Who did ye place her with?"

"Maxene. I thought it best all-around considering her loss yesterday."

Ander nodded thoughtfully. "Good choice, I think. Maxene could use the help with the children, even if only until we reach the next village." He looked down the line and saw Maxene already folding Lily into her family. The children flocked to their new adopted aunt, who smiled shyly at the attention.

&●

Early the next morning, a gentle rain fell as the Fairmen resumed their trek toward the village of New Dodge. Jack found the name unusual among the towns of Asher, but Ander had explained that Offlanders founded the village when they could not find a place where they felt at home after arriving on Eldriko. Jack wondered how much it might resemble Earth.

The wagons rolled on, leaving the scattered trees behind. The road bent toward a slow-moving river that widened as they neared the coast. Jack and Scott returned to their self-appointed positions as pickets, unwilling to risk a repeat of the previous day's tragedy. Jack hated burial detail; he had no desire to face it again anytime soon.

He watched the perimeter carefully. Only wildlife scattered before the wagons, and a few distant predators shadowed the caravan without drawing near.

As midday approached, Jack spotted the lop-eared coyote he called Loki trotting about twenty-five paces away, keeping pace with him.

"I see you came back." Jack spoke in his normal voice. "I hope that doesn't mean you are bringing me another warning. I don't think we could handle another attack."

Loki darted toward the river and vanished from sight, but she reappeared an hour later just before the wagons halted for a short meal. Jack sat with Ander, though his eyes continued to sweep the perimeter. Loki dropped to the ground less than ten paces away and tilted her head. Jack chuckled and tossed her a piece of jerky.

Ander watched the exchange. "Are ye sure ye wanna do that?" he asked. "They dinnae act well around people."

Jack smiled. "We seem to have created a bond between us." He tossed another piece of jerky. "I think he adopted me."

"She," Ander corrected. "Dinnae dae see the alpha males fighting over her earlier?"

Jack looked up. "She? I didn't see males out there. How did you know?"

"One smaller coyote with three larger coyotes in chase? That is a bitch in heat." Ander took a bite of bread, amused.

Jack looked at the coyote. "Loki?" Her head snapped up. "I guess I saddled you with a wrong name, but it looks like you adopted it." Loki lowered her head and rested near them.

Ander chuckled. "Maybe I am wrong. She seems pleased as part of your band."

When the meal ended and the banter faded, the Fairmen resumed their journey. By midafternoon, the low buildings of New Dodge came into view. Ander scanned the outskirts for a place to camp. As they drew within half a mile, the children broke into a run toward the colorful wagons despite adults calling for them to wait.

After the brigand attack, Ander decided the company needed several days to rest and recover. He arranged the wagons in two facing rows with a walkway between them, festival-style. Family tents rose behind the wagons, and the children tended their chores while the adults set up shop. Their well-practiced routine raised a temporary hamlet in short order.

Ander formally asked the mayor for permission to draw water from the town well—a courtesy no village had ever denied. He believed such gestures kept the wheels of commerce turning smoothly.

Early the next morning, villagers made their way to the temporary market by the river, and trading began in earnest. Both sides sought good bargains, though Fairmen were known for fair dealing and spirited haggling rather than exploitation.

As the Offlanders wandered through the booths, Ander noticed someone out of place—a man in a dark green robe. He recognized the Manos monk immediately. He flashed a discreet signal to Jack, who approached quietly.

Still smiling and greeting customers, Ander spoke softly. "Ye told me ye are heading to the Manos archives, dinnae ye?"

Jack nodded. "I did, yes. Why?"

Ander inclined his head toward the robed figure. "See the lad in the green robe?" Jack nodded. "Ye might want to speak with him. He is a Manos monk. He will know the archives well enough."

"Do you think he would help us, Ander?"

"Ye have the letter from the Council, correct? Show it to him. Once he sees Teyr's signature, he will help ye."

Jack scanned the camp for Asta and found her quickly. "Asta, I need your help," he said quietly. "Ander said there is a Manos monk in New Dodge. He may be able to point us to the closest archive." His excitement was unmistakable.

Asta chuckled—a rare sound. "Alright Jack, let us go see the monk you found." She shook her head, smiling. "Where is he?"

Jack pointed. Asta followed his gesture, then laughed softly. "I have to compliment you, when you have luck, it is a full share."

Jack blinked. "What do you mean?"

"That is Kialin Lyrien, the Arch-Monk of his order." She saw Jack's confusion. "Jack, he is the head of the archivists across Eldriko. Have you spoken with him yet?"

Jack shook his head. "Ander just pointed him out to me. I looked for you hoping you could introduce me." He realized he had never heard Asta laugh like this.

"Yes, Jack, I will introduce you." She walked directly to the monk. "Kialin, what are you doing in New Dodge? I thought you were down in Alderg to straighten out that mess."

He turned, startled. "My goodness and blessings, what are you doing here, Asta?" His eyes sparkled. "I was down there, but I got it figured out quicker than I thought it would take." He lowered his voice conspiratorially. "I told them if they can't keep records straight and in order that I would send them to the Ostorn archives. It's amazing how cooperative monks can become when you threaten them with a seven-month winter." He grinned.

"My, you have been away from the Motherhouse a long time, have you not?" Asta laughed with him. "I cannot remember the last time you spoke so informally in a public forum."

They walked toward his wagon at the edge of the Fairmen camp, Jack trailing behind. After a moment, Kialin glanced over his shoulder. "We have a tail, my dear."

Asta looked back. "Oh, I'm so sorry. Kialin, this is Jack Marshall; Jack, this is Kialin Lyrien, Arch-Monk of the Manos archives." She winced slightly. "I guess I told you that already, did I not Jack?"

Jack saw the warmth in both their expressions and felt accepted almost immediately. The three fell into conversation about Jack's journey and Teyr's directive, forgetting the bustle around them.

In the shadow of a nearby wagon, a young man dressed like the Offlanders of New Dodge lingered close enough to hear fragments of their discussion. He pressed himself against the wagon's side, hidden from view, weighing his next move.

Kialin's laughter rose above the din of bartering and conversation around the Fairmen wagons. Asta caught a flicker of movement along a nearby wagon—the same young Offlander she had noticed earlier. She shifted her stance, turning her back to the wagon and speaking quietly to Jack.

"Jack," she murmured, "look over my shoulder. Do you see the lad in the shadows there?"

Jack nodded without breaking stride in his laughter at one of Kialin's stories.

Asta stepped past them. "I need to check about something. I will not be long. Excuse me, Kialin—Jack."

Jack watched her disappear around Ander's wagon. Kialin continued talking, barely noticing her departure. Jack kept the conversation going, glancing occasionally toward the Offlander. A few minutes later, he saw Asta circling behind the young man. Jack waited, knowing she could handle whatever she started.

"It is impolite to spy on others." Asta's voice was firm.

The young man jumped, startled. He bolted, but Jack had anticipated the move and stepped in to block his escape. Jack grabbed his arm. "Hold it right there, buddy."

Kialin crossed the distance quickly. "What have we here? Who are you and what do you mean listening to our conference?" His voice carried an authority the Offlander had never encountered.

"I-I'm sorry. I didn't mean to interrupt. It's just that I heard something about a journey and, well, it's boring in this village." Jack could see the boy posed no threat—only curiosity and restlessness.

"Who are you, boy?" Kialin asked, his tone commanding.

"My name is Casey O'Neal. My father is a merchant in town, but..." Casey drew a breath. "I'm a spare. My older brother will inherit Father's business. I will have to work for my brother, join one of the religious organizations, or find my own way in the world." He looked up at Jack. "Sir, you spoke of a journey to accomplish something of importance. Would you need an apprentice or squire on your adventure?"

Jack glanced at Asta. Seeing her grin, he nodded. "Alright, sure, you can join us. I don't know in what role, but we will call it a squire for now."

Casey's face lit with a quick smile. "Thank you! Let me get my things." He sprinted toward the village.

Jack called after him, "We're traveling light!"

"Travel light, right, I got it!" Casey shouted over his shoulder before vanishing into the crowd.

Jack shook his head. "Lord, what have I done now?"

Kialin laughed, and Asta grinned knowingly. She chuckled. "You have a squire, Sir Jack."

Jack gave a crooked smile. "What am I supposed to do with a squire?" He looked at Kialin for help.

"Do not look at me. I have never been a knight." Kialin grinned and returned to his wagon. He and Asta began preparing for their departure the next morning.

Kialin knew the roads and trails to the archive Jack needed. He had interned there ninety years earlier as an apprentice. Now, as Master Archivist of the Manos libraries, he carried a confidence he lacked at eighty-seven. Ironically, his old master still oversaw that archive.

Jack checked with each member of his team, ensuring they would be ready at first light. As he rearranged his pack, Casey returned—with his father in tow.

The older man wore a stern expression. "What's this I hear about you taking my boy on some damned fool adventure?" He ignored all courtesies.

Jack turned toward him. "You must be O'Neal. What can I do for you?" His tone shifted into the clipped authority of his Army days.

O'Neal stopped short. "W-What can you...? You can tell my son to forget this fool's mission. He is my boy, and you are a charlatan."

Jack looked at Casey, who seemed ready to melt into the shadows. "Casey, how old are you?"

"Two and twenty years this past winter, Jack."

Jack nodded. "In your culture, when do you become a man, Casey?"

"We are expected to follow our own path, as a man or a woman, at age eighteen."

Jack turned back to O'Neal. "Have you raised an incompetent son, even one who has been a man under your cultural dictates for more than four years?"

O'Neal blinked, looking between them. "My son is no idiot. He just makes poor choices at times."

Jack softened. "Didn't we all at his age? Or are you telling me you never screwed up?" He tilted his head. "O'Neal, I didn't trap Casey into coming along. In fact, he begged me to let him join us. Begged me."

O'Neal looked at Casey. "Is that true, son? You sought him out?"

"Yes, Father. I have no future in New Dodge. You wanted me to work for you as the second son or join a monastery. Neither option appeals to me. I overheard Jack speaking with the Manos archivist, and I felt drawn to join them." He grinned. "I don't think he wanted to take me at first, but... I can be convincing at times."

O'Neal laughed. "Yes, you are just like your mother in that sense." He sighed and turned to Jack. "Don't let him get killed, will you?"

Jack's expression softened. "I can't promise you that, O'Neal, but I won't let him walk into obvious danger."

O'Neal nodded. "Fair enough." He turned to Casey. "This man seems like a fair judge of men, and I believe he won't put you in danger if it is up to him." He paused. "He's right, you know—you are a man. I'm proud of the man you became." He started to leave, then looked back. "If you get yourself killed, your mother will never forgive me." He winked and walked toward the village.

Jack woke before dawn, the sky still a muted gray beneath the high clouds. He moved through the camp, rousing his companions and making sure each was packed for the three-day trek southeast. After heartfelt farewells to their Fairmen friends, Jack rode out at the head of the column with Asta beside him and Scott bringing up the rear with Kendra. Kialin guided his wagon in the center, listening to the easy banter of a family still forming around shared purpose.

Ronan rode as he always did—drifting up and down the line like a seasoned cattle herder, making sure no one fell behind. Nathan, newly mounted on a horse gifted by Casey's father, rode just ahead of Scott, drawing on the fragments of cultural training he carried from Earth to make sense of this new world. Casey rode his own horse, granted as a boon by his father. Lily, who had never ridden anything more demanding than public transportation, accepted Kialin's offer to ride in his wagon.

They followed the trade road for half the day before turning onto a lesser-used path that angled southeast. The trail was narrower, the ground marked with old prints—large cats, the occasional bear, and the more common deer. In places, hardened mud showed no tracks at all.

Kialin flicked the reins lightly, keeping his draft ponies in step with the group. He smiled as he encouraged them, though they rarely needed urging. His wagon—his "landship," as he called it—was sturdy but light, crafted from strong pale wood painted loamy brown with forest-green trim. The sage-dyed canvas kept the interior cool in summer. Inside, he carried only what he needed: a chest of papers, a small bed platform, and storage drawers.

"Have you ridden in a wagon like mine, Miss Lily?"

Lily smiled, remembering carriage rides in the park on Earth. Her memories were more intact than most Offlanders'. "I haven't ridden in a wagon like this, Kialin. It is beautiful and rides well."

Kialin grinned at the praise. "You can sleep inside the wagon. I have a swinging bed I hang below it during the summer heat." He glanced at her. "What about horses—do you ride, Miss Lily?"

She shook her head. "I never had the chance to try."

"You can learn in the evenings after we make camp. We have some gentle horses with us."

Jack found a suitable campsite just off the road where a sweet spring fed a small pool. After consulting with Scott, he called a halt. They chose their sleeping spots near a shared fire. Lily settled into Kialin's wagon; Kialin slung his hammock beneath it. They ate a simple meal from their New Dodge supplies and talked around the fire with the ease of companions growing into friendship. As the night deepened, the laughter faded and exhaustion claimed them. Jack stoked the fire, pulled a cloak over his bedroll, and drifted into sleep.

The night shattered.

A deep growl tore through the darkness. Jack bolted upright, scanning the edges of the firelight. Something moved in the black beyond. A cry rang out—Casey stumbling toward the fire. A sharp yip followed, then a louder growl. A heartbeat of silence, then a yelp of pain Jack recognized instantly. Loki burst through the firelight, pursued by a bear.

Scott reacted as quickly as Jack. Jack reached for his bow; Scott stepped into a defensive stance with his sword. Loki streaked past them. Scott thrust his blade as Jack released an arrow. The arrow struck the bear's chest near the heart; Scott's blade found flesh a moment later. The bear collapsed at Scott's feet, exhaling one final breath.

Jack sprinted to Casey, who lay bleeding where the bear had struck him. "Kendra, get over here now. Casey got mauled!" Jack pressed his hands to the wound, trying to slow down the blood.

Kendra rushed over with her herb pouch. She pressed a mixture of herbs to the wound and pushed Jack's hand back into place. "Keep pressure on it here until I tell you otherwise."

Kialin dropped from his sling bed, short sword in hand, standing guard beside his wagon. Lily peeked out from the back flap, eyes wide at the chaos.

Ronan checked the bear to ensure it was dead. "Scott, this bear has a lot of meat on her. What do you think?"

Scott knelt beside the carcass. "Looks like a thick fur too. Let's get her skinned and butchered." He began working the hide. "Ronan, why don't you cure the skin while I butcher her up?"

Kendra tended Casey while Jack and Asta circled the camp's edge, checking for further threats. Nathan calmed the horses and secured them. Lily climbed down from the wagon, wanting to help but unsure how. She assisted Kendra where she could, though she had few practical skills for survival on Eldriko. Kendra noticed the determined look on Lily's face and resolved to help her find a place—a purpose—within their growing band.

·

Chapter Thirteen

*Hope is being able to see that there is light
despite all of the darkness.*

—DESMOND TUTU

T he storm swept in from the sea and drove hard into the
mountains west of Alderg. Alaster rode behind Dietz,
keeping close to Brother Amets whenever the narrow trail
allowed. Walter Lewis brought up the rear, leading two pack
horses. Alaster had hired Lewis the night before they set out,
trusting the man's steady competence for the difficult terrain
ahead.

Dietz had found the cavern three years earlier during an
early autumn snowstorm. Trapped there for two days, he had
waited out the cold before escaping back down the mountain.
Now he led Alaster's small band toward the same place, hoping
memory would guide him to the narrow trail he had stumbled
upon in terror.

Rain stung Alaster's face from the northwest. His patience
thinned with every soaked hour. "Dietz, are you sure this is the

trail you took?" He wanted answers—and shelter. Even a cold cavern would be better than the wind and the relentless downpour.

"Just up har' a little more, Boss. I remember that crooked tree we passed when we took this trail."

Dietz sounded certain. Alaster had heard similar assurances three times already that morning, but this time the old prospector's conviction felt different.

"Yes, yes. Here we are. See? See that holly thicket? I'd ne'er forget that. It cut me so mercilessly that I didn't mind hiding out in that cave for two days until I could heal." Dietz swung down from his horse and crawled under the holly toward the rock wall. "Here it is. I knew this was it." He stuck his head back out, grinning. "Come on, there is a gap next to the rock face. The horses will fit past the holly. We'll hobble them inside."

Alaster dismounted and examined the wall. "Well, I'll be damned." He had nearly given up on the old man. He led his horse through the low mouth of the cavern and felt a faint draft— a suggestion of another entrance deeper within. "Bring these horses inside and get a fire going. I'm cold and wet."

Amets hobbled his horse and gathered the small pile of branches left from an earlier camp. He placed tinder on the old ashes and struck steel to flint. Sparks fell into the doss, and the tinder caught. He coaxed the flame until the cavern warmed slightly.

As the chill eased, Alaster looked around the small chamber. "Where are the papers you said you found, Dietz?"

Dietz led him around a stone pillar. A sack leaned against the wall beside a skull, as though its owner had used it for a pillow before the cold claimed him. Alaster crouched. "Did you look in the sack?"

"Just enough to know that he was a poor monk. A few coppers, which I pocketed, and several scrolls and two bound records of no use to me."

Alaster pulled the sack into the firelight and sorted through the contents. "There is a map in here. Did you see that?" He spread the map on the cavern floor. "Look at this, would you? You didn't think this map might be important? Damn!" Pencil dots marked a trail that ended in the mountains. "Does this line lead to this ravine?"

Dietz squinted. "I'll be damned! It sure looks like it does."

Alaster sifted through the remaining papers. "All I see are mundane records. Storage inventories, annual tithe reports, outgoing correspondence to monasteries, and an index of archival holdings. Amets, get over here, will you?" He pointed at the map. "Is that a temple archive?"

Amets studied the margins. "It does seem to be. Look here at this note. It mentions the Noset archive, but..." He moved the map into better light. "It can't be. That was always just a legend. It didn't exist."

Alaster's frustration sharpened. "What didn't exist?"

"In ancient Aneglur folk tales, they spoke of the oldest Aneglur temple and archive located at Noset. All monks know the story, but none believed it. It told of hidden parchments stored in the Noset archives." Amets shook his head. "Nobody knew where it was. The tales said a landquake buried the temple, but the records had been moved into a vast cavern system before the disaster. They never found it."

Alaster turned to Dietz. "You know these mountains. Do you think you could lead me to the trailhead on this map?"

Dietz studied the age-yellowed parchment. "I believe I could put us close." He looked up. "Ya have to understand these mountain trails get tricky, especially if the map makers are, how do I say this, confused with their landmarks."

Alaster and Amets exchanged a long look. Was it possible? The fabled temple and archive of the ancient Aneglurian scribes?

Wind howled through the ravines, driving rain into the cavern mouth. Alaster exhaled sharply. "I guess that means you will not show me the way to the ravine today."

Dietz and Amets shared a worried glance.

"I suppose we have to stay here at least until morning," Alaster said, fighting his irritation.

They fed the horses travel rations and settled near the fire, sheltered from the worst of the storm. With no chance to hunt, supper was jerky and oats. Lewis added the last of the dry wood to the flames before they tried to sleep.

By first light, the rain had eased. Alaster ordered them forward, following Dietz's interpretation of the centuries-old map. Lewis doused the fire and stirred the ashes before they led the horses out into the gray morning.

Once mounted, Dietz reminded them of the danger. "One slip of yer horse and ya both go over the edge to yer death, so keep a close hand on yer mount. If ya are unsure, dismount and walk him. Better to lose one horse than both pony and rider."

The men nodded. Alaster drew a steadying breath. "Mount up, men, and be careful. We don't want any screwups this deep in the mountains."

෴

Jack could not find sleep after the bear attack. Restlessness after combat had become a constant companion since his tour of duty. He could usually settle enough to steal a few hours of fitful rest only after confirming that those under his protection faced no further threat. Whether the danger came from an enemy in the field or a startled bear in the night, the result was the same: Jack rose and walked the perimeter until his mind eased.

He moved through the quiet camp, thinking of how to keep his companions safe. He had never planned on leading anyone again after his medical discharge, yet people seemed to feel safer when he took command. Responsibility had a way of finding him.

He was halfway around the camp when a calm voice drifted from behind a pair of trees.

"It's hard to be responsible for the safety of others, isn't it?"

Jack stopped. A man stepped from the shadows—simple trousers, a tunic, a wide-brimmed hat. The firelight caught him just enough to outline his shape.

"It is a duty that I thought I had left behind." Jack chose his words carefully.

The man kept his distance. "Duty comes with rewards; don't you find it so?"

"What is your point, mister?" Irritation crept into Jack's voice—partly from the interruption, partly from the stranger's familiarity.

The man smiled. "On Eldriko, there are ways to secure one's needs that are, shall we say, more foreign than on Earth."

Jack's instinct sharpened instantly. "How did you know...?"

"You served in the army, assuring the safety of your men, the best you could under the circumstances." The man took a single step forward. "I could assure the safety of those who put their lives in your hands here on Eldriko. I could grant you the power to assure their safety. I would lead you to the riches to hold onto that power."

He paused, watching Jack's expression shift.

Jack's interest flickered for only a heartbeat. "Mister, I don't know who you are, but I know what you are. I read a lot on my tour of duty. I recognize what you are offering, whether you can produce it or not. I also understand that there ain't no such thing as a free lunch. You better be gone. Don't come back to my camp."

Scott approached from behind Jack. "Everything okay, LT?"

Jack didn't turn. "Just peachy, Scott."

When he looked back toward the stranger, the man was gone—vanished into the night as the wind whispered a single name—Julleg.

The rich aroma of roasting bear meat drifted through the camp. Asta and Ronan tended the shoulder roast, turning it slowly on a fresh wooden spit and basting it with care. While the meat cooked, Kialin rummaged through his wagon and emerged with a small keg of ale. He moved around the fire, filling mugs and lifting spirits. The scent of fresh meat and the taste of Fandos ale eased the tension that had lingered since the attack.

Jack, however, couldn't shake the feeling that Casey's injuries were somehow his fault. Scott caught his eye across the fire and gave a small shake of his head—a silent reminder that Jack wasn't responsible for everything that happened under the stars.

Kendra knelt beside Casey, checking whether the bleeding had stopped enough to apply herb-infused raw honey. She whispered the incantation Jalianna had taught her for animal bites and scrapes. Casey drifted into a magic-induced sleep while the meat roasted.

Jack had calmed Loki long enough for Kendra to examine her glancing wound. She determined it would heal in a few days, though she coated it with honey to be safe. Loki trotted over afterward and curled beside Jack near the fire.

Kialin set the keg down and lowered himself to the ground beside Jack. "You know, the bear is a symbol of Julleg. I wonder if that is why the bear attacked." He stared at the fire, lost in thought.

Jack looked up, brow furrowed. "Julleg? What or who is Julleg?"

Kialin chuckled and shook his head. "I'm sorry, Jack, I keep forgetting you are not from our world." He took a sip of ale. "Julleg is one of the gods on Eldriko. He reigns over the realm of chaos. The bear is Julleg's symbol in the visible world."

"You have gods here?" Jack perked up, the conversation taking an unexpected turn.

"Of course, dear Jack. Doesn't your world have gods?" Kialin grinned, already knowing the answer.

Jack shrugged and grinned. "I guess we do, for some more than others."

"Your world has many gods?" Kialin leaned in, genuinely curious.

Jack laughed. "In the way you mean it, we have a couple of gods. There is one big one that three different religions fight over. However, some would say my world has many gods. The god of food, of pleasure, of women or men, of wealth, of health. The list can go on and on."

Kialin considered this. "Do your gods force the people in your world to do things?"

Jack stared into the fire for a long moment. His voice softened. "Some would say that many gods force us to do things. And the one big god? Some would say he has absolute control over us in everything." He sighed. "Still others claim gods have no control over anything at all."

He fell silent, drifting into memories—the faith he'd found on the farm, the faith he'd lost in the foxholes. Some said there were no atheists in a foxhole. Jack knew better.

Kialin gently broke the silence. "The gods on Eldriko are, as I understand Offlander gods, more emotional. It appears to me that Eratha gods are like some type of exalted Eratha though still retaining all the faults of the everyday beings in the world. Some gods are loving, some angry, some frustrated or paranoid, some well controlled and some embracing chaos. The god I suspect, Julleg, is the pinnacle of chaos."

Jack gave him an amused look. "It sounds like the old Greek gods on Earth. They were always up to some kind of mischief, often involving people on Earth."

Kialin nodded. "I have heard of your Greek gods, and they sound much like our gods on Eldriko. You don't suppose there is some commonality between the two communities of gods, do you?"

Jack laughed. "Wouldn't that be something? We would all be in a lot of trouble if they ever got together."

Kialin smiled. "We have enough trouble with some of our own gods. We do not need any help from Earth. Take Julleg, for example. That is one chaotic god. He likes nothing better than to stir up our plans on this plane. We used to have a well-balanced world. There are tales of seeing past the clouds and rain many times a year." He looked up at the sky. "Julleg got bored with such a world. He may have been responsible for the loss of that balance." His gaze sharpened. "You seek the Heart of Sheol."

Jack looked quickly at Asta. She shrugged with a half-smile. "He overheard me talking with Kendra. Sorry, Jack."

Jack leaned closer to Kialin and whispered. "Can we keep this to ourselves? I've collected too large of a following to keep secrets from being too widely known."

Kialin chuckled and nodded. "I was a priest before I ascended to the office of Arch-Monk. I'm good with secrets. Where are you going first?"

Jack glanced southeast. "Teyr suggested an archives in that direction. Asher sports hundreds of archives, and Teyr knows only a few."

Kialin's grin widened. "You are truly fortunate, my friend. My duties require me to be intimate with all the archives in the Manos system. I also made sure that I stopped at as many libraries and Temples in Erathian Orthodoxy as possible. I will be your guide." He slapped Jack's shoulder. "Have some more ale."

ٮ٭

Kendra finished tending the wounded and slipped away toward the nearby spring at the edge of the woods. The spring fed a small pond that stretched back beneath the trees, its surface rippling softly in the evening breeze. Herbs grew thick along the water's edge, and Kendra knelt to examine them. Some she recognized instantly; others were unfamiliar, their shapes and scents beyond anything she had learned in Mistdale.

As she followed the pond's curve into the forest, a rustling to her right made her pause. A soft glow flickered between the trees—not firelight, not moonlight. Someone sat on a fallen trunk.

"I have been waiting for you, Kendra Hess."

A young woman in a long, flowing chiton sat upon the downed tree. The glow Kendra had noticed radiated from her.

"Who are you?" Kendra stopped short. "And how do you know my name?"

The woman straightened, though she remained seated. "We have had our eye on you for some time, Kendra. We watched your introduction to herbalism; we eased your path to the Manos. Lovely race, the Manos. They treat our world with absolute respect. The Manos are excellent guardians of our realm." She rose and stepped towards Kendra. "My name is Taimi Wyndra of the Talue. I am the Master Healer of my clan."

The glow of Taimi's chiton drew Kendra's gaze and unsettled her. She looked away from the unnatural radiance. Taimi noticed.

"I am sorry." Her voice was gentle, almost melodic. "I forget how sensitive humans can be to our natural appearance." The glow softened to a faint aura. "Is that better?"

A surprised Kendra nodded. "Yes, thank you." She tilted her head. "What are you?"

Taimi smiled, as though she had heard the question a thousand times. "We have many names among the races. We are guardians and guides to those who seek guidance and share our fervor for all you see." She lifted her arms, turning slowly, as if presenting the entire forest to Kendra.

Kendra followed her gaze. The trees, the pond, the moss, the flowers—everything seemed sharper, more vivid, as though she were seeing the world for the first time. Awe loosened her breath.

"Ohhhh..." The sound escaped her without thinking.

Taimi faced her again. "We know your potential and we know the kernel of power deep in your core waiting and hoping to spring forth. That is why I was created and sent." Her smile was tender. "I am to be your guide should you elect to follow that path."

Kendra's breathing quickened. "You want me as an apprentice?"

Taimi shook her head. "Not an apprentice, but as a peer." She saw confusion flicker across Kendra's face. "Kendra, you have the skills. The Manos prepared you adequately as a Healer. Unfortunately, their knowledge is as limited as their vision. It is as good as their narrow scope can take them. You have so much more potential, and on this quest that you follow, you will need any guidance I can offer."

Kendra swallowed. "I-I am a full Healer already? How is that possible? I left Mistdale less than a fortnight ago."

Taimi smiled. "You were a Healer before you met Madam Emeria and..." She paused. "She knew that you possessed all the skills needed as a Master Healer. You only need guidance. Mine, if you will allow it."

A calmness washed over Kendra—not forced, not magical, but deeply familiar, like a truth she had always known but never named. Her instincts whispered that accepting Taimi's offer would shape not only this journey with Jack and the others, but the rest of her life. Taimi's presence radiated confidence and serenity, and Kendra felt it settling into her own spirit.

For the first time, she sensed her genuine self—not the apprentice, not the student, but the Healer she had always been becoming.

Chapter Fourteen

Each of us has a unique part to play
in the healing of the world.

—MARIANNE WILLIAMSON

Jack leaned over the end of the large worktable in the Edows archive of the port city of Edhearn. Stacks of parchment lay in loose, precarious order across its surface. One end had been cleared so Jack could take notes while Kialin translated the ancient text into the common tongue. The hanging lamps flickered, and Jack reached up to expose more of the wick.

"Slow down some, Kialin. I missed that last part."

He still hadn't mastered the archivists' ink pens. If he only had to write, he could keep pace with the Master Archivist—but dipping the nib into the inkwell slowed him more than he liked.

"Apologies, my friend." Kialin's embarrassment showed plainly. "I got so excited examining these particular parchments that I could not control myself." He shook his head. "I never had reason to examine the Temple inventories from the Tirast

Dynasty. Boring stuff, those endless lists of beans, dried meats, wines, and spirits kept by the monks."

Jack grinned. He had watched Kialin pore over those lists as if they were an epic tale. To an archivist, perhaps they were.

"I'm glad you found that door behind that cart. We never would have found these notes. What was his name?"

"Let me see...." Kialin shuffled through the parchments. "Here it is. The archivist's name was Eddin Berbow." He shook his head. "I cannot get used to those Tirast names. I'm glad we got past them."

Kialin translated the next parchment. Jack glanced at the writing while Kialin read silently before dictating the next passage.

"I think I'm beginning to recognize some of Berbow's words there," Jack said.

"This language has been out of style for almost two thousand years," Kialin replied. "It is not that far removed from the common tongue, but unrecognizable for most who see it. We will work on your recognition every day."

"You said something about Berbow being transferred to another archives. What do you mean?"

Kialin set the parchment down. "In those days, archivists moved about every eight to ten years. The Arch-Monk wanted fresh eyes on scrolls and parchments that a long tenure would not facilitate." He selected a previously read sheet. "Yes, here it is. Berbow had to relocate to another archive. Let's see where that was." He scanned the page. "Oh my, I missed this before."

Jack looked up. "What is it?"

"Berbow was assigned to Noset." Kialin checked the front of the sheet. "Here it is. I thought by this date that all contact with Noset had been lost, but he was ordered there before harvest." He dug through the stack. "Well, I'll be." He looked up with a smile. "We are both in for a treat, my friend. Berbow left written descriptions and a crude map to the lost archive of Noset."

Jack's curiosity sharpened. "Where did he get a map?"

"It seems the Arch-Monk who ordered him to Noset included a courier pouch with the old map and instruction from two centuries before." Kialin's excitement was contagious. Jack's eyes widened. "Jack, we cannot leave yet. There is more to uncover before embarking on what looks like a perilous journey."

Jack tried to steady his breathing. "I have to say that it sounds so exciting, but you know what we still need to do. What's next for us?"

Kialin stood and turned toward the stacks. "It looks like I must find some different scrolls and pages. I will not be long." He took one of the lamps and disappeared into a vault to the left.

Jack reviewed his transcription of Kialin's translation, then slid the sheets into the leather pouch they used to protect their research. Kialin's voice echoed faintly from the stacks—a one-sided lecture delivered to no one in particular. Occasionally he asked Jack a question that turned out to be rhetorical.

Eventually, his voice grew louder as he returned, still speaking as though continuing a lesson.

"Here we are, my friend. I thought this was back there somewhere." Kialin set a thick stack of parchment on the corner of the table. "It's from Berbow's dark period."

"Dark period?" Jack's eyes widened.

"Yes. The story is that Berbow did not want the posting here. He had been here about two years when he sank into a deep melancholia that lasted two and one-half years." Kialin sorted through the pages. "His assistant feared for his safety and his mortal being. The Central House sent a healer to make sure Berbow would not harm himself."

Jack's mouth dropped open. "How many archivists served here at that time?"

"About twenty-five monks caring for the collection."

"And they couldn't take care of his mental health?"

Kialin paused. "That is a term I have not heard. I assume it means making sure he was right up here?" He tapped his temple.

Jack nodded. "That is what we call it on my world."

Kialin smiled. "Mental health—I like that. I think I am going to steal that from you, my friend."

Jack grinned. "Be my guest. How much longer do you think we will need to dig through the stacks to get what we need?"

"I think we are close now. This last stack provided precious little to advance our search." Kialin straightened the pages. "We leave in a day or two, unless you have need of further subjects."

"I think I must rely on your knowledge of the archives to figure out if we need more time or not. I would like to see how Kendra is getting along with her research in the healing stacks. I don't think she even came out to eat, and I suspect she turned to sleeping on the worktable to get right to her studies as soon as she woke."

Kialin chuckled. "My sources tell me that our Kendra has not left the stacks since I took her down to the science archivist. I think the best we can hope for is to inform her that the time in the archives must end when we leave. I think she would stay here a decade if I allowed it."

6♦

Kendra walked through the dusty hallways of the Edows Archive. From the worn stone and the age-darkened beams, she could tell the place dated back more than three centuries. Kialin had handed her an oil lamp and a simple hand-drawn map to the Healers' stacks in the lower catacombs. She followed the instructions for nearly a quarter hour before spotting the same symbol on the wall that Kialin had sketched—a pole crossed by a series of curves.

She stepped through the doorway. Her lamp cast a warm circle of light over a central study table, with narrow passages branching off in several directions. She peered down the first corridor: shelves lined with scrolls on both sides, stretching into darkness. Returning to the table, she found an index box listing subjects and symbols for each hallway.

The herb catalog appeared near the front. She matched the symbol to the correct corridor and walked only a short distance before finding the first scrolls on herbal identification. Some herbs she recognized immediately; others were entirely new to her—names she had never heard, descriptions she had never seen.

Herbal cures fell into familiar categories: remedies, formulas, distillates. Remedies she had learned as a child. Formulas she had studied in Mistdale. Distillates—pure concentrates—she had only recently begun to understand.

In Mistdale, she had also learned that healing could be more than physical. Jalianna Emeria had taught her that magic could infuse herbs with deeper potency. Madam Emeria had pushed her beyond the simple knowledge she brought from Hadon, urging her toward the deeper truths of healing.

Now, in the Edows archive, Kendra felt her education shift again. The parchments spoke of distilling herbal fermentations into concentrated cures and potions. She wondered whether the healers of Edows had merely studied these methods or practiced them until mastery. She knew she needed to move from theory to practice before they left.

She slipped back into the stacks, searching for a manual of procedures. She found recipes—some familiar, some strange— and even one every young girl whispered about: a simple love potion. For a fleeting moment she imagined distilling it to catch someone's attention. Her thoughts flickered toward Jack before she shook the idea away, cheeks warming.

She forced herself back to the healing texts. As she reached for another scroll, one fell from an upper shelf. She unrolled it and read carefully, following the instructions until she reached an obscure reference to a tome in "the vault." Which vault? She reread the passage twice more, then left the scroll open on the table and returned to the aisle where she had found it, walking deeper into the dim passage.

When she looked back, only a faint flicker of lamplight marked the distant study table.

The corridor curved slightly left, and Kendra found herself facing a large oak door, standing slightly ajar. She pushed it open. A larger table sat within, covered in yellowed parchments. As she stepped inside, the door drifted back toward its original position.

Her lamp illuminated the top sheet:

SPELL OF HEALING No. 267
Bone Knitting for Fractures—Complex

The words struck her like a revelation. Healing magic was not merely passive—not merely supportive. It could be active, intentional, transformative.

And she felt, deep in her core, that this was the path she had always been moving toward.

&❧

Kendra stared at the top of the sheet. The words seemed to leap from the parchment, striking her like a sudden gale. Her mind was flooded with questions.

Were Manos healers using magic to cure diseases and mend broken bones? Why had Madam Emeria spoken only of magic enhancing herbs, never of magic acting alone? How could Kendra learn more if she couldn't yet wield magic herself?

The implications swirled through her thoughts, dizzying and exhilarating.

The heavy oak door slammed open, crashing against the stone wall.

"Who the hell are you and what are you doing in my vault?"

The woman's voice boomed through the chamber. Kendra spun toward the sound and stumbled back from the table.

"I-I'm sorry. I didn't know..." She struggled for words as the imposing woman strode toward her, the door easing shut behind her.

"I asked you a question. Who are you, and what are you doing here?"

The tall, stocky woman towered over Kendra's small frame. "Well? Have you no tongue?"

Kendra's throat tightened. "I-I was sent down here." She held out the map Kialin had given her.

The woman snatched it and scanned the page. "Where did you get this? Who gave it to you?"

"K-Kialin, the Archivist." Her voice dropped to a whisper.

"Master Kialin gave you...." Confusion flickered across the woman's face.

The door creaked open again. A head poked in. "Haeria? Is there a problem?"

Both Haeria and Kendra began speaking at once, each trying to explain themselves to Kialin. Hearing the familiarity in the other's tone, they both fell silent.

Kialin looked between them. "Ladies, are we having a problem?" Neither answered. "Haeria, what happened?"

"I was trying to find the cause of the latest rumors I heard last week. I had the sheets I needed and went to the stacks for more files." She drew a breath. "When I returned, this woman was standing over my table, reading the parchments. Thank the gods she was not touching any of them."

Kendra bristled. "I would never touch old files like that. I'm not stupid."

Kialin shook his head. "Calm down, both of you. No harm done. Haeria, I sent Kendra down to research some of our healing techniques. You could help her find what she needs." He turned to Kendra. "And you will follow the Master Healer's directions, will you not, little one?"

Kendra lowered her gaze. "I'm sorry I invaded your research, Haeria. I didn't know. Please forgive me."

Haeria sighed. "Perhaps I overreacted. I take my craft seriously and finding you looking over my current work—well, I worried you might have shuffled the parchments." She glanced at Kialin, then smiled at Kendra. "What is your interest in the healing arts?"

"Back home, I learned some of the local herbs and their benefits. When we passed through Mistdale, I had a chance to learn more from Madam Emeria."

Haeria's expression softened. "You met Jalianna, did you? She is a sweetheart, and a true master in the arts of healing. I learned so much under her watchful eye."

Kendra smiled. "I was terrified when she made me identify all the herbs in her lab. I had four, no, five days with her while Jack met with the Council."

Haeria's eyebrows rose. "Someone in your band met with the council?"

Kendra nodded. "The reason we were in Mistdale was because the head of the council, Teyr, wanted to meet Jack for some reason." She smiled. "While Teyr met with Jack, I sought the healer in Mistdale to learn as much as I could."

"What did Jalianna teach you?"

Kendra chuckled. "At first, I thought she was just going to review the local herbs, but she went past that. I learned that magic could enhance the effects of herbal remedies. I thought I had learned all there is to learn until I stumbled into your vault. I had no idea magic heals apart from herbs."

Haeria studied her for a long moment. "There is much to learn about the healing arts. Not many are willing to take the steps needed as a healer." She paused. "There are thousands of herbalists across the world. Some of those herbalists will learn of infusions. Fewer still are taught the distillation of herbal remedies. Very few ever learn to use simple magic to enhance those herbal remedies."

Kendra nodded toward the parchment-covered table. "And then there is that...."

Haeria's expression grew solemn. "Yes, there is that. That is something most outside of Manos circles have never even considered, let alone knowing it exists." She hesitated. "I hope I can count on you to keep what you learned here safe."

She glanced toward the door. "Since Kialin vouched for you, I assume there is no question of your trustworthiness." She studied Kendra's face. "You are intrigued in the arts of magical healing, are you not?"

Kendra nodded eagerly. "I would love to learn those skills."

A sad smile touched Haeria's lips. "Kendra, you need to know about the effects of using magical healing arts. It is not as simple as waving your hands and speaking some ancient language. Practitioners pay a cost. You must understand that cost and consciously accept the responsibility and consequences of becoming a Master Healer."

She led Kendra down the hall to her sitting room and offered her a rich, bold tea. Kendra sat.

"For the herbalist," Haeria began, "the largest problem arises from a customer who thinks the herbalist gave them the wrong remedy. I have heard of the occasional herbalist punched in the nose because a treatment failed to provide the desired effect." She chuckled. "That is usually from a young lass wanting a love potion to capture the heart of some unsuspecting lad, and it just did not bring him around."

Her tone shifted. "Healers, especially Master Healers, are in a class of their own. All true Healers touch the flow of magic at some point in their healings." She watched Kendra closely. "Personally, when I heal some malady, my cost is usually extreme exhaustion. Other Healers suffer their own response. Some are quite severe—extreme pain, or even a loss of the ability to think for several hours. Each healer learns their costs after they touch the flow for the first time."

Kendra's eyes widened. "If I wanted to learn magical healing skills, I would be affected like that?"

"Most certainly. The only unanswered question is to what degree and in what form your cost will exhibit itself. You must decide if it is worth the cost to practice healing at that level."

Kendra looked down, thinking. When she spoke, her voice was soft. "I think I want to learn. I'll deal with the cost later."

Haeria sighed. She had seen this before—the hopeful, the gifted, the ones who either rose or broke. "Before you make that decision, I need to determine if you possess the spark that allows you to touch the flow." She dimmed the lamp. "I will look into your eyes now, looking for that magical spark necessary to become a Master Healer. Are you ready?"

Kendra nodded.

Haeria placed her hands over Kendra's ears and looked into her eyes. She began to hum a low, minor melody. As she hummed, Kendra felt something inside her open—a door she had never known existed.

Finally, Haeria whispered, "There it is." She leaned back, smiling. "More than a spark, I see in you. You have the gift to be a great healer if you can meet the price."

ℰ♦

After a long day in the stacks with Kialin, Jack finally made his way back to the guest quarters. Reading ancient histories and prophecies drained him more than he ever expected. Kialin always seemed to know exactly where to find the next clue, but every answer uncovered three new questions. Jack had hoped their stay would last a week. Now it looked like two or three.

The last four days had been a blur of research. Jack only managed to catch up with Scott in the evenings over a mug of ale. Scott, meanwhile, had settled easily into life at Edows. Nathan was teaching Lily to ride. Ronan had taken Casey under his wing, drilling him in wilderness defense. Asta and Scott sparred late each afternoon, steel ringing against steel.

Jack rounded the corner toward his room and nearly collided with Kendra as she stepped out of hers.

"Kendra, I haven't seen you for three days. Those healing files must have you weighed down."

Kendra gave him a crooked smile. "You have no idea how much." She tilted her head. "Have you eaten this evening?"

Jack laughed. "Is it evening? I haven't been outside since we got here at Edows. Kialin just had meals brought to the stacks. I finally had to get away for a few hours."

Kendra nodded toward the kitchen. "Want to join me? I took the night off."

"Sure, why not? We can catch up over whatever they are serving."

They walked through the quiet hallways to the kitchen—a place Jack hadn't yet seen. It turned out to be closer to midnight than evening, but archivists kept odd hours, and hot food was always available. A pot of lamb stew simmered over a low fire. They filled bowls, grabbed sourdough bread and pints of mead, and settled at a corner table.

Jack dipped his bread into the stew. "How is your research going down in the Healers' stacks? Are you finding anything we can use when we leave here?"

Kendra took a swallow of mead. "Actually, more than I could hope." She ate a spoonful of stew. "I had just stumbled across something astonishing when I had an even bigger surprise. More of a shock. It turns out I was in the private research vault of the Master Healer Archivist."

Jack choked. "Oh, damn. She walked in on you?"

Kendra grinned. "She did. She was not happy at all that I was reading her material. I don't know what would have happened if Kialin hadn't stopped by at just that moment." She chuckled. "Both of us were yelling at each other. That is until Kialin walked in. It quickly got quiet when that happened. I don't know who was more embarrassed." She laughed. "Kialin was quite amused, I think."

"What happened after Kialin left you?" Jack leaned forward.

"What else could happen? I apologized for invading her space; she apologized for overreacting." Kendra smiled. "Then we talked business. She is a Master Healer. I would be a fool not to ask her questions."

Jack could see something unsettled behind her eyes. "Kendra? What else happened? It feels like you are holding back."

She met his gaze. "I always thought that herbs were our means of healing, and they do have their place. But as much as I was right about that, I was wrong about so much else."

"Wrong about what?"

"Did I tell you about my experience with the Mistdale healer?" He shook his head. "She told me about the use of magic to enhance the healing effect of herbs. I thought I had reached the mountain summit. Whoever thought that you could use magic to fortify herbal remedies." She shook her head. "That first day in the stacks, my world turned over." She looked at Jack. "Healers can use pure magic to heal diseases and mend bones. The effect is instant. No waiting for herbs to get into the system. The correct words in the original language and poof! Healed."

Jack's eyes widened. "Wait, just like that? No medicine or splints? Nothing?"

She shook her head. "Nothing, just words obscura."

"There must be a trick to it. I mean, is magic real here?"

"Apparently magic is very real on Eldriko." Kendra stared into the dim hall. "I always thought magic was just a tale to saddle Manos with or to make Fairmen seem more exotic, but..."

She sighed. "What is even more extraordinary is that Madam Haeria believes I have the ability to learn magical healing."

Jack stared. "Like a wizard or something?"

Kendra tilted her head. "I don't know that term. Is that from your world, Jack?"

Jack chuckled. "I guess it is. My memory still has some holes in it, but that term seems so familiar to me, and I am sure it's a term applied to someone who uses magic."

Kendra smiled. "Then I suppose I am a—what was that term? Wizard?"

She held her mug, her smile fading into contemplation. Jack watched her expression shift, her thoughts turning inward. Something about the idea unsettled and excited her at once.

Jack found himself drifting too—not toward magic, but toward her. Toward the space she had begun to occupy in his thoughts without permission.

Kendra's eyes returned to him. "What are you smiling at, Jack?"

He snapped back and covered the truth with a quick lie. "I just imagined you as a wizard from Middle-Earth." He grinned, proud of the deflection.

But the thought lingered: When did she take up that much room in your mind, Jack? Her place in his thoughts had begun to shift—from friend to something he didn't yet dare name.

Chapter Fifteen

*Two roads diverged in a wood and I - I took the
one less traveled by, and that has made all the
difference.*

—Robert Frost

The sky held a high, pale overcast—the kind that
promised a good traveling day. The Union, as they had
begun calling themselves, let Kialin lead as they entered the
mountain passes marked on the ancient map. One of the Edows
archivists had carefully replicated the fragile original onto fresh
vellum, and Kialin referred to it often, hoping it would guide
them to the long-lost archive of Noset.

They had camped at the mouth of the pass the night before.
Now, early in the morning, they turned into the narrowing
canyon. Kialin knew the correct pass would be wide enough for
a wagon like his to navigate. He and Jack had spent hours
discussing the natural markers described in the old records—
landmarks that had survived millennia of storms and shifting
stone.

As midday approached, Kialin pointed toward a granite pinnacle rising opposite a narrow trail that angled northeast.

Jack rode up beside the wagon. "That's the marker, isn't it?"

Kialin nodded. "I believe it is, my friend. The signs are there, even with the tight trail leading back to the northeast." He eyed the path. "The record claimed that they could get supply wagons up this trail. I hope they did not exaggerate the accessibility of the road."

The trail bore the hardened surface of centuries of wagon traffic, though brush had begun reclaiming it. Jack spotted a sagebrush crowding the right side of the path. He leaned over, grabbed Kialin's axe, and strode ahead.

"I'll take care of that."

A few quick swings widened the trail enough for the wagon.

They continued until the canyon narrowed to a bottleneck, then opened into a natural courtyard—a place where supply wagons once turned before heading back down the mountain. But as Jack looked deeper into the canyon, his excitement faltered. Where the entrance to Noset should have been, a massive rockslide blocked the way. Rubble filled the entire face of the cliff.

"Kialin, look…"

Kialin followed his gaze and sighed. He studied the map again. "This must be the archive, but from the looks of things, I can see why the charter house lost contact with the monks. Strange that the records at Edows made no mention of this. They surely would have sent someone to investigate when they quit receiving dispatches."

Jack examined the rubble. "I think it was a sudden slide. I don't think anyone got out when this hit, especially if there was no report of the disaster."

Kialin frowned at the map. "Jack, look here." He pointed to a sparsely marked section. "Right here, about a quarter mile along the main trail, the archivist added another path with some markings. See here?" Jack nodded. "That is an incredibly old rune meaning horses. I think that could be the archive stables. It is worth a look."

Jack studied the symbol. Kialin saw hope where none seemed to exist. "Let's check it out, Kialin. It's only a little time."

Kialin stepped down from the wagon. "I think the Union could use a rest and some food. You and I can ride up ahead and see what that might look like. If it is nothing, we can ride back and decide what to do next. Does that sound fair?"

Jack agreed. The Union gathered for a midday meal while he and Kialin took food to eat on the ride. They reached the northwest trail quickly. Like the first, it ended in a rockslide— but this time, Jack spotted the top edge of a doorway protruding from the rubble.

"Kialin, do you see that?"

Jack scrambled up the rocks. The lintel rose just above the debris. He shifted a few stones—they moved more easily than expected. Kialin joined him, and together they cleared enough rubble to reveal the top half of a doorway. The rocks had spilled inward, down into a dark hallway.

"Did you bring the lamp?" Jack asked.

Kialin grinned. "I always carry a bullseye lamp with me."

He lit it and handed it up. Jack shone the beam into the darkness.

"I'm going to check it out, Kialin."

He slipped down into the hall. The beam revealed branching corridors, dust thick on the floor, the air still and untouched. Jack explored only twenty paces before returning.

"That might be the archive. Do you think your wagon can get up this path?"

Kialin considered. "I think I could back it in ten paces. We should talk it over with the others."

They returned to camp. Jack explained what they had found, and the group discussed their options. Kendra favored staying near the hidden entrance. Scott located a mountain spring. Asta and Ronan hunted for game. Lily continued her riding lessons with Nathan. Everyone worked to make camp comfortable for a longer stay.

The next morning, Jack and Kialin returned to the hidden entrance, Kendra joining them to explore the healing files. Each carried a lamp and spare oil. Jack showed Kendra the safest way to climb into the inner passages. Kialin pointed toward what he believed to be the Healers' route. Jack and Kialin watched her disappear into the dark with only her lamp to guide her.

Kialin led Jack to the restricted stacks—rooms no unauthorized researcher had entered in nearly two thousand years. Jack lit the lamp over the dusty workbench and wiped down the chairs while Kialin vanished into the shelves. He returned with three tomes and seven scrolls.

"You have a handful, Kialin. Anything look promising?"

Kialin set the materials down carefully. "Jack, be careful when handling these documents. They are thousands of years old and several of the scrolls already show signs of age-related damage." He slid the hand-bound books toward Jack. "These are in somewhat better shape, so I will examine the scrolls while you see what the tomes contain."

Jack opened the top book. It held myths, legends, and folklore collected two millennia earlier. A section on lost relics caught his eye.

"Kialin? I think I just found something." Jack flipped pages. "There is a reference to a rare magic infused gem that disappeared... let's see... here. This is it. It went missing about eight thousand years ago. They found it missing one early morning with one of their monks unaccounted for, and they assumed he stole it. Nobody has seen that gem since."

"Does it have anything else of importance?"

Jack turned more pages. "Not anything I can put my finger on, but there is one other thing that may be important." He flipped back. "Yes, right here. Before the gem disappeared, there are some weather reports. Sunrises, sunsets, severe storms, cloudless days. Mostly normal stuff. But then, after the gem disappeared, the weather altered beyond anything the Manos had ever seen. Days and nights alike turned foggy, misty, stormy—good days consisted of overcast skies or light rain." He scanned the other books. "From that point to when the archivists died from the rockslide, the weather stayed the same. Their weather became what you have now every day."

Kialin stared at him. "The scrolls are in pitiful shape. I think the books were scribed on vellum while the scrolls are recorded on some pulp sheets. They planned to transfer them to the vellum pages within a few years. The rockslide altered those plans. My guess is that the scrolls were recorded just before the disaster. What I can read spoke of teams sent out to find that gemstone to set things right. They may have discovered its location, but..."

Jack leaned in. "But what? What did they find?"

"That is the thing. That part of the scroll was rolled on the outside. I cannot tell if it is insect or rodent damage. Trying to read such an old document is complicated by the pest damage. Through natural happenstance, the scrolls survived since the rocks trapped the archivists in this makeshift tomb."

&♥

The library deep within the Aneglur Temple made Alaster uneasy, though Brother Amets insisted that the most obscure records on ancient relics were kept here. Amets had left him to read through the Third Age volumes—collected soon after the disappearance of the relic Alaster sought. Alaster had just finished the second volume when Amets returned, carrying a crate filled with loose sheets.

"Did you find anything interesting in the memoirs of the bishops?" Amets dropped the crate onto the study table with a thud.

"These are memoirs? I thought memoirs were supposed to be interesting." Alaster sighed. This was their third library, and the results were no better than the last two.

Amets chuckled and gathered the faded volumes. "These scrolls should give you some more fertile ground to plow. I selected those books simply on the chance we might get lucky with an obvious clue." He pulled a scroll from the top of the pile.

"These are very brittle, so be careful. This one is more than five thousand years old."

Alaster grumbled but pulled on the soft gloves Amets had given him. "Is it safe to handle? I don't want an angry priest after me because it crumbled in my hands."

Amets shot him a glare. "Just be careful."

He donned his own gloves and gently unrolled the scroll he had chosen. Small sandbags held the corners flat. He traced the lines with the tip of an archivist's quill, the feather barely brushing the vellum.

He reached the fourth paragraph, stopped, returned to the beginning of the section, and read it again—slower, more deliberate.

"What have we here..."

Alaster straightened immediately. "What did you find, Amets? Is it the location of the relic?"

"One would hope so, but I fear it will not be that simple." Amets continued reading, his expression tightening with frustration.

Alaster moved beside him and read over his shoulder. "What do you mean?"

"Crafty lot, they were, those Aneglur priests." Amets sighed. "They feared the secret would find the light of day, so they divided the secrets of the Heart and scattered the clues across the land. If I read this dialect correctly, they divided the clues among the Twelve Great Houses of Aneglur to hide as they each saw fit." He shook his head. "This house thought it best to hide the clue in seven parts, and only the Arch-Deaconess of this house knew each location of those seven parts of the clue. Thankfully, she thought ahead enough to keep those locations in her journal, but in what they called 'The Southern Dialect'."

Alaster's frustration spiked. "You do speak that dialect, don't you?"

"By the gods, of course I do. Do you think I am a simple cleric?" Amets bristled. "I understand perfectly, but there are twelve houses, and each prefect would have decided his or her own way to safeguard the clues delivered to them. The Twelve Houses had members from all over Eldriko, from diverse cultures and mythologies. I'm afraid this task just became much more difficult than either of us expected."

Alaster's panic rose. "That could take years!"

Amets softened slightly. "Take it easy. The Aneglur monks spread across the face of the world. I will get Carriers to send the messages out to the Charter houses. They will spread the word, and by next week, my house will be searching for the secrets of the Heart."

Alaster blinked. "What are Carriers?"

"We have priests who have the ability, through Temple magic, to send messages to all our Charter Houses. It isn't perfect, but most of the messages get through."

"Can these Carriers be trusted?"

Amets straightened, jaw set. "I would trust them with my life."

Alaster realized he had pushed too far. He took a breath and forced a smile. "Forgive me, my friend. I lost my head. You know how important this is to me personally." He hesitated, then added, "And I know you have gold in your eyes when you think of the Heart of Sheol."

Amets chuckled, though the heat behind Alaster's words lingered. "True, that." He began writing messages to his Aneglur brothers and sisters. Within the hour, concise dispatches were delivered to the Carriers, who sent them before the midday break.

Later that night, Alaster sat by the fire with Amets. Smoke curled from his carved bone pipe as he drew in the sweet burn of bacca leaves. "How many ancient dialects exist on Eldriko?"

Amets considered. "Hundreds, at least. Many were lost in the Dark Days. We can only pray none of the prefects decided to code their part of the secret with the lost tongues."

"And if they did? Then what?" Alaster's voice rose with the fear he hadn't voiced until now.

Amets waved a hand. "Those languages are lost due to the death of anyone who spoke those ancient tongues. If those volumes still exist, we could try to translate them."

Alaster couldn't say the answer made him feel any better.

§❧

Jack refilled the wooden bowl they had found in the deserted kitchen. *Deserted* didn't feel like the right word. The archivists of Noset hadn't abandoned anything—they had been trapped, sealed in by rockslides with no hope of rescue, left to starve in the dark halls they once tended with devotion.

He returned to the table where Kialin, Kendra, and Asta waited. The others had left earlier to pack for their morning departure. Kendra was recounting her frustrations in the Healers' section.

"It's almost like the archivists never heard of magical healings." She sipped her ale. "I saw shelf after shelf of documents about finding, preparing, and even distilling herbs, but nothing at all about spells for healing. In fact, I didn't even see references to using magic for enhancing herbal cures."

Kialin lifted a hand. "These archivists died two millennia ago. You must remember that magic in healing only began to appear two millennia ago. When Noset reigned as the jewel of the budding archival system, herbal treatments offered the only cure and were often mingled with mythology and folklore."

Asta shook her head. "I did not know that the science of magic appeared so late in our history."

Kialin grinned. "The science of magic is very young compared to the art of magic."

Jack looked at him. "Science of magic, art of magic? Aren't they the same thing?"

Kialin's expression shifted into that of a patient mentor. "Jack, do you have epic tales in your world? Stories?"

"Yes, of course."

"And you have physical sciences, I expect? Things driven by hard proven research?"

Jack nodded. "Many types of sciences."

Kialin pressed gently. "Was there a time in your history where science and art comingled? Is there still some type of proven science that feels more like art than science?"

Jack understood. "I suppose the field of psychology could fall into a field of both hard science and the art of application."

Kialin smiled. "On Eldriko, magic is your psychology. Parts of magic can be proven, trials repeated, results confirmed. Other parts—the application, the nuance—are art. There are records of two different practitioners in the same period using the exact same spell, and through an unintended inflection of voice, resulting in dramatically different outcomes."

Kendra leaned forward. "Then the healing magic just hadn't been separated from the art of healing into the science of today?"

"Hard to fathom, isn't it, Kendra?" Kialin chuckled. "We have come a long way scientifically since these poor souls starved to death under tons of rock and dirt."

Their conversation softened into easy banter as they ate. Jack took a bite of the venison Asta had brought in earlier. He smiled at how naturally the nine of them functioned as a team. Scott had told him the night before that it felt like their old company on Earth—when working together meant the difference between life and death.

Jack's thoughts drifted. A lake he didn't know. A stretch of plains beyond the mountains. The sensation was familiar— Loki's sight, shared through whatever strange bond had formed between them. He sensed no danger, only reconnaissance. The coyote was mapping the land ahead, and Jack felt the shape of their near future through her eyes.

"Jack!" A hand shook his arm. "Jack, are you listening? Where is our next stop?" Asta's tone held its usual deference to his leadership.

"I'm sorry. My mind just wandered." Jack grinned, shaking off the vision. "Kialin said we need to stop in Alderg at the Southern Chapter House."

Kialin nodded. "I saw an obscure reference in a dialect I haven't read in thirty years. I would like to confer with an old colleague of mine from our training days. He oversees the language studies in Alderg, and he can help me translate it accurately. We can rest for a week while I get what I need. Then we will have our direction." He grinned. "Do you think the rest of the crew will mind a week in the city?"

They all laughed at the absurdity of anyone resisting a warm bed and a real inn.

Kendra and Kialin left the kitchen still debating the recordkeeping habits of long-dead archivists. Asta lingered as Jack rinsed his bowl and set it aside with the same care the monks would have used centuries earlier.

"Jack? A word if you please."

Jack dried his hands and joined her at the table. "What's on your mind, Asta?"

She stared into her mug before speaking. "Jack, you know they all look up to you. It is obvious Scott would walk into a score of demons with a spoon to protect you. What relationship did you two have in your other world?"

Jack had expected the question someday. "We depended on each other for our survival."

Asta nodded slowly. "I thought as much. Everything about how he deferred to you suggested you were his general."

Jack laughed. "Well, not that high a rank, but he did report to me. What is your point, Asta?"

"I can understand Scott obeying you, and I am bound to follow you while keeping you safe. You know, orders from Mother." She paused. "It is the others that I think about. Every one of them has some unexplainable devotion to your cause. And such a varied company: Eratha, Offlander, Manos—even the Fairmen seem to support you."

She hesitated, then smiled faintly. "It is not just Mother, either. I knew there was something about you I could not explain, even before Mother told me you are my half-brother." Her eyes flashed. "Let us keep that between us, shall we?"

Jack froze.

Asta leaned closer. "Jack, they will all follow you into the unknown and the shadow of death." Her gaze locked onto his. "Do not waste their lives. I fear they would, to a body, sacrifice their lives to assure you achieve Mother's task for you."

She stepped forward and gave him a brief, fierce embrace. "Bring us home safely, if it is in your power to do so."

Then she turned and walked out, leaving Jack alone in the quiet kitchen—confused, shaken, and carrying a weight he had never asked for.

Loki trotted along the lakeshore, hunger sharpening every instinct. Her mind held only one thought: need food. She caught the scent of a marmot among the rocks and circled downwind, slipping through tall grass. The marmot foraged, alert but unaware. When it turned away, Loki struck, killing it cleanly.

She tore into the fresh kill, satisfying the primal need that ruled her kind. But as the blood warmed her tongue, another thought crept into her mind—one that was not her own. It had brushed her consciousness before, faint and fleeting. Now it pressed in with shape and intention.

I found the secret to possess the mind of this creature.

Julleg looked out through the coyote's eyes.

The god of chaos watched with wry amusement as Loki continued eating, driven by instincts Julleg had not anticipated. Julleg had influenced Loki for months, nudging her closer to Jack, but this was the first time she had taken full possession. She had not expected the animal's raw impulses to continue unabated.

Loki finished her meal and licked the blood from her muzzle. Julleg tested her new vessel, guiding Loki toward the lake. The coyote obeyed easily at first, trotting to the water's edge. Together they explored the countryside, Julleg adjusting to the strange balance of directing a creature whose mind was built for scent, sound, and instinct rather than thought.

But control was not absolute. When Loki was startled or tired, her primal emotions surged, and Julleg struggled to steer her.

A distant howl echoed across the lake.

Loki froze, ears pricked. Another coyote. A male.

Julleg felt the shift immediately—the pull of instinct, the surge of something deeper than hunger. Loki trotted toward the sound, ignoring Julleg's attempts to redirect her.

What are you doing? Julleg demanded.

Loki did not hear. The howl grew louder. Loki's thoughts narrowed to a single, ancient purpose.

A large male emerged from the woods and began following her. Loki stopped to mark the ground. The male sniffed, marked over it, and closed the distance. Julleg understood too late.

She tried to seize control.

No! Stop!

Loki did not stop.

Nature drowned out divinity.

The two coyotes circled, danced, and yielded to the ageless ritual of their kind. Loki paused, looked back at the male, and accepted him. Julleg screamed inside her mind, powerless. The god of chaos became an unwilling passenger in the most primal of acts.

When it was over, Julleg felt shaken—not by the physicality, but by the loss of control. The divine and the animal collided, and the animal had won. Loki's chaotic nature had surpassed even Julleg's own.

The experience was unbearable.

Julleg withdrew, relinquishing her hold on the coyote. But before she left, she planted a final suggestion deep in Loki's mind—a whisper urging her to use her natural unpredictability to keep Jack off balance.

Then Julleg drifted free of the coyote's body, hovering nearby as she struggled to regain her equilibrium, before fading back into the unseen places where gods brood.

Chapter Sixteen

One ought to hold on to one's heart; for if one lets it go, one soon loses control of the head too.

—FRIEDRICH NIETZSCHE

Once they broke free of the narrow mountain trails, the Union found themselves riding across high, rolling hills that sloped gently toward the gulf outside Alderg. Kialin estimated they would reach the city before dark if they kept their current pace. The land grew more settled—family farms, grazing fields, and small villages dotted the countryside, a clear sign they were approaching the capital. Their band of nine kept a watchful eye on the road, though Scott quickly realized the danger here was far less than in the mountains.

He cantered up beside Asta at the front. "See anything out there?"

Asta scanned the fields with her usual vigilance. "It is calm out there. Just farmers and their families doing what farmers do. Have you noticed anything of concern?"

Scott chuckled. "Peaceful as a Temple during the high holy days." He watched her for a moment. "I think you can relax a little bit, Asta. I saw some capital patrols a little bit ago. I think they try to keep the roads safe around here." He grinned. "Good for commerce, you know what I mean?"

Asta nodded. "Yes, too much rowdiness discourages travel, and less travel results in fewer sales. An effective way for the duke to be separated from his head."

Scott blinked at the bluntness of the consequence. Even after a year in Asher, he still wasn't used to how direct the stakes could be. He was already imagining a warm bed and a pub meal once they reached Alderg. "I can almost feel the bed in one of the inns in Alderg, can't you?"

Asta glanced at him. "If you say so. Cities make me feel uncomfortable."

"I love them. They make me think of home, you know— before." Scott smiled at the memory of the Big Easy: beignets, shrimp étouffée, the music drifting through the French Quarter. He never wanted to live there, but a few days of escape from farm work had always lifted his spirits.

Asta shook her head. "I do not feel the same. A city is the one place where anxiety crushes my spirit." She gestured around them. "Out here, I can see whatever danger exists around me and meet the threat. In the cities, threats appear from around any building. I can only react to the sudden threats, not prepare for the specific foe appearing."

Scott could feel her tension rising just from the thought of Alderg. The city wasn't even close to the size of New Orleans, but to Asta it might as well have been. "We can face any threats together."

"This is the capital city, Scott, it is so large." She drew a deep breath.

Scott frowned. "Just how many people are in Alderg, Asta?"

"I have heard that there are over twenty-five thousand souls living in Alderg."

Scott laughed before he could stop himself. "I'm sorry, Asta, I didn't mean to react that way." He looked embarrassed. "The city I spent time in as a young man is called New Orleans and its population stands at more than ten times that of Alderg. It may house more than three hundred thousand people by now. And things can get rowdy on any given night in those streets."

Asta turned sharply toward him. "Did you say ten times larger than Alderg? By the gods, I could not enter such a place."

Scott grinned. "Tell you what, I'll stay with you in this little city. Besides, can you imagine how big an attacking mob would need to be to succeed against you and I?"

Asta studied him for a moment before chuckling. "It would have to be a sizable force to overwhelm the two of us. To be safe, when we stop at midday for our meal, would you spar with me? The thought of the city makes me feel edgy."

"Do you mean with live steel sparring or wooden gatka?" Scott hoped she chose the wooden swords.

Asta smiled. "I will take it easy on you. Gatka is fine. Did you pack them in Kialin's wagon?"

Scott grinned. "Hey, I was a Boy Scout." Her puzzled look made him laugh. "I'm always prepared. I packed them, although I expected to use them with Nathan and Casey more than with you."

"I would not want to interfere with your special time with the boys." Her eyes betrayed the humor beneath her serious expression.

Scott shook his head. "You almost got me there." He chuckled. "I'll get the gatkas from Kialin's wagon when we stop."

They rode in companionable silence for a while before Asta spoke again.

"May I ask a question, Scott?"

"Of course. What's on your mind?"

She hesitated. "You speak of your former world, although usually with Jack. In that world, did you have a mate?"

The question caught him off guard. "I dated, but never anything serious."

"I assume you had no offspring."

Scott laughed. "Well, none that I know of." He glanced at her. "Do you have a point to these questions?"

Asta looked ahead, choosing her words. "There has never been anything of a serious nature for me either. I traveled so much as a ranger and a messenger for Mother when she needed me. I just never found the time to consider any man as someone to settle down with." She paused. "I never met a man who could share my chosen lifestyle."

Scott considered her carefully. "Do I understand that you might consider the possibility of pursuing a relationship with me?"

His directness startled her. She had tried to ask indirectly, but Scott saw through it. "I did not mean to suggest..."

"What did you mean to suggest?" he asked gently.

Asta's heart pounded. "I just... I mean, we are both alone and maybe we could spend some time together. If that time turns into something more, who would it hurt?"

Scott softened. "I would like to spend more time with you. We have much in common with each other, if you can discount the difference in the worlds of our birth."

Asta relaxed, smiling. "I would like to see where it might take us. Mother keeps writing to me that it is time to consider a serious union." She grinned. "Who says that it must always be serious? There is nothing wrong with a little fun along the way. If it turns to more, I am willing to pass that ford when I come to it."

&

Nathan watched Lily trot across the field on his horse. "That's it, you're doing beautifully. Gently turn her and ride back to me."

Lily guided the horse into a smooth left turn and brought her back. For several days now, Nathan had been giving her lessons, helping her grow comfortable in the saddle. She had ridden in Kialin's wagon since leaving New Dodge, but each day she grew more confident. Nathan knew she was ready. Asta had told her that Alderg held a large weekly livestock auction, and she was certain they could find a gentle mare for Lily.

Nathan smiled as he took hold of his horse's halter. "How did that feel today? I must tell you that you looked good out there."

Lily slid down and patted the mare's neck. "It felt wonderful. I can't believe it took so long for me to want to learn to ride." She glanced at Nathan. "Back home, many girls took riding lessons, and I thought they were crazy. Boy, was I wrong."

"Have you thought of what kind of horse you would like to get in Alderg?" Nathan led his horse toward the others.

Lily walked beside him, comfortable in his presence. Unlike the bullies who had greeted her when she first arrived on Eldriko, Nathan had a gentle, patient way about him. When he realized she feared horses, he never pushed. Instead, he invited her to walk with him each evening, always—somehow—ending up near the horses. He claimed he needed to curry and feed them, though Lily doubted the excuse. Still, he never forced her to touch them. She simply watched him work and eventually found herself stroking the neck and face of his mare.

"She's a gentle mare. She won't hurt you." Nathan had smiled at her breakthrough. "Do you want one like mine, or does one of the other horses appeal to you?"

Lily looked down the line and grinned. "I can't believe I'm saying this, but that horse of Kialin's is a big gentle teddy bear. He is so much bigger than the riding horses."

Nathan laughed. "He is large, isn't he? He's one of the breeds that's both a light draft and a riding horse. What makes him so appealing to you?"

Lily studied the horse again. "I don't know. I just feel safe riding him, even with his size."

"He's a gentle giant, that one. We can find one like him in Alderg." Nathan enjoyed every moment he spent with her.

As evening settled over the camp, Lily walked with Nathan through the center of their little settlement. "How long have you been here, Nathan?"

"Not that long. I woke here a few weeks before we met you." His steps drifted closer to her before he pulled back to a polite distance.

Lily noticed—and smiled.

"Lily, do you know how you died?" Nathan asked quietly.

She walked in silence before answering. "I know from hearing Jack and Kendra talking that I must have died on Earth, but I have no memory of that. I was walking across campus one minute and standing in a strange meadow the next with no idea how I got there." She glanced at him. "What about you?"

Nathan's discomfort was immediate. He took a breath. "I was at an event with my horse. I was riding her to a cross-country course that I entered when some pick-up came speeding through the field like some drunk. He hit us–hard. And here I am, talking with you in a new world." He tried to smile.

Lily took his hand. "I'm so sorry, Nathan. That had to be hard for you, since you obviously love horses."

Nathan looked away. "There's no way that she could've survived that collision." Tears slipped down his face. He wiped them quickly and walked with Lily to Kialin's horse, who stood a little taller than the others.

She stroked the horse's neck. "You are a beautiful beast." She turned to Nathan. "Are all of this breed as gentle as he is?"

Nathan smiled. "If this breed is like his Earth equivalent, then would I have to say yes, they are an easy-going breed. Why don't you climb up on him to see how you feel about his size."

He offered his hand, and Lily climbed up bareback. She wobbled at first on the broad back of the stout wagon horse. "Oh, wow. He's magnificent. How is his ride?"

"I don't think Kialin would mind a little walk around the camp to try him out." Nathan clipped a halter to the bridle and led the horse around the camp's edge. Lily held the mane to steady herself. Nathan picked up his pace, and the horse trotted behind him.

"Hey!" Lily yelped. "Not so fast." She grabbed the mane with both hands.

"It's just a trot. You did that with my horse. How does it feel?"

Lily considered. "Okay, I guess that he's so wide that I felt like I couldn't hold on. It feels better now." Soon she relaxed into the movement. "Nathan? I think I like riding this big guy. Do you really think we could find one like him in Alderg?"

Nathan grinned. "I'm sure we can. I'll talk to Kialin. He'll know who carries this breed for sale."

He watched her with quiet happiness—seeing her take the final steps from fear to confidence, from passenger to rider, from uncertainty to wanting a horse of her own.

Chapter Seventeen

*Whoever is careless with the truth in small
matters cannot be trusted with important
matters.*

—ALBERT EINSTEIN

The pub bustled with a full clientele that evening. Alaster had discovered that the Boar and Crow served the best food in this part of Alderg, and he had fallen into the habit of spending most nights in its smoky, noisy warmth. A wench led the four of them to a table tucked into a quieter corner near the back, where conversation was possible without shouting.

They ordered the night's special and a round of drinks— mead for Alaster, ale for the others. Dietz and Lewis dug into their stew immediately. Amets and Alaster, however, slipped back into their ongoing discussion about relics, myths, and the maddeningly incomplete records of Eldriko. Amets had found a few promising references, but the slow pace of discovery gnawed at him. Alaster listened, though his mind kept drifting to the documents he had uncovered late in the day. He tried to contain his excitement while Amets lectured on the linguistic complexities of the morning's finds. To Amets, every scroll was an academic pilgrimage.

At last, Amets leaned back with a satisfied smile, having solved some obscure scholarly riddle. He turned to Alaster. "Did those holdings in the back prove useful at all?"

"The only important references to the Heart of Sheol points back to the Noset archive," Alaster said carefully, "but you told me that the Noset holdings were lost years ago."

Amets set down his ale, his smile fading. "Back to Noset, is it? Hopefully, we can find our way around that roadblock."

He ordered another ale—more out of need than desire after hearing Alaster's news. "Noset was the gleaming gem of the Manos archival system. It held all the most important documents they gathered over the centuries. If possible, they would have cleared the gateway to those archives and reopened them. That the Manos simply stopped referring to that archive, and its holdings, tells me they could never regain access to those documents."

"Is that it, then? Are you telling me to just give up?" Alaster's shock sharpened into anger.

Amets nursed his ale. "Using the Manos archives, yes. The Orthodox or the Aneglur holdings might have similar documents, but the Noset was the best possibility we had. We could try the Aneglur library at DragonPass. They have the most critical documents my order collected since the great schism twenty-five hundred years ago."

Alaster's mouth fell open. "D-Dragon—DragonPass? There aren't any real…"

Amets waved a hand. "Oh, there haven't been any sightings in years." He returned to his stew. "But it is quite a journey from here. Up in the Blade Mountains near Pirate Bay." He paused. "We could reach it in twenty days."

"Twenty days?" Alaster's voice cracked with disbelief.

Amets nodded. "On horseback, yes." Then he noticed a table of sailors near the door. A slow grin spread across his face. "Do you get motion sickness?"

Alaster stared. "You don't mean…"

Amets nodded, delighted. "We could be there in less than half of a fortnight."

Alaster grimaced at the thought of boarding a ship. "Fine, but if that ship sinks and you survive, I will find a way to haunt you for the rest of your life."

Amets chuckled and clapped him on the shoulder. "You won't die. You may wish you could die if the motion affects you, but you won't."

Alaster groaned, tempted to wipe the grin off the monk's face. "I'll get you for this. I will." He stood. "Let's go."

Amets shook his head at the land-lover merchant. "You will have a short reprieve. We need to ride up to Blackhaven first. I hear there are some intriguing tomes from the Third Age in their holdings."

Alaster started toward the door, glancing at two young men seated nearby. The darker of the two nudged his companion, nodded toward the exit, and said only, "Jack." They stood, dropped coins on the table, and followed.

Alaster couldn't tell whether they had overheard the conversation—the tables were uncomfortably close for privacy. As he rushed out, he shoved the oddly dressed dark stranger aside.

"Damn Offlanders. You can't get away from them."

ᔔ

"I don't know who he was, but I heard him plainly even over the dinner crowd at the Boar and Crow." Scott's firm voice snapped Kendra's attention toward him. "I heard him say he is hunting something called the Heart, and he was disappointed when the other guy told him the place called Noset didn't exist anymore." He turned to Jack. "That place up in the mountains, didn't you call that Noset?"

Kendra felt the tension in Scott's voice—a blend of anger and something she rarely saw in him: fear.

Jack looked to Kialin for guidance, but Kendra answered first. "Yes, that was the name of the old archive. It was so dirty, and parts of the ceiling caved into what was left of it. And I swear I could smell the death hanging throughout the hallways, even after all those years."

Scott scowled. "Great! So, now we have to look over our shoulders while we chase this ancient stone?" He glanced at Asta and shook his head. "Looks like we are on guard duty from here on out." He moved to the corner window and scanned the street below.

Kialin turned to Jack. "What else did they say, these guys at the Boar and Crow?"

"Once the older guy got over his disappointment, he asked where else they could get the same information that Noset held. The guy that looked like a monk told him of another library way up north somewhere. He said it would take three weeks by horse to get there." Jack looked at Scott. "Look, if they head that far north, we won't have to worry about them at all, right?"

Scott shook his head. "Not right now, but they could pop up anywhere while we are out searching for whatever we need to find. If that happens, we could be in a pile of shit."

Kendra felt her own anxiety rising. What if these men caught up with them on a lonely stretch of road? What if they were already nearby? Did they know she and the others sought the same treasure?

Ronan stepped forward. "Listen, Scott, we can keep a vigil. I'll help you and Asta guard our flanks. I can teach Nathan and Casey how to spot trouble, too. It will be just like when we put that crew together back home. A couple of them were so green I wasn't sure they could make it through the week. You know how they turned out. They are the cream now and we trusted them to keep things working when we joined Jack."

Before Jack could speak, Scott answered. "Okay, Ronan, I will make you responsible for training these greenhorns. Our lives could count on them staying alert on the trail." He softened his tone. "I'm counting on you, Ronan. These are our friends, not just some cattle going to market."

"How long do you see us in Alderg, Kialin?" Jack asked, already planning their next steps.

Kialin paused. "I would say another fortnight to exhaust the research needs in these archives and libraries. The rest of the team can pick up supplies while you, Kendra, and I finish with the records."

Kendra frowned. "What did this man look like, Jack?" Something about the description tugged at her memory.

"I don't know. A little shorter than I am, and a little stocky for a man his age and height."

"How old was he? Hair, eyes?" Kendra pressed.

"Scott? Did you get a good look at him?"

Scott took a breath. "Yeah, LT, I did. Graying hair and steely eyes." He paused. "Oh, and he was a piece of work too. When he was rushing out of the Boar and Crow, he ran into some guy who seemed a little off in the way he was dressed. Mr. Congeniality elbowed him and made a comment about—Oh my God! It was one of us—an Offlander. That guy's comment left little doubt that he does not like Offlanders at all."

Kendra's breath caught. "I think I know who this guy is. What is he doing this far from home?"

Jack turned to her. "You know him?"

"I think so. I ran into him at a pub back in Hadon, near my uncle's farm. That guy had an attitude toward anyone not born on Eldriko. I heard later that an Offlander molested and killed his daughter. Reason enough to hate someone, but this fellow already hated Offlanders just for hatred's sake. Once his daughter died, he applied his hatred to every Offlander he met. Our neighbor felt his ire even though Charlie lived next to my uncle for fifteen years. It didn't matter to that guy." She paused. "Kempe, Alaster Kempe was his name. I knew his daughter Donia. Nice girl. She didn't deserve what happened to her."

Asta looked at her. "How did you know her?"

"We lived in a small town. Everybody knew everyone's business. She was about ten years younger than me, but I saw her when I shopped in her father's store. She was sweet, despite who her father was."

Jack nodded to Scott. "Okay, we will keep a close watch in our immediate vicinity when we are traveling and in town. Please be aware of your surroundings. I always hate losing those entrusted to my care."

Scott nodded. "You know you always have my support." He smirked. "Just like in the Middle East, right LT?"

Jack shook his head with a faint smile. "I do wish you would cut the LT crap, Sergeant."

Scott chuckled. "Yes, Sir, your worship."

"Oh God, you will never change, will you?" Jack laughed. "All right, we have two weeks to get things set and back on the road. Just be careful and pray that guy heads north soon—very soon."

&♦

Scott spent much of the next morning checking his gear. He ground a fresh edge onto his sword, finishing it with his whetstone until the blade gleamed with a razor sheen. When he was satisfied, he moved on to the bow Jack had given him. Even after days of practice on the Alderg parade grounds, the arrowheads needed only a light touch of the stone to bring them back to perfection.

He noticed Casey watching from the edge of the field.

"Casey, would you like to take a ride with me this morning?"

The young man jumped to his feet. "Yes, sir, I would like that very much." He started toward Scott at a run.

"Where is your sword? You don't want to forget that." Scott shook his head, amused. The boy needed training before he got himself killed.

Casey returned with a well-used longsword. "Father gave me this old sword before we left New Dodge." He hesitated. "I've never used it though."

Scott sighed. "Well, carry it anyway and I can teach you how to use it later. We will try to stay out of trouble today, but better safe, you know?" He glanced around. "Do you have a bow? Have you ever used one?"

"No, sir, I've never even picked one up."

Scott shook his head. "I should have noticed that earlier. We will find you one you can use before we leave. I should be able to get at least a used longbow for you. If I'm lucky, we can secure a war-bow for you. It is easier to carry and has more power."

Casey's eyes widened at the prospect.

Scott strapped on his sword, grabbed his bow, and headed toward the stables. "Let's go saddle up and get going."

Casey trotted to keep up. "Where are we going?"

"In a couple of weeks, we are heading up the coast road," Scott said over his shoulder. "I don't want any surprises. We will ride about two hours up the road reconnoitering for ambush or choke points along the road."

They saddled their horses and soon passed through the north gate of Alderg. The road curved gently northeast, the plains rising into foothills. A southeast bend kept the road low until the eastern sea came into view. From there, the road followed the coastline north. For more than an hour, the corridor was wide and safe.

Then the shoulders narrowed.

Scott spotted the first trouble point. "See that thicket, Casey? That is the type of thing we want to watch out for." The brush nearly touched the road. "Brigands could easily find cover there to attack unsuspecting travelers. We are not such travelers."

He smiled at Casey—and caught himself. He needed to stop thinking of him as a boy. Casey had chosen to leave the safety of the city and join their band. That was a man's choice.

Casey pointed ahead. "What about that narrowing where the boulders almost reach the road? Would that be a place for an ambush too?"

Scott smiled. *Yes, this boy is more man than boy.* "Good eyes, Casey. If I were setting a trap, that is just where I would hide."

They continued their survey, marking every dangerous stretch for their odd collection of healers, scholars, rangers, warriors, and amateur adventurers. Scott also kept an eye on the soft ground beside the packed road.

"Look here, Casey. See that print? What would you say that is from?"

Casey dismounted and examined the large paw print. "Too big to be a dog, but I think it is in that family." He looked up. "Wolf, maybe?"

"Nice guess, and close, but not quite." Scott dismounted and drew in the dirt. "This is the size of a dog paw print." Then he drew another. "This is a wolf-sized print. See the difference?"

Casey nodded, comparing the shapes.

"I would guess that this is either a yearling wolf or a coyote," Scott continued. "Since I have not seen any young wolves out here—too early in the season—I would say that it is not a young wolf print. That leaves my choice to an adult coyote."

"I am impressed that you know the prints so accurately." Casey grinned, genuinely awed.

Scott chuckled. "Well, that and I saw the coyote back down the road behind us about a quarter of an hour ago."

Casey's head snapped around, and Scott laughed.

He scanned the area again and caught the faint scent of old smoke. He led his horse to a cold campfire and held his hand above the ashes. "Still a little warm. We are not alone out here. We best head back before we find ourselves in a world of hurt."

They mounted, turning back toward Alderg at an unhurried pace. Scott kept his gaze forward. Casey began to glance back.

"Don't look back," Scott warned softly. "I don't think they are still around, but if they are and they see us looking back, they will be on us in a flash. We will hear them chasing after us in time to defend ourselves if they want a fight. Otherwise, I don't want to invite one."

They rode in tense silence for half an hour. When the road bent west, Scott risked a look behind them. No shadows followed.

He exhaled. "We are in the clear now. I don't think they want to risk raiding travelers this close to Alderg."

Casey relaxed slightly. "Were they really back there?"

"Maybe, but I didn't see anything of them." Scott kept his voice honest. Casey deserved that. "Still, when we get back in the city, you and I are going to get you some training with that sword of yours, and we will find you a bow to practice with."

Casey smiled—a quiet, proud smile. Scott saw it and knew the truth: the boy had earned his place today. And Scott would treat him like the man he was becoming.

Chapter Eighteen

Be still with yourself
Until the object of your attention
Affirms your presence

—Minor White

When Jack arrived in Alderg, he fell into the habit of walking along the river at dusk to clear his mind and plan for the next day. Tonight, a light fog rose from the water, spreading across the fields on both sides of the slow-moving river. The walk to the old willow and back gave him the space he needed to push away self-doubt. Even through the fog, he watched geese paddling in the current, diving for moss. Evening birds called from the trees. A soft wind stirred the deepening mist as darkness settled over the fields. He still had enough light to reach the gate—if he didn't linger too long in the quiet that the city walls could never offer.

From the distance, he heard the familiar call from the gate guard. "Master Marshall, don't get lost. That water is cold this time of year."

The guard had called the same warning every evening since Jack's third night. Jack waved in acknowledgment and continued along the bank.

As he neared the willow, a sudden lightheadedness washed over him—sharp, familiar, unwelcome. It reminded him of the hours after he first arrived on Eldriko.

"No, not now," he muttered.

His world went black. Sound vanished. His heart hammered in his chest, the pulse echoing in his ears. Slowly, faintly, the sound of the river returned—warped, distant, as though heard through a cavern.

His vision returned next, but wrong. Colors were muted, washed in a pale brown tint. The world looked faded, as if seen through an old lens with darkened edges. Nothing came into sharp focus. Even the geese and otters moving along the river seemed blurred at the edges.

He wondered if he needed glasses—and whether Eldriko even had such things.

Something nudged his leg. He looked down and found Loki staring up at him. Relief flickered through him.

"It's nice seeing something normal, though I wish I could see you clearer."

"This is all part of your visions, Jack."

Jack froze. "D-Did you just speak?"

Loki danced across his path and stopped before him. "Do not think so much, Jack. I am here to bring you signs of what may be and what may not be. What you see is aimed at your gut, not your mind. I am blocked from sharing concise images of what may come. The future is not fixed but rather fluid. You will see what it could be, but in many ways. Your choices dictate your future and the future of your companions, close and distant alike."

The words hit him like a blow. He stared at the coyote—familiar, yet suddenly vast and unknowable. "Am I alive?"

Loki laughed softly. "You are between life and death. Dead to all who knew you on Earth; alive to all who love and count on you on Eldriko." She tilted her head. "Your future holds many choices that define your life, or death, in the world where you now live. The choices are yours alone and affect your loved ones."

Jack's thoughts leapt to the people he had met—people he cared for more deeply than he had realized. His voice dropped. "Show me what I am fated to see."

Loki nodded and trotted left. "Follow me but keep up."

Jack lengthened his stride, following her into the thickening fog. As the mist lifted, the world shifted. Colors softened into a muted, sepia-like palette—something between Dorothy Gale's Kansas and the first glimpse of Oz.

Before him stood the house he grew up in.

His parents stood on the porch, young again, untouched by time. His mother's beauty matched the photograph that once hung in the living room. His stepfather stood strong and confident. Near the barn, Jack saw a blurred version of himself—years younger, long before enlistment. And at the edge of the drive, shimmering like a memory half-remembered, stood his ex-wife.

Loki turned down the path toward the woods behind the barn. "You remember this, don't you?"

"I don't want to go back there. I cannot stand to see what is there." Jack hesitated on the trail leading to the place of his death.

"You must follow the path before you," Loki urged. "You have already taken the first steps to fulfilling your fate. Keep up."

Jack wanted to stop, but his feet carried him forward. The woods dissolved. The sky brightened to a high overcast. He stood in a field of wildflowers in full summer bloom. Figures surrounded him—some tall, some short, all blurred but familiar. They looked to him for guidance, standing ready to protect him.

Across the field stood an obelisk, the only thing in perfect focus, glowing with blinding light. A sound rose from it—cicada calls woven with soft symphonic tones. Without Loki's prompting, Jack walked toward it. The blurred figures encouraged him. He reached within twenty-five paces when the scene shifted again.

Darkness. Mist. A burned field where the wildflowers had been. The obelisk still stood, close enough to touch. The blurred figures followed, but now some glowed faintly while others deepened into shadow, losing all distinguishing features—except one. A single figure stood apart, wrapped in a dull glow and mist. Her outline tugged at Jack's memory, familiar yet unreachable.

Then the world changed again.

Jack stood in a vast, empty building. Light filtered through high openings. The floor was hard-packed dirt. Loki trotted to him.

"I cannot make your decision for you," she said. "Roads that you choose lead to various outcomes. I can see the possible outcomes, but I am restricted from directly influencing your choices." She sat beside him. "I am more than coyote, although her traits match me well."

"Can I speak with you again after this vision ends?" Jack asked, though he already knew.

Loki shook her head. "This is a one-time allowance by the other gods. They allowed me to show shadowy hints of what may be to you without speaking clear directions. When this vision, this prophecy, fades I will only appear as this simple coyote—with a personality."

Jack's confusion deepened. "But what if I need answers?"

The room darkened. Loki dissolved into mist, her voice echoing through the blackness. "You have a wise council in your companions. Trust their judgement."

Silence swallowed everything.

Then a voice shattered it. "Master Marshall, it is time to come back into the city."

Jack blinked. The guard from the gate approached him. In the distance, the torches burned bright, marking the safety of Alderg.

Jack looked back into the darkness behind him and wondered: Is there any safety for me anywhere in this world?

Jack made his way toward the pub beside the inn on Alderg's edge. The guards were lighting the street torches, pushing back the night with warm halos of flame. Jack walked lost in the tangle of his thoughts—the vision outside the city gates, Loki's voice, the shifting scenes, the obelisk, the blurred figures. *What could it all mean? Where will this journey lead me? How will I get there? Why couldn't Loki just tell me the path?*

He shook his head, trying to scatter the questions, but one clung stubbornly: *How did Loki speak unless I've finally slipped into madness?*

Inside the pub, he ordered a tall mug of mead and retreated to a table in the back, away from the noise. From there he spotted a small group of his companions—Scott, Asta, Nathan, and Lily— sharing food and drink near the gaming room. He tried to slip past unnoticed, but Lily's eyes caught his just as he sat. She held his gaze for a heartbeat before turning back to her conversation.

Jack nursed his mead for nearly half an hour before Lily rose from her table and walked toward him. He sighed inwardly. *Busted.* She sat across from him without asking and motioned for a mug of ale. Jack watched her over the rim of his drink as she sat in silence, studying him.

After several minutes, Jack said, "Care to join me, Lily?"

"I don't mind if I do, Jack." She didn't look away. "Are you having food with that or are you just trying to get lost in the mug?"

Jack sighed. "Okay, I'll try their lamb stew with brandy."

Lily chuckled. "Good choice, Jack."

The serving girl brought the stew and dark bread. Lily tore a piece and nibbled thoughtfully. Jack poked at the stew, taking occasional bites—just enough to keep Lily from scolding him.

After half an hour of his slow picking, Lily finally spoke. "Where were you this evening, Jack? I know you go for walks before they close the city gates, but you were out later than usual."

Jack stirred the stew and glanced at her intent gaze, then toward Scott's table where Nathan kept glancing between them. Jack looked back at Lily. "I'm still trying to make sense of what happened out there."

Lily caught Nathan's eye and gave a small shake of her head before turning back to Jack. "You might feel better talking about it."

Jack watched Scott's group pay their bill and leave, Nathan giving Lily one last look. When the door closed behind them, Jack exhaled. "Lily, I didn't plan to tell anybody about this, but maybe you are right—if you promise to keep it to yourself."

With her quiet assurance, Jack told her everything he dared. The unnatural darkness. Loki speaking. The vision of his parents and the ghostlike presence of his ex-wife. The field of wildflowers. The glowing obelisk. The burned world. The vast empty building. Loki's final warning. He held back the parts he didn't understand—he didn't want to burden Lily with more than she could carry.

When he finished, he realized he did feel lighter.

Lily's ale sat untouched. "I see why you looked a little shook up now," she said softly. "I won't tell any of the others unless you want me to let them know. But Jack, I'm here if you need to talk anymore. That is such a dark, troubling story."

"I appreciate that, Lily. It did help for me to tell someone."
Jack took a long drink of his warming mead.

Lily shifted the conversation, gently pulling him back
toward steadier ground. "Are you and Kialin finished with your
research? I mean, how long will we stay here?"

Jack smiled, recognizing the kindness in her pivot. "We are
close to having what this archive can give us. Kendra may need
one more day. I would say we should move on by the end of the
week."

"Then I guess I better get some sleep." Lily finished her ale.
"I have some things to buy tomorrow, and I need to check my
bags before the week's end." She stood and looked at him. "Are
you coming with me? Or are you going to have me walk these
dark streets all by myself?"

Jack laughed, dropped coins on the table, and rose. "I would
never put you in danger. Let's go."

&♦

Alaster had arrived at DragonPass with Amets and the
others only two days earlier, and his frustration had already
reached a breaking point. Amets had told him that DragonPass
held the most important Aneglur documents in safekeeping. He
had not mentioned that the Nyehtor monks curated and
controlled access to the archive with suffocating rigidity. It took
Amets two full days to secure permission for Alaster to enter—
and even then, only as Amets's assistant.

Alaster took petty satisfaction in watching Amets don the
orthodox Nyehtor robes required for entry into the restricted
chambers, while he himself wore only the plain clerical robes of
an apprentice.

As they descended deeper into the catacombs, Alaster's irritation boiled over. "What the hell am I even doing here? I can't read any of these documents. You Aneglurian monks record everything in code that nobody else can read."

Amets hissed, "Will you keep your voice down! Sounds carry through these stone corridors easily." He glanced around to ensure they were alone. "You are here as my assistant, as anyone of my assumed station would require. Someone of your assumed station would do what he is told and keep his mouth shut. Can you do that, or do you wish to abandon this fools' pursuit you dragged me into?"

Alaster glared at the back of Amets's robes. "Alright, I understand, but I don't like it," he muttered through clenched teeth. "This better give us something. I'm getting tired of all the blind ends and false trails these libraries have given us."

They turned down a new corridor toward a vault they had not yet visited.

"A tome yesterday suggested a prophecy down here contains an interesting possibility," Amets said.

Alaster's temper snapped. "Another possibility? That's what I mean. Why can't we find a book that says, 'look behind this rock and find the gem wrapped in a velvet cloth'?"

Amets stopped and gave him a withering look. "Do you really believe it will be that easy?" He shook his head. "You can't be that stupid."

Alaster sighed. "No, I know we won't find a map with an 'X' on it telling where to dig. I'm just getting tired of all the books. I want to see the treasure."

Amets laughed. "My friend, these books are the treasures. The gem is just the symbol that the true treasure brought us to." He checked the runes etched into the walls where the corridors branched, then chose the left passage. Twenty paces later, they reached an oak door blocking the way. "I think this is it."

He pushed through into a large vault lined with shelves of books, tomes, and scrolls. "Yes, yes—this looks like the right time frame."

Alaster set down the bundle Amets had made him carry. "What do you want me to do?"

"Make sure the lamps have enough oil for several hours' work, and dust that table off. It has been decades since anyone needed any of these resources." Amets's voice faded into muttering as he disappeared into the stacks, searching for the volume mentioned in a dead monk's notes.

Alaster prepared the workspace, still simmering. In his mind, Amets's station fell far below his own—yet he needed the monk's ability to read the cryptic Aneglurian codes. He had looked into one of the codices the day before and found only numbers, symbols, and letters from an alphabet he didn't recognize.

"Aha! Here it is." Amets emerged from the far aisle carrying a thick, dusty, leather-bound book. He set it on the table and looked up at the lamps. "Alaster, do we have any other lamps? One on a stand?"

Alaster searched, but the only spare was the bullseye lamp in Amets's bundle. "I'm afraid this is all you brought with you." His tone carried a thinly veiled accusation, which Amets ignored.

"Here it is. The reference is to 'him who is tasked with the discovery of relic of balance'—a seeker and speaks of the hero of the relic. The wording is unusual. Hero, yes, but the meaning seems more." Amets flipped through his notes. "Aha, yes, here we go. That notation suggests hero or keeper—it is used interchangeably in this context." He tucked the notes away. "The hero, being essential to the seeker, drives the journey forward into perilous lands. Hazards that lead to the grasping of the—what is this word?" He adjusted the lamp.

Alaster leaned in, though he couldn't read a single symbol. His head blocked the light.

"Do you mind?" Amets snapped. When Alaster stepped back, he continued. "Oh, very clever. It is an archaic term for an amulet of some type. This seeker will discover the object of his task or his quest, if you will, and reap the rewards of his perilous journey."

"Is that it? No new clues or directions?" Alaster's frustration surged again.

"This is a major discovery," Amets said.

"How so? I don't see that this helps us." Alaster's face reddened. His head had begun to ache an hour earlier, and now his heart pounded hard enough to frighten him. He felt as though something inside him was slipping out of his control.

Amets sighed. "You can't see it, can you? You will meet this hero who will direct your journey to the relic. You are the seeker, aren't you?" His tone was that of a teacher guiding a slow student toward an obvious conclusion.

Alaster's anger erupted. "How dare you treat me as some adolescent dolt! I am Alaster Kempe. I hired you to find a lost relic, and all you can do is treat me as one of your dense students." His outburst stunned Amets into silence.

Alaster turned away, breathing hard, fighting to regain control before he did something he couldn't undo. After several deep breaths, he faced the monk again. Amets stood rigid, hands trembling slightly from the shock of Alaster's rage.

"You need to find what I hired you to find," Alaster said, voice low and dangerous. "My time is running out. I don't care how you do it but find the location of that relic—and soon."

᠖᠙

Alaster decided he needed a break and left Amets buried in the temple library. He wandered through the deeper vaults without direction, irritation simmering beneath his skin. The stone corridors twisted and branched, each one colder and more silent than the last.

He turned a corner and collided hard with a Nyehtor monk. The impact knocked the breath from his lungs.

"Fool! Watch where you are..." Then he realized who he had struck. "I'm sorry, brother. You caught me by surprise."

The familiar voice froze him. "You should be more careful, Kempe."

"Julleg! Where have you been? It's been weeks, dammit."

Julleg glanced sharply down the corridor. "Hush! Don't use my name around the monks. We aren't on the best of terms. Besides, you have been doing well. I've kept my eye on you and your cohorts."

"You've been watching me?" Alaster couldn't hide his surprise.

Julleg pulled him into a narrow alcove, shadows swallowing them both. "Of course. I have an investment in you. More importantly, I have information that Amets has yet to discover."

Alaster's eyes widened. "What information?"

Julleg peeked down the hall in both directions before speaking. "This keeper that Amets found reference of—be careful of him. He is not what you wish for him, but he can be helpful. It is true many prophecies exist referring to him, but many of those scrolls conflict." He checked the corridor again, as though expecting a spy to materialize from the stone. "Just remember, prophecies are fluid. They can mean one thing today and something else tomorrow. I cannot tell you more but watch every clue for its genuineness and timeliness. Both aspects decide the validity of the ancient statements."

With that, Julleg stepped out of the alcove and walked down the hallway, robes whispering against the stone.

Alaster called after him, "When will I see you again?"

Without turning, Julleg replied, "When the need is great."

He rounded the corner and vanished.

Chapter Nineteen

Beginnings are easy, but after that,
happiness takes some work

—Liz Thebart

Jack took an evening walk to clear his head before the team left for Blackhaven. He followed the curve of the small lake north of Alderg, where the river widened before flowing south into the bay. A young couple sat close together on the shore, absorbed in each other. Jack continued on, but the sight stirred thoughts he had avoided for years. His last relationship had withered while he served overseas, and the ache of that loss had followed him even into death.

He glanced back—and recognized the couple. Nathan and Lily. Jack smiled. Their closeness made sense now. Nathan's patient riding lessons, Lily's trust, the quiet evenings near the horses—it had all been leading here.

Their connection mirrored what he saw forming between Scott and Asta. Jack suspected the other men would soon seek companionship of their own.

When he first arrived on Eldriko, confusion had smothered any thought of companionship. Yet he had never truly been alone. From the beginning, Kendra had been there—steady, present, grounding.

His thoughts snapped back as Scott approached from behind. "There you are. Are we all set to leave in the morning?"

"I think we are ready—if you did your job." Jack smiled as Scott feigned shock.

"When have I ever not been ready to move out, LT?"

"If you keep calling me LT, I'm going to short-sheet your bed." Jack shook his head, amused by the familiar banter. He glanced back at Nathan and Lily, and Scott followed his gaze.

"They have been getting closer almost daily."

"I noticed that. It's sad for me to say it, but I just noticed it today." Jack watched them a moment longer. "They are a lucky pair."

Scott looked at him. "No luckier than you are."

Jack turned. "I'm sure I don't know what you mean."

"Oh, please, Jack. We can all see it. Day after day, you and Kendra are close."

"Come on, Scott, we are just friends." Jack felt his breath quicken.

Scott laughed. "Just keep telling yourself that, Jack. You might even convince yourself. But I'll tell you this," he said, suddenly serious, "if you let her get away, you are a damned fool and deserve to live a miserable and lonely life."

He started toward the gate, then turned back. "I mean it, Jack. She will find someone else if you don't tell her how you feel. Even a healer needs someone in her bed to keep her warm." He walked away without looking back. Jack watched him join Asta, and together they headed toward the pub.

Jack had much to think about as he made for the inn. He considered stopping for a drink but decided sleep was wiser. Four restless hours later, he regretted skipping the ale—the pub had long since closed.

Morning came too soon. Jack knew the long ride would exhaust him. By the time he reached the training grounds, Scott had already organized the group.

"You ready, boss?" Scott grinned, noting the dark circles under Jack's eyes. He knew Jack would perform, but he also knew he'd be dragging.

Scott led their mixed company eastward. Their chatter filled the road—everyone except Jack, who drifted between exhaustion and the echo of Scott's words.

An hour into the journey, Jack made his decision. He spotted Kendra riding beside Kialin's wagon, slightly behind the others. He reined back, crossed the road, and eased up beside her.

Kendra glanced at him. "You know, Jack, you really need to get some sleep when you find a bed."

Jack chuckled. "You're right, of course. I just had a lot on my mind last night."

Kendra studied him. "Anything you want to talk about?"

Jack rode in silence for several paces. "I never thanked you for coming to my aid when I first came to Asher. You were a lifesaver."

She waited, sensing more.

"You have been a welcomed companion as my journey dragged you along with me. Even as we gained followers, you remained someone I depended on."

"What are you saying, Jack?"

"I realized that you are important to me. You are essential to my well-being. You've healed me, treated my injuries, and talked me out of my loneliness."

Kendra frowned. "Jack, get to the point, will you? You are taking me all around the mountain to get down the meadow."

"Kendra..." Jack sighed. "I realized last night that feelings for you have been building since we left Mistdale, perhaps before that."

Kendra smiled and eased her horse closer. "You aren't alone in those feelings. I'm glad you were able to admit them."

Jack's eyes widened. "What? You knew?"

Kendra nodded. "I suspected. You spend most of your free time with me. It was hard to not see that you had an interest in me."

Jack laughed loudly enough that several companions turned. Scott glanced back, smiled, winked, and nudged his horse forward.

Kendra looked at Jack, who shook his head. "He already guessed." Jack laughed again.

᧡

Teyr woke from the vision drenched in sweat. As with all her visions, no clear prediction emerged—only the force of the warning and the unmistakable subject of it. Jack had appeared prominently again, just as he had ever since arriving at the archive in Riven. Communication from Riven had ceased nearly a year ago with no explanation. Teyr had chosen to leave the matter in Kialin's hands as Arch-Monk, but the vision she'd just endured made her reconsider that decision.

In her dream, she saw Jack arrive at the Riven archive, only to be blocked by the aide to the Lead Archivist. She saw Kialin attempt to intervene, but the local monks barred him as well. The vision darkened beneath the shadow of a bear. A ghostly shape slipped unnoticed into the vaults, gliding through the passages until it paused before a door marked with a bow repeated three times. Then it dissolved into mist.

The mist cleared, and Teyr saw the aide seated behind the Lead Archivist's desk, signing orders with practiced ease. Monks came and went, carrying documents bearing the aide's signature. Teyr's perspective shifted, drifting into the private chambers of the Lead Archivist. There she found the man himself—restless, unconscious, trapped in a fevered sleep.

The aide entered the room as Teyr's vantage lowered from the corner. He poured a liquid into a glass of water, lifted the archivist's head, and trickled the mixture past his lips. The archivist's agitation eased almost immediately. The aide smiled, set the cup aside, and locked the door behind him as he left.

The memory of the vision struck Teyr with renewed force. She dressed quickly, threw open her chamber door, and strode into the corridor.

"Get Delon Oakel to my office before the hour. And send for the Master of Arms."

The guard stared at her, wide-eyed.

Teyr snapped, "By the gods, NOW!"

❧

Since arriving in the village of Blackhaven, Kendra found herself ill at ease. In some ways, the name of the village revealed more than just the darkness she felt. She wondered what convinced the early settlers to name their home with such a dark name. Even the temple, found on the outskirts of the community, suggested a negative view of the orthodox religion symbolized by the twin spires rising above the nearby squat residences.

When she, Jack, and Kialin approached the monks of the temple for access, they begrudgingly granted it due to Kialin's reputation. Kendra found her way to the Healers' vault to continue her ongoing, multifaceted research while Jack and Kialin descended to the lower-level restricted stacks. Even though the Healers' archive had multiple windows, it felt dark to Kendra. The temple itself had gained a dark tint over the years, both inside and out. Kendra found that the lamps hanging in the archive provided only nominal light for her research and she requested more oil lamps so not to stress her eyes.

She found her thoughts divided while looking for references to healing relics. She wasn't sure what she would find about the often dismissed, as mythical, items. She pored over the texts that she happily found in Common Tongue as well as Healer Codex,

240

which she began to understand at a basic level while in Mistdale. Most of the healers recorded their records in Common Tongue since many had risen from the life of village herbalists before learning the magical arts of the Healers.

Late on the second day of her research, she stumbled upon the most unique looking tome she had seen in the archives. It measured a span by a span-and-a-half, and a half-span thick, with rich parchment pages bound with fine leather. She took it to the workbench and began to leaf through the yellowed sheets. She quickly discovered the volume held, according to the introductory notes, the journals of a highly respected Master Healer named Reena Galsen who lived from more than a century earlier. The healer described her journey from a simple farm girl to a highly skilled healer in the employment of the Manos.

Her notes revealed some of the healing magic she learned as a novice and the spells she researched and recorded later in life. Kendra took careful notes as she methodically read the historical account and continued into the next day, picking up where she left off.

As midday approached, she came across a reference that shook her. Amid the spells and potions systematically recorded, she stumbled upon the words 'Hope of Asher'. Reading those words brought an echo of the significance of the relic. She stared at the words trying to remember if she had ever seen that term before, but a resonance of recognition surged from her very core. It seemed familiar, but she couldn't place its source. Yet the words filled her essence with a deep understanding beyond any training she could remember. She tried to dismiss the thoughts that flooded her mind—Healing and Love. She looked at the following pages for a deeper description of what that term meant to Reena Galsen.

Kendra found other references to the Hope of Asher with regards to Reena's rise to power in the healing community. According to her journal, Reena had possession of the Hope of Asher during the later years of her life. One reference near the end of the volume revealed Reena's anxiety over the disposition of the Hope of Asher upon her death. The last line speaking of the relic expressed her desire for the Hope of Asher to select its future wielder: 'The Hope' cannot fall into unreasonable hands. I have searched for a means to ensure it only speaks to its rightful heir. With that line, Reena fell silent on the subject in her journal, and Kendra suspected that Reena Galsen fell silent in life.

Kendra spent the rest of the day exploring Reena's journals, but the rest of the volume focused on potion recipes and wording of incantations in the Common Tongue. Kendra recognized some of the spells, but most reached a level of ability that she only aspired to reach one day. She kept meticulous notes of what she read and wished she could persuade the monks to loan the volume to her for an extended time so she could have it copied.

She reached the end of Reena's journals and turned the last page of the journal only to find one final page of text without any other notations. That page had words that Kendra could not understand:

> *Bydded i Geidwad cyfiawn Hope brofi'n deilwng o'r cyfrifoldeb a'r canlyniadau.*

Kendra recognized a rune of protection embossed over the unknown words. Below the cryptic words, Kendra saw the handwritten notation in the shaky pen of one of the elder healers in the Common Tongue. It read:

*May the rightful keeper of Hope prove worthy
of the responsibility and consequences.*

The note, whether a comment or a translation Kendra did not know, ended with the shaky signature of Reena Galsen, and the final words: *The gods be with whoever accepts this charge.*

Kendra looked at the foreign text, sounding out the words in her mind several times, trying to get into the mind of Reena Galsen. On the final reciting of the text on the page, Kendra unconsciously spoke the words softly aloud.

She just finished the phrase when she felt a frigid wind rush past her, and a moan of relief filled the room. Kendra shuddered and looked around the room, which had since fallen silent, but words still found her deepest thoughts: *Finally, the heir found the path to me.*

☙

Kendra's discomfort in Blackhaven discouraged her from walking in the surrounding fields as had become her habit since embarking on the quest with Jack. However, the temple kept a walled garden that served as a substitute for Kendra while pursuing her studies in the dismal mountain village. Evening light began to fade as Kendra entered the torch-lit enclosure. Her mind wandered as she explored the surprising variety of the flora kept by the monks of the temple.

Kendra sat on a bench by the garden pond located behind the compact herbal patch at the back of the garden. Frogs began their evening ritual chorus drifting over the calm water. Kendra felt a presence behind her even before she noticed the soft glow invading the misplaced oasis.

"The writings of Reena Galsen touched you today." The soft, melodic voice both startled and calmed Kendra. "She lived a life much like your own, Kendra."

"Taimi, is that you?" The sudden appearance of her intermittent mentor caught her off guard. "I thought you had left me on my own."

Taimi seemed to glide through the garden as she approached Kendra. "We waited for you to stumble onto Reena's journals, although their discovery was more by design than chance."

Taimi stood beside the calm pond rather than taking a seat on the garden bench. "We directed Reena's journey centuries ago. Now, we will guide your journey."

"You directed Reena?" Kendra tried to understand Taimi's meaning in her words.

A slight smile crossed Taimi's lips as she gazed into the pond. "Not really directed. We gently nudged her field of studies. The times allowed for a subtler hand with Master Galsen." Taimi turned to face Kendra. "We do not have that luxury now with you, Kendra Hess. We will allow your natural progression to continue, but I will step in when you need specific direction."

Kendra quickly thought. "And now is one of those times for direct action by your kind?"

Taimi smiled as she glanced at Kendra. "Not direct action exactly, but we would not want you to miss important writings." Taimi thought for a long minute. "Now that you found Master Galsen's journals, do not take them lightly." Taimi turned to face Kendra directly. "Have you heard thoughts not your own since reading her writings?"

Kendra remembered her experience after finding the cryptic text in Reena's journal. A puzzled look crossed her face. "What is the keeper of Hope?"

Chapter Twenty

Rumours die out faster than they are born, and
I'm prepared for them.

—Rana Daggubati

Jack's chamber was dim, lit only by the soft ambient glow of the torches outside the southern window. The rope-mattress bed offered more comfort than anything he had slept on since arriving on Eldriko. The cool seasonal air made the room pleasant, and Jack drifted into a deep, restful sleep.

A shadow gathered in the high corner above the door. The temperature dipped, as though the darkness itself had drawn the warmth from the room. Jack shifted under the quilt, pulling it closer as he sank into a deep REM sleep. The shadow thickened as his dream deepened.

Jack found himself walking along the river toward a calm pool at a bend in the water. Thick fog clung to the far bank, hiding everything beyond the first few paces. Bullfrogs called from somewhere within the mist. About eight paces out, a faint glow revealed a roil in the pool. A figure rose slowly from the water, as though lifted from the riverbed.

A head emerged first—golden hair framing a face of impossible beauty. The figure continued to rise, not stepping, simply ascending. Shoulders broke the surface, and Jack realized she wore nothing but her own skin. When her feet reached the surface, she walked across the water as if it were stone.

Jack's breath caught as she introduced herself as Caria. Her beauty surpassed anything he had known on Earth or Eldriko. He felt himself drawn to her, compelled to please her. She smiled coyly and reached for him. Jack felt no resistance to her charm. She offered herself to him—if he would only listen to her god, Julleg. Jack felt a deeper pull, a desire to obey whatever Julleg wished.

A blue-white orb appeared behind him. Caria's expression twisted—fear and hatred mingled in her eyes. The shadow from Jack's room descended from the treetops of the dreamworld.

A voice broke from the shadow. "You have no right to be here, Sebin. He must choose of his own free will."

The orb spoke, its swirling light shifting across its surface. "Julleg, you know you cannot use Caria to tempt what I have claimed when he came to us. Back off or face the consequences."

Julleg howled softly, the sound stretching like a threat. "NO! You cannot have him."

As the two forces clashed, Caria's form changed. The innocent beauty melted away, replaced by a colder, older presence—still beautiful, but sharpened, calculating. Jack stepped back, seeing her now as a puppet of the gods, sent to ensnare him. Her power over him broke. With a scream, she dissolved into the fog.

Julleg, seeing his plan unravel, retreated into the trees in his shadowed form. "You cannot protect him all the time, Sebin. I will find a way to have him. You wait and see; he will be mine." His voice faded with the darkness.

Jack jolted awake from the nightmare of gods and demons. His heart pounded, breath ragged. It took long moments before he could push the dream aside. Eventually, exhaustion reclaimed him, and he drifted into a restless sleep until the rooster crowed.

§♦

Jack took the morning off in Blackhaven, leaving Kialin to explore the temple's modest holdings alone. He still struggled to make sense of the vision he'd had on his last night in Alderg. In the days leading up to it, Loki had been absent, avoiding the city as if its walls repelled her. But once they left for Blackhaven, the coyote reappeared and stayed close. Jack couldn't decide whether she was watching him, guarding him, or simply following her own inscrutable instincts. Most of her behavior had been a mystery since his final days on Earth.

He wandered through the narrow byways of the small town, wondering how its merchants survived in such a grim, unimpressive place. Blackhaven maintained a single public space that served as green, market, and grazing pasture all at once. As Jack approached it, the area felt unexpectedly peaceful.

Near the center of the green, Asta practiced her shadow-fencing. Jack stopped about ten paces away, watching the fluid precision of her movements. Her routine resembled a martial dance—thrust, parry, slash, riposte—advancing, retreating, circling through the compass points. Her blade flowed through high and low guards before she returned to her opening stance.

Asta finished her circuit and noticed Jack watching with a faint smile. She took a resting position and wiped her blade as though she had just dispatched an unseen foe.

"Good morning, Jack." She gave him a puzzled look. "Did they lock you out of the temple?"

Jack shook his head. "I just took a day off." He glanced around the green. "This is the only peaceful part of this town."

Asta sheathed her blade. "It is peaceful enough to get my meditative practice in before too many people interrupt me."

"Oh, I didn't mean to disturb your exercise." Jack's remorse was genuine.

Asta waved a hand. "No harm. I was nearly finished."

Jack stood in silence for several moments, lost in thought. "Jack, are you alright?" Asta had never seen him so withdrawn.

He met her eyes. "Can we talk a little—in private, I mean?"

She gestured for him to lead. Jack walked to the far side of the green where a rough bench sat beside a small copse of young trees.

"What is wrong, Jack?" Asta asked, concern softening her voice.

He took a deep breath. "The other night, evening really, I saw something not quite real, yet so compelling just the same."

"You have my complete attention, Jack."

Jack explained the vision in detail. Asta listened closely, asking precise questions about what he saw, how it felt, and who appeared. Jack answered as honestly as he could.

250

Her final question surprised him. "Did you have Targonith on your belt when you walked outside the gates?"

"What does that have to do with what I saw and heard?" Jack didn't understand.

Asta simply raised an eyebrow.

"Okay, yes, I had my sword on. It isn't always safe at dusk outside the gates." Jack still didn't see where she was going.

"I suspected as much." Asta paused, choosing her next words carefully. "Jack, Mother should have informed you of the attributes of that sword. It now falls to me."

Jack opened his mouth, but no words came. His mind was still trying to catch up.

Asta lifted her hand. "Let me tell you about that sword before you ask your questions." She waited for his nod. "Targonith accompanied our father and his ancestors for several centuries. I did not say Targonith belonged to anyone, because she does not. She offered her services to our ancestors in a time of extreme despair for our world." Asta glanced at the sword on Jack's belt. "Good, I see you have her with you now. Never be without her. It could mean the difference between life and death for any of us."

Jack's hand drifted to the hilt. "She?"

Asta smiled. "Yes, Targonith is a 'she,' and you need to remember that. How long has it been since Teyr presented Targonith to you?"

Jack thought. "I don't know. Maybe a few months. It was spring when we got to Mistdale, I think."

"That sounds about right." Asta nodded. "I expect you have felt Targonith trying to reach out to your thoughts in different ways. Have you?"

Jack hesitated. "Are you saying that vision could have been Targonith trying to contact me?"

"That is one possibility." Asta's grin was small but knowing. "In that vision, you mentioned a name. I do not mean when you refer to Loki. We know about her well enough. You only used the other name once. I think you mentioned Julleg, did you not?"

Jack replayed the memory. "Yes, that was a name that Loki mentioned to me. And Kialin told me the history of Julleg. What do you know about Julleg?"

Asta took a steadying breath. "The family tale suggested that Julleg formed Targonith to hold a presence with an influential Manos family such as ours. Julleg is a chaotic god who relies on the end justifying how she achieves such ends. Two other gods contributed to the forging of Targonith with a more controlled influence over her actions—most of the time. Father mentioned that Targonith still follows that chaotic path occasionally."

Jack tried to process this. "Do you mean that this sword will force my behavior?"

Asta shook her head. "Far from it. However, Targonith may influence your thinking and decision-making. She has her own agenda that you must constantly realize exists. Your strength in wielding a sword like Targonith is that of your companions. We can provide council to balance both the chaotic and the harmonious influences of Targonith."

Jack sat in silence, trying to make sense of it. *Great. Now I have a sword in my head,* he thought.

A voice answered him—distinctly feminine, unmistakably present. *Yes, we are of one mind now.*

᠖᠉

Amets helped Alaster find a cart-full of Common Tongue histories that might hold clues to the mystic relic they sought. He instructed Alaster to study the histories in the upper workroom of the library's historic catacombs while he descended three floors deeper into the restricted vaults to examine the older codices open only to trained Aneglur monks and librarians.

Alaster leafed through the tomes one by one, struggling to stay focused. His mind kept drifting back to the journey from Blackhaven. Amets had assured him the voyage would be short and easy in late summer. Alaster boarded the cargo ship expecting a week-long trip on gentle swells to the northern bay below the mountainside Aneglur castle-library. But expectations fell victim to a freak gale out of the northeast. The one-week trip along the eastern Asher coast became a battle to stay off the shoals. The captain and crew fought the winds and house-sized waves with grim determination, inching their way toward the bay—a sanctuary from the hellish typhoon.

As a landlocked merchant, Alaster had never experienced true sea travel. Rivers and lakes were all he knew. When the storm hit, he learned quickly how different the high seas were. His stomach rebelled whether he had eaten or not. He retreated to his cabin, but the waves followed him. The bucket provided by the crew proved useless as the swells tipped it over, filling the cabin with a pungent stench. He tried to go topside, but the moment he opened the hatch, the ship lurched and threw him down the stairs. He returned to his cabin, choosing the foul air over the deadly deck. He was certain he would die when the storm finally claimed the ship.

Alaster shuddered at the memory of the harrowing voyage that stretched to just over a fortnight. When the ship finally entered the choppy waters of the bay, it felt like a mirror-still lake. Once docked, he dragged himself onto the pier and spent three days trying to regain his land-legs and coax his stomach into accepting the blandest fare the inn could offer.

He forced those thoughts aside and returned to the material Amets had left him. Much of it read like the dry histories archivists favored. Common Tongue volumes tended to attract readers who found the older texts too intellectual, but Alaster trusted Amets's judgment that something important might be hidden among them.

He pulled the next book from the cart: *Recent Discoveries of the Second Age of Althaeon General Practitioners*, by Brother Jorvik Moran. He had never heard the term "Second Age," and curiosity nudged him to open it. The contents read like a census—citizens, livestock, lands owned and rented, professions, and the nobility governing each principality of Asher.

Alaster skimmed the dry material until he reached a section titled "Known Relics, Amulets, and Icons." He slowed, hoping for a reference to the relic he sought. Several items caught his attention, but he pressed on, searching for the one relic that had consumed his thoughts for months.

Then he saw it—a reference to the Heart of Sheol. Moran listed it among "lost relics" and considered it more myth than fact. He included a translation of an old record that some monks regarded as prophecy. The words leapt from the page:

The product of the gods' intent to balance the lands and seas, forged and formed with their cooperation and single-mindedness, rested in the core of the mountain of the gods for millennia undisturbed.

In time, the gods squabbled over the proper caretakers of the Heart of Sheol in the First Age. When the year-end council met in the core of the mountain, the unwelcomed discovery of the empty nest of the Heart raised the accusations of the gods that drove a wedge between their classes.

As the gods departed the core of the mountain, the Chaotic god declared that the Heart could only be located and returned by the hand and direction of the Seeker in the time of outside upheaval.

Alaster stared at the page, unsure whether to take the text literally or figuratively. The rest of the book had been factual and straightforward, but this section felt out of place—as though it existed outside time. Something about it lodged itself in his mind.

At that moment, Amets called up from the vaults below. "Alaster! I think I found it. Get down here, quickly."

Alaster doubted Amets had found anything as important as what he had just discovered. He scribbled the prophecy onto a scrap of parchment and shouted back, "I will be down after I copy this text. Won't be a minute." He wrote feverishly, reread the copy, and satisfied with its accuracy, bounded down the stairs.

He found Amets in the third vault to the left and thrust the parchment toward him. "I found it." Alaster grinned, breathless, as Amets read the note. When Amets looked up, Alaster blurted, "I'm the Seeker. I just know it."

Amets slowly nodded and handed the parchment back. "Could be, my friend, if there is only one Seeker."

Alaster stared at him, shocked. "What do you mean? I copied it straight from a two-hundred-year-old book. I copied it faithfully."

"I didn't mean to imply you made some mistake." Amets chose his words carefully. "I found a similar text in Codex, but..."

Alaster cut him off. "But what?"

"In Codex, this text is word for word the same, with one difference." Amets pointed to the Codex Alaster could not read. "Right here, it also used the word for seeker, but the Codex word was more ambiguous. Where the Common Tongue said, or implies, the seeker, the Codex clearly used the word for seeker that intended to suggest a seeker or more than one seeker. The context was intentionally unclear." He let the meaning settle. "Alaster, there may be other seekers of the Heart. The hero we read about in Alderg may not be our hero."

§♦

Jack found the last few weeks exhausting, both physically and emotionally. By the time they reached Tavenshell, he knew he needed a few days of rest to think clearly again. Kialin knew the archives well but needed an assistant to sift through the stacks for references to both the Hope of Asher and the Heart of Sheol. He suspected that notes about the Heart would be scarce in any archive. Asta agreed to help Kialin and Kendra, leaving Jack free to explore the mountains along the eastern seacoast.

Jack's only experience with a seacoast came from his deployment in the Middle East before his unit moved inland. The shore near Tavenshell offered a welcome respite. He even stripped down to skinny-dip in a secluded cove south of the academic town. Tavenshell, he learned, held not only a major Manos archive but a university as well. Kialin had secured the help of an elder student who felt honored to work with the Arch-Monk, even temporarily.

On the second evening after Kialin and Asta began sorting through the older documents, the Union gathered at the only pub in Tavenshell to share their day. Kialin, well-known to the pubkeeper, arranged for a large table in the back meeting room. They arrived later than the usual university crowd. The pubkeeper personally escorted them to the private room and closed the double doors before shouting orders to the servers. Within minutes, bowls of cubed beef, root vegetables, steamed greens, and pitchers of ale filled the center of the ten-span table. The Union dug in, filling the room with excited chatter.

Jack picked at his plate while listening to his intentional family. Each of them had come to him in a different way. Scott came first, from the same world. Jack had learned to trust him, mourn him, and reconnect with him—the best warrior he had ever known. Kendra had found him when he was still trying to understand this new world. Asta was the strangest addition, sharing blood with him despite coming from another world entirely. Ronan had arrived as part of Scott's story, a man Scott had mentored after arriving on Eldriko.

The newest members came quickly but blended seamlessly. Kialin, the Arch-Monk, felt an immediate kinship with Jack and helped him navigate the chaotic archives. Nathan and Lily had been abandoned on Eldriko like Jack. Casey, the youngest, had left his merchant life to join the Union and find his own path.

And then there was Loki—the most unusual member of all. She had joined him before he died on Earth and had become a regular, though not constant, companion. She always seemed to appear when Jack needed her most and vanish when he entered a large town. Over the last eight weeks, Jack noticed she had grown rounder. When she disappeared into a thicket, he realized she must be carrying a litter and would be gone for a while.

Jack tried to follow the overlapping conversations. He smiled at the rapid-fire exchanges and the celebrations of their discoveries. Kendra couldn't stop praising the orderly records of the healing arts and the Master Healer who supervised the cataloguing. Kialin and Asta discussed their findings in the restricted section. Jack chuckled at how easily Kialin gained access to the vaults he needed. On the first day, an apprentice archivist tried to block him and quickly found himself mucking out stables for the next month.

As the conversation continued, Jack noticed Kendra being drawn into Kialin's and Asta's discussion. Soon the three of them were deep in conversation about the excellent curation of the volumes and scrolls they had examined. Kendra excitedly shared her discovery of references to the Hope of Asher. Kialin and Asta chimed in with similar findings. Kendra's excitement grew when she learned her topic appeared in at least three separate sections of the archives. Plans formed quickly for the three of them to combine their efforts.

Scott and Nathan planned a hunt in the mountains the next morning, much to Lily's disappointment. She had grown used to her morning rides with Nathan. He soothed her with a promise of an afternoon ride along the seashore. Ronan, who had lived far from the sea, wanted to explore the coves south of Tavenshell and invited Lily and Casey to join him.

Jack listened to the lively banter and felt his thoughts pulled into each of their lives—the people he now called family. He loved each of them in a way he had never felt for those outside blood. As he listened to Kialin, Asta, and Kendra discuss their literary treasure hunt, he felt a pull of his own—a desire to explore the stacks alone, following only his instincts. He would have to wait until Kialin descended into the deep vaults before slipping away.

Everyone made plans to explore different parts of the university town. Only Jack planned a solitary morning. He grabbed his bow and slipped away for a quiet hunt, hoping for fresh venison while the others researched. As the evening wound down, Jack's plan solidified. He would either need to reach the deep stacks before Kialin began his work or wait until Kialin was fully absorbed in his search.

Morning would decide for him.

&

A thick fog embraced the forest of the lower mountains. Scott and Nathan were used to the usual mist that clung to Eldriko, but this fog pressed in with a claustrophobic weight that unsettled Scott. Nathan handled it better for reasons Scott couldn't name. A light wind swirled the fog into shifting pockets, opening brief shooting lanes where deer appeared and vanished before either man could draw a bow.

As morning light strengthened, the wind thinned the fog to a lingering mist. Wildlife began to stir. Scott moved into a patch where the underbrush opened. He caught movement through the brush but couldn't make out the creature approaching. His eyes tracked the shifting shape until a deer stepped into view, exposing its head and neck.

A twig snapped to the right of the deer.

The deer's head jerked up, then back, and it bolted into the thicket. Scott and Nathan exchanged a look before turning toward the sound of something pushing through the brush.

When the creature emerged, all three froze, struggling to understand what stood before them.

Scott towered beside Nathan with his usual commanding presence. At six-foot-five, muscular, and carrying the strength of his Louisiana ancestry, he had always seemed larger than life. Nathan, though strong and broad-shouldered, carried the leaner build of his indigenous New York ancestors. He was competent with a bow, but his sword was more ornament than weapon despite training with Scott and Asta.

Neither man was prepared for the creature that stepped into the clearing.

It stood nearly six-foot-seven—a man with the head of a wolf, holding a compact bow. It locked eyes with Scott, dropped the bow, and drew a broadsword.

Scott mirrored the motion, drawing his longsword and taking a defensive stance. Nathan hesitated, then followed Scott's lead.

The standoff ended in an instant. The creature growled and charged Nathan. Nathan swung too early and missed. The creature did not. Its blade slashed Nathan's right shoulder, dropping him to the ground and out of the fight.

Scott seized the opening and struck the creature's shoulder, but his blade bounced off armor. They squared off, exchanging parries and testing defenses. Scott landed a minor hit on the creature's off-arm but took a shallow chest wound in return. Their blades clashed in a rhythm of thrusts, slashes, and guarded retreats. Scott could hear the creature's breathing grow ragged, matching his own.

Scott stepped back and growled, "What the hell are you?"

The creature cocked its head and replied, "I'm not from hell. I am a Son of Adam."

Scott's mouth fell open. "You spoke."

"As did you, human." The creature held its sword defensively but no longer advanced.

Scott noticed the ichthys hanging from a leather cord around its neck. "Where did you get that?" he asked, pointing to the wooden fish.

The man-wolf looked down and tucked the carving into his tunic. "It is a symbol of my faith."

Scott lowered his blade slightly. "That is also a symbol in my faith, or it was centuries ago. One of the earliest symbols."

The wolf head tilted. "You follow The Way?"

Scott's mind spun. He remembered that early Christians had been called followers of the Way. He nodded slowly. "I am, though it has been a while since I met other followers."

The man-wolf lowered his sword. "Then we are brothers, and I cannot fight you. My name is Kyneos Ashstone, late of Alemara before the expulsion and genocide two hundred years ago."

Scott lowered his sword to match him. "I'm Scott Boudreau of Louisiana."

Kyneos glanced at Nathan, who lay clutching his shoulder. "Your companion needs tending. Do you have a healer with you?"

"We do, but not out here." Scott pulled a crude roll of bandages from his pack. "I'll bind it up, then we need to get him to the city, to our healer."

Kyneos opened a pouch. "Let me sprinkle this on the wound, or it will fester." Scott nodded, and Kyneos applied a generous coating before Scott bound the injury.

Scott looked toward the city hidden by the forest. "We decided to walk out here this morning for our hunt. I'll have to carry him back."

Kyneos followed his gaze. "I'll carry him. It was my blade that caused the wound." He hesitated. "I cannot enter your city. Humans have hunted my kind for centuries. That is how I came to be in this world."

Scott helped him lift Nathan gently. "What do you mean?"

Kyneos began walking. "You are an Offlander, are you not? You do not carry yourself as an Eratha, and you certainly are no Manos or Fairmen."

"You are right, I'm from Earth—before I died, that is." Scott tried to read Kyneos' expression, but the wolf features made it difficult.

"My race originated on Earth. We spread from North Africa across to India. Some traveled further. In the fourth century, my people found solace and hope in following The Way. We coexisted with the orthodox Church for decades, more successfully in the Indian provinces than the western empire." Kyneos paused. "In 364 Anno Domini, the Church, despite Augustine's treatise, declared my race not sons of Adam, and therefore not recipients of Grace." His voice tightened. "They ordered our destruction, but not before the conversion of many of us. I hoped some of my brethren escaped the sword, but many found themselves here in this world with me. We continue the work of the Way with limited success."

Scott walked beside him, absorbing the tale—a story of faith, exile, and survival across worlds. He felt a growing kinship with the warrior who, like him, was out of place in two worlds.

Chapter Twenty-One

I think everybody encounters difficulty.
It's just more pitched in some people.

—JULIA CAMERON

Jack returned to the archives of Tavenshell after taking a few days away from the research he and Kialin had begun weeks earlier in Edhearn. Kialin possessed an intellectual endurance Jack could only admire from a distance. After a short break, Jack felt clear-headed again and ready to rejoin the work. They started early, heading into the vaults just after Scott and Nathan left for their morning hunt. Jack wished he could have gone with them, but the search for any reference to the Heart of Sheol weighed on him. Kialin pointed him toward shelves containing Common Tongue tomes that might prove useful.

Jack worked through the volumes for over an hour before a familiar sensation washed over him.

"Not now," he hissed under his breath.

He had no control over Loki's visions. His sight blurred, colors muted, and suddenly he was seeing through Loki's eyes— the forested mountainside outside Tavenshell. Scott and Nathan were preparing for a shot as a deer stepped from the brush. The deer snapped its head toward something unseen and bolted. Loki's competitive instinct surged as she prepared to confront another predator encroaching on her hunt.

Then the creature stepped from the forest.

Loki's confidence vanished. Fear overtook her, and she slipped into the brush, glancing back once. Through that final glance, Jack saw the creature facing Scott and Nathan. He saw Nathan fall. Then Loki fled deeper into the woods, and the vision ended.

Jack's sight snapped back to the piles of books. His heart hammered. He stood and hurried down to the vaults where Kialin worked.

"Kialin, I just had a vision."

Kialin looked up sharply. "What was that? Your coyote sight?"

Jack nodded. "I'm afraid so. I saw Scott facing off with a— well, I don't know what it was. All I know is that it scared Loki quickly."

"Loki ran from it?" Kialin's eyebrow arched. "That is serious. What did it look like?"

Jack described the tall figure with a man's body and a wolf's head. "Scott is very stout, but this thing had Scott beat."

Kialin stared. "I cannot believe it." He shook his head. "I have heard tales, of course. Who hasn't? But nobody believes them. They're stories to scare children."

Jack frowned. "Heard about what? Are Scott and Nathan in danger?"

"Most likely, yes, if the tales are accurate." Kialin rifled through the shelves until he found a leather-bound volume. "Here we go. The Complete Guide to the Mythical Creatures of Asher. I thought it was here." He flipped pages. "Yes. The Kethan—part man, part beast. Often with the head of a dire wolf. First sighted fifteen hundred years ago. Rare. Dangerous."

Jack's anxiety spiked. "And they were dangerous?"

"Oh, most certainly. Any Manos foolish enough to face one ceased to exist." Kialin scanned further. "Your sighting is the first in two centuries. Not good news."

"Good God, we need to find Scott and Nathan before it's too late."

Kialin closed the book. "Son, it may already be too late unless they are extremely lucky—or the gods smiled on them."

At that moment, Asta burst through the door. "Jack, you need to come—now! Scott and Nathan were attacked. Nathan does not look well. Kendra is tending to him."

Jack bolted for the door. "Show me." He shouted back, "Kialin, I've got to go!"

"I am behind you, Jack. These books can wait."

They sprinted through the vaults and into the fresh air of the city green. Jack spotted Scott standing over Kendra as she worked on Nathan. She pressed down on the wound through layers of cloth.

"You did a good job, Scott," Kendra said. "I don't know what you put on it, but it stemmed the flow. He won't be lifting or hunting soon, but he'll live."

Lily rushed in, but Kendra held her back gently. "He needs rest. He will recover, I promise. You can sit with him when we get him inside. You can even hold his hand."

Jack turned to Scott, scanning him for injuries. Seeing nothing serious, he snapped into command mode. "What the hell happened out there?"

Scott pulled him aside. "Um, you need to come with me, LT."

Jack followed him through the city gates toward a copse of trees. Before they reached it, Scott stopped.

"I just want to prepare you for what you're about to see."

"What are you talking about?"

"Just keep an open mind, Jack."

Scott stepped into the trees toward a figure sitting by a fire. "Jack, this is Kyneos."

Kyneos rose and turned. Jack felt Loki's fear surge through him again. "Oh my God, what is that?" He drew his sword.

Scott jumped between them. "Stand down, Jack. There was a misunderstanding. I got it worked out."

"I saw him attack Nathan. I thought you both were dead."

"Jack, we all reacted on instinct. Nathan swung too early. Honestly, I think Kyneos pulled back to avoid beheading him." Scott kept his voice calm. "Nathan will be fine. Kendra said so."

Kyneos spoke. "Scott is correct. My strikes were defensive with the young man." He nodded toward Scott. "It was different with that one. I fought with all my skill to stay untouched. He is an accomplished swordsman. I am glad I will not have to face him again."

Jack looked between them. "What am I missing here?"

Scott answered. "It's like this, Jack. Kyneos is a brother. I couldn't fight him again." Seeing Jack's confusion, he added, "Kyneos, show him."

Kyneos reached into his tunic and pulled out the fish-shaped symbol.

Jack stared. "Is that a…"

Kyneos nodded. "It is a symbol of my chosen faith. I follow The Way. All my people have for almost two thousand years. We were martyred for it on Earth. Landing on Eldriko did not separate us from our beliefs."

Jack finally understood. Scott accepted Kyneos as a brother of faith.

Asta took her turn at point as they rode up the mountain valley toward the archive at Riven. Kialin had warned Jack earlier that he didn't know what to expect when they reached the gate. The archivist charter house had lost contact with Riven months before. As they passed the one-mile marker, Kialin guided his wagon toward the front of the procession so he could see the situation as soon as the gatehouse came into view. Asta rode beside him, watching the road ahead while chatting casually with the Arch-Monk.

She spotted the squat towers of the gatehouse as the road curved. She slowed her horse, studying the figures gathered there. "Kialin, we may have a problem. Look up there. I see at least a dozen armed men at the gate. Is that standard for an archive?"

Kialin slowed his team. "No, it is not. No more than a pair of guards is normal in a time of peace." He eased the wagon forward until they were a dozen paces from the gate, set the brake, and jumped down. He called out with a practiced, friendly authority, "Hello, the gate."

One of the guards straightened and turned. "We are not looking to trade today. Move along." He turned his back and walked toward the gate.

Asta felt Kialin bristle at the dismissal. "Now see here, pip. Do you know who I am?"

The guard turned again with a scowl. "Yes, you are some poor Fairmen trader, and I told you to move on. Now leave."

Kialin strode forward. "Paddle off and inform Mator Orender that Kialin Lyrien demands an audience with him—immediately!"

The guard reached for his sword. "Master Orander no longer takes visitors. And do you think that name means anything around here?"

Kialin sputtered with indignation. "Y-You will be sleeping in the woods tonight, you arrogant..." His face reddened as he fought for words.

A monk in fine robes appeared at the gate. "Zalon, what is the meaning of this? You were told to admit no one to the archives until Master Orander himself rescinded that order."

"Yes, sir, I know. We did not admit him, but he is becoming insistent."

The monk turned on Kialin. "Sir, whoever you are, we are not accepting visitors currently. Please move along before we resort to force."

Kialin straightened to his full height, his voice carrying the weight of his office. "I don't know who you are, but they view you as having some authority. I am Kialin Lyrien, Arch-Monk of the Archives of Asher, and I demand entry at once."

The monk's face drained of color. "I-I am so sorry. I did not know." He swallowed. "My name is Joron Vantil, Master Orander's aide. Master Orander has been unwell. We closed the archive for the duration of his recovery."

"I expect that you mean you closed it to standard researchers," Kialin said, jaw tightening.

"No, Master Lyrien, to everyone. Including you."

Kialin stepped forward. "Including me? The Arch-Monk of your order? The man you work for?"

Vantil faltered. "I'm sorry, but yes."

Asta prepared to intervene, but a voice rang out behind her. "Stand aside for the personal guard of Teyr Elenya, Madam Chief of the Manos of Asher."

Asta turned to see Delon Oakel advancing with a dozen heavily armed council guards, swords drawn. "Stand down immediately, monk."

Vantil stiffened. "Field Marshall, I cannot allow even you through these gates."

Delon nodded to his aide. A bugle call echoed down the valley. Moments later, the clatter of armor filled the air as Oakel's company trotted into view. Vantil's guards were outnumbered eight to one. He stood down.

Kialin pushed through the line of guards and strode into the archive. He pointed at Vantil. "You! Take me to Orander, now!"

"But Sir, like I told you, he is unwell." Vantil's voice wavered.

Kialin's eyes narrowed. "How long have you been Orander's aide?"

"I ascended to that position eight months ago."

"What were your duties before that?"

Vantil swallowed. "I worked in the stables."

"If you wish to return to the stables, keep blocking my access to my Lead Archivist."

Vantil broke under the force of Kialin's stare. "Y-Yes, Sir. This way if you please."

He led Kialin and Asta through the winding passages, wondering how he could control a man with such presence.

Kialin pushed past him into Orander's quarters. The Lead Archivist lay bedbound, barely moving, breaths shallow.

"What happened to him?" Kialin demanded.

"We do not know," Vantil said—and the lie was obvious.

Kialin examined Orander quickly: chest, skin, heartbeat, temperature. Then he turned to a guard. "Run to the gate and quickly escort the young woman Kendra here. Tell her to bring her Healer bag and to be quick. Your archivist's very life is endangered."

The guard sprinted away and returned within a quarter hour with Kendra and Lily. "Here she is, but she would not come without this other one."

Kialin waved him off. "It is fine, son. You did well."

The guard relaxed. Kendra moved to the bedside and began tending to the ailing archivist while Asta kept a close watch on Vantil.

§❧

Delon Oakel reestablished order in the archive with practiced efficiency. Once the gate was secured, he presented Asta with a courier pouch bearing the seal of Teyr, her mother. He then moved his personal guard into the armory just inside the gate, displacing the archive guards and billeting them in field tents outside with the rest of his company.

Delon had already read his sealed orders upon securing the gate and had carried out Teyr's first directive: Joron Vantil was placed under arrest and escorted to the cells that had not been used in eighty years. Vantil protested loudly as he was led away, but it made no difference.

"What are you going to do with him?" Asta asked.

Delon chuckled. "I will ship him back to face Teyr. I am tempted to tell him what awaits him before he leaves under guard, but that would be too cruel. Still, I would love to see his face when he learns that his fate depends on Teyr herself."

Asta took the pouch to the guard captain's office, broke the seal, and read through the multipage directive. When she returned to the great room just inside the security gate, she said, "Delon, would you send for all of Jack's Union to meet me here? My mother has thoughts for all of them."

Delon nodded sharply, recognizing her authority as Teyr's representative. He dispatched a guard to gather everyone who had traveled with Jack. Within half an hour, the Union assembled. Kendra arrived last, explaining she wanted to ensure her patient was stable before leaving his side.

Asta waited until they all gathered. "The Madam Chief of Mistdale sends her greetings and her hopes that we are all well and safe. She sent missives to the seven members of our Union that she knew about. I opened mine and read my orders before I sent for you. Officially, she views me as her representative on this journey, even though she recognizes Jack as the commander of our band."

She looked over the faces of her companions—her friends, her intentional family. "Three weeks ago, Teyr had a vision recognizing a danger here at Riven." Murmurs rippled through the group. "I am happy to say that Kialin, with Delon Oakel's assistance, handled that peril effectively."

She lifted the pouch. "Please step forward when I call your name. To those of you who joined us after we left Mistdale, I'm sorry, but Teyr has no knowledge of you, so there are no orders at this time. I will inform her of our current complement."

One by one, Asta handed out the sealed missives. Each recipient broke the wax and read Teyr's words. Asta could almost read the tone of each letter by the expressions that followed.

Jack immediately pulled Kialin aside, the two of them whispering in animated discussion.

Kendra and Lily compared their notes with quiet, knowing smiles.

Scott and Ronan exchanged glances—their orders clearly reinforcing their tactical partnership.

Nathan read his notice with guarded caution. Whatever Teyr had written, he wasn't ready to share it. He slipped the parchment into his pouch and waited silently.

Asta surveyed the room. "Okay, that is all for now. I think we will stay at least four days, right Jack?"

Jack jerked his head up from his conversation. "Huh? What? Oh, yes, yes. At least four days." He immediately returned to his discussion with Kialin.

Asta turned to Scott, Ronan, and Delon. "Before you three leave, a word, if you please."

As the others drifted into their own thoughts, the three warriors remained. Asta led them into the captain's office. "We need to plan how we move forward. Teyr anticipates a more perilous journey ahead of us."

Delon, though commander of the Mistdale detachment, deferred to Asta as the Council's representative. The four of them gathered around the table.

"I want your thoughts," Asta said, "on how to protect the archives while we are here—and how to defend ourselves on the trail."

❧

Jack's and Kialin's discussion stayed intense long after the others drifted out of the great room. Only when their voices echoed back at them did Jack realize they were alone.

"Well, we must have been some fun hosts to this party." He laughed, and Kialin joined him, the sound bouncing off the stone walls.

Kialin shuffled through the papers on the worktable, as though searching for something to anchor his thoughts. "Jack, is there something going on between your man Scott and Asta?"

Jack's head snapped up. "What about Asta and Scott?"

Kialin looked genuinely perplexed. "I am not sure. Just that they have spent a lot of time together these last few weeks. It must be my mind playing tricks on me. Forget I said anything."

Jack chuckled. "That would be their affair, wouldn't it?"

"That it would, my friend." Kialin shook his head, amused at himself.

Jack drew a long breath. "I think we have some searching to do in the vaults if Teyr is right."

Kialin nodded. "She must have found something she thinks we need. How could I have missed that?"

Jack grinned. "We've been a little busy since we left Mistdale. Teyr only had her own people to oversee."

Kialin snorted. "I will not tell Madam Chief you said that. She might not see the humor." He started toward the hallway leading to the grand stairs. "Are you coming, my friend?"

Jack fell in behind him.

They descended into the lower stacks, searching for the section Teyr had indicated. The ancient journals of the Manos Chiefs were stored here, tucked away in Riven's deep vaults. Kialin finally located the scrolls he wanted. Together, he and Jack sifted through them, hunting for the timeframe of the prophecies and the writings of the philosophers who had shaped them.

The first dozen scrolls were useless. They pressed on into the second hour, Jack working through the Common Tongue texts while Kialin wrestled with the older languages.

Then Kialin let out a low "Hmmm."

Jack looked up. "Did you find something?"

Kialin didn't answer immediately. He kept reading, unrolling more of the scroll. "Could be, my friend. It could well be. Hold on."

Jack set aside his unhelpful scroll and waited.

"Uh-huh, yes, I see." Kialin muttered as he read. "Yes, yes." Finally, he looked up. "I think I have what Teyr wanted us to find."

"Well, what is it? Don't leave me hanging here."

Kialin set the scroll down. "First, they did not say where to find the Heart, but there appear to be references in every archive to where the next clue is located. This archive is no different, but it is the first we've found. That is the easy part. It is not that hard to find the Heart of Sheol. The problem is how to fulfill the prophecy to set things right."

Jack leaned in. "What kind of riddle?"

"That is the thing. There are clues scattered throughout Eldriko. The solution to the two parts of the prophecy will keep us traveling before we have it all put together." Kialin raised his eyes. "It is not just about the relics you collect. It is about who has each of those relics and the order in which they stand when trying to invoke them. Jack, you are the keystone to this as the one suggested in the prophecy in Mistdale. You gather your companions, and they collect the relics."

Jack whispered, "Me?"

Kialin nodded. "Jack, it also says the gods will fight about you—some for and some against."

Jack's temper flared. "I refuse to be anybody's damn puppet, even a god's."

"Not a puppet, Jack." Kialin softened his tone. "How can I say this? You are more like the fulcrum. Without you, nobody else has the power, or the means, to affect the return to balance. The other nine—including myself, if I am reading this correctly— will direct their acquired power through you to restore balance to Eldriko. And Jack? This prophecy does not rule out injury for any of us as part of this journey. The possibility of death for any of us, other than you, also exists."

Chapter Twenty-Two

The harder the conflict,
the more glorious the triumph.

—THOMAS PAINE

J ack sat across the table from Kialin in a state of shock. "I know we have run into some problems with brigands and wildlife, but that paper is saying some of us might die?"

Kialin saw the fear and frustration in Jack's face and nodded. "Yes, Jack, that is what the prophecy suggests. We must remember, though, that prophecies are shadows of what might happen rather than declarations of what will happen. This prophecy seems more concerned about the overall goal of your journey rather than the details of the daily risks we all may face."

Jack stared at the parchment in Kialin's hand. "This is getting harder than I thought. The injuries to our group were hard enough, but you are saying that one or more of us may be maimed or killed?"

Kialin understood the weight settling on Jack's shoulders. His own life had been spent among scrolls, not battlefields. He chose a different angle. "Jack, you said you commanded warriors on your previous world, did you not?"

Jack nodded slowly. "I did. What is your point?"

"Did any in your command die due to your leadership?"

Jack froze. He hadn't let himself think about that in depth since reuniting with Scott on Eldriko. "Yes, I lost men."

Kialin pressed gently. "I believe that Scott was one of those men you lost."

The truth hit Jack like a physical blow. His voice failed him. Tears slid down his cheeks as he nodded.

Kialin let the silence sit, giving Jack space to face the memory he had buried. When he finally spoke, his voice was soft. "Did Scott ever blame you for what cost his life on your world?"

Jack shook his head. "Scott understood the consequences of the decision to enlist. He was, he is, a professional soldier. He never questioned my command, and he didn't blame me for his injuries that killed him."

Kialin lowered his voice further. "Jack, do you not think the rest of us knew what we faced when we decided to follow you on this journey?"

Jack shook his head. "How could they know this could kill or maim them? They weren't trained for any of this."

Kialin's grin was small but warm. "You think they have not trained? Have you bothered to look out there whenever we stop for a rest? Asta is sparring with anyone willing. Nathan is teaching Lily to ride. Scott offers hand-to-hand combat with anyone—though he claims it is for his own practice, we both know what he is doing. And Kendra? She devours every healing text she can find. At every archive, she studies how to save lives and treat battle wounds. You do not think they know what might happen on this journey? You think they have not thought about the death of a friend, or of themselves?"

Jack realized he hadn't truly seen them—not as individuals preparing for danger, but as people quietly choosing courage. "You're right. I didn't give it much thought. Each of them has been preparing in their own way. I was so focused on the task Teyr gave me; I didn't stop to notice."

Kialin nodded, pleased. "Trust them, Jack. They all are playing a vital role in this drama that Teyr laid out before us."

Jack took a deep breath, steadying himself. "They are good companions. I know I wouldn't have gone this far without them. Even Kyneos found his place among us." He looked at Kialin. "Kyneos is fitting in with the rest of them, isn't he?"

"He is getting there," Kialin said carefully. "Most have never even heard of the Kethan, let alone met one. They are such a solitary race that most scholars relegate them to myths and legends. Even I was happily surprised to make his acquaintance."

Jack grinned. "You were surprised? I'll have to write today's date down in my journal. I don't want to forget the day that surprised the Arch-Monk of Archives."

Kialin shook his head with a smile. "Take care, my friend, I may have additional surprises for you."

Their banter eased the tension, but the truth lingered. Jack's role in Eldriko's unfolding story pressed on him like a weight he could no longer ignore.

He thought of the journey as a play. Teyr had produced it. He and his companions acted the parts. Today, Kialin became the director. But who had written the script? Ancient prophets had penned the words, but Jack now understood the gods had authored the thoughts behind them.

And the ending was unwritten.

Jack's decisions—his leadership, his courage, his failures— would write the final scenes. His choice to accept Teyr's task bound him to the journey's end. The path ahead would either restore Eldriko to its former balance... or doom it to the perpetual gloom that had become its shadowed state.

€

Jack rode in silence, listening to the banter among the Union. Even Kyneos joined in from time to time. Everyone took Scott's playful teasing as a natural part of his personality. Kialin kept up a steady stream of conversation with anyone who rode near his wagon, and Jack recognized it for what it was—an informal check on everyone's emotional state. Weeks on the road wore on a person, mentally and physically. The stops at libraries and archives had become essential moments of rest for most of the group.

The road north toward DragonPass was well traveled, with occasional pull-offs and mountain pastures used by Fairmen caravans. Jack assumed it served as a major trade route, though calling it a "highway" would have been generous by Earth standards. Asta estimated the trek would take a fortnight at a steady pace. They had left Riven five days earlier, and Jack felt good about their progress.

Just after their midday stop, they encountered an old man walking south. He waved them down. "'Ello, mate! 'Eding up DragonPass way, then? Ain't exactly the safest route, know what I mean?"

Jack halted his horse and glanced at Scott before answering. "Hello, old-timer. Did you say the road isn't safe?"

The man leaned on his staff. "Not for the last half 'ear, mate. Bandits've been causin' trouble since early spring."

Jack looked to Kialin for confirmation. Kialin shrugged. "This road runs in cycles. Some months are safe, others hazardous. Word usually spreads when it is best to take an alternate route."

Jack sighed. "Great. We're five days in, and now we need to divert to avoid bandits."

The old man tapped his staff. "Take the ridge trail, mate. Fewer bandits bother wi' it. T'ain't as profitable up 'igh."

Kendra offered him food and water while Jack conferred with Scott and Kialin. They agreed the ridge trail might not be faster, but it would likely be safer.

The old man described a large boulder hidden behind scrub trees—the marker for the turnoff.

Jack nodded. "You may have saved us from brigands. Thank you." He studied the man. "What is your name? You seem familiar to me."

The old man smiled and turned south again. "My name is Nadre, mate. Farewell, Jack." He disappeared around a bend.

Kialin took the lead up the incline. The rest followed, guiding the horses carefully. They had been climbing for nearly fifteen minutes when Jack suddenly realized Nadre had called him by name. No one had mentioned it in the old man's presence. It wasn't dangerous—just strange.

The trail grew steeper, forcing the men to dismount and help push Kialin's wagon at intervals. By late afternoon, the forest thinned as they neared the tree line. They found an alpine meadow suitable for camp. The clouds had lifted into a high overcast, revealing the mountains to the east and the valleys to the west. Ground squirrels darted through the grass, and mountain sheep grazed at the meadow's edge, unbothered by the newcomers.

Jack looked north. The trail followed the ridge, level for now. He hoped it would stay that way for a day or two before descending toward DragonPass.

As he turned to speak with Kialin, he noticed a bank of clouds forming to the east. Towering columns rose into the sky— thunderstorm clouds, unmistakable.

Oh, great. Just what we need out in the open.

He hurried back to camp. "Okay, everybody, if you look to the east, I think you'll agree we're in for an interesting night and maybe tomorrow as well."

Before he could say more, Scott took over. "Let's get this camp secure. Hobble the horses. Stake your tents tight. We're not moving before dark, so let's be ready for that storm."

Jack smiled at the familiar tone—his sergeant doing what he did best. He gave the clouds one last look and joined Nathan in securing the horses.

Scott finished staking his tent and immediately headed below the tree line to gather fallen branches for a fire. Kialin parked his wagon on level ground and set the brake. The rest of the Union arranged their bedrolls around the firepit. Scott returned with an armful of branches and sent Casey and Nathan back down the trail for more wood to last the night.

✦

Alaster stepped from the security of the stone archive at DragonPass, as had become his evening habit. The daily study of the records left him drained, and the solitary walks outside the Aneglur repository gave him a chance to breathe before retreating to his chambers. The evening fog thinned as darkness settled across the high valley that cradled the archive.

Even traveling with Amets, Dietz, and Lewis, Alaster often felt a deep loneliness. A year ago, his life had been entirely different. His world revolved around his wife, his children, and his business. One fateful decision by a damned Offlander had cost him almost everything. His business survived only because his son—the last of his family—managed it in his absence. Alaster missed them all with an ache that never dulled. If he could find the miraculous relic, if the legend proved true, he could restore his family. He believed, without hesitation, that the Heart would resurrect his daughter if only he could locate it.

As he walked along the garden wall, a familiar voice broke the silence.

"We must speak, Alaster Kempe."

Alaster turned and found the source—a monk's robe, less than ten paces away. "Do you have more news for me?" He remembered Julleg's warning not to speak his name in public.

Julleg stepped from the shadows into the torchlight. "You might call it news. You could identify it as part warning and part encouragement." He began walking along the garden path, expecting Alaster to fall in beside him.

"What warning do you bring me?" Alaster asked, curiosity tightening his voice.

Julleg continued at a measured pace. "The Keeper your man learned of is a threat to your goal. You must move to eliminate the Keeper and his plans for the Heart."

Alaster felt his heart drop. He had known there might be competition for the relic, but Julleg's words confirmed not only a rival—but a rival whose success would destroy Alaster's last hope of restoring his family. He had never felt more alone. Amets helped him search for clues, but no one understood what he carried. Each passing day brought him closer to the relic, yet each passing mile left him more isolated.

He slowed, then quickened his pace to match Julleg's. "I have no idea where to find this Keeper. How can I rid myself of him?"

"You will move your research to the Manos archival retreat of Riven along the western slopes of the eastern mountains. Hire mercenaries before moving south." Julleg stopped at an overlook above the valley. "Along the western mountain road to the south, you will come upon a mixed party of less than a dozen. Dispose of them—every one of them."

Alaster turned toward him. "And your encouragement?"

Julleg gazed out over the valley. "Do not drag your feet. Time has become essential for our success." He turned and walked down the lower garden path. "Leave no later than midday on the morrow."

Julleg faded into the evening fog, leaving Alaster standing alone.

δ♦

Alaster still felt anxious after the rushed departure from DragonPass following his encounter with Julleg. Julleg's appearances always surprised and confused him. The demand for immediate departure—to ambush a competitor he had never met—went against Alaster's nature of careful planning. Yet the thought that the Heart of Sheol might finally be within reach stirred a dangerous excitement in him.

Within hours, Alaster and Dietz had found and hired five ruffians armed well enough to carry out Julleg's instructions. Alaster had succeeded in business through negotiation and persistence, never through hired blades. The prospect of killing a competitor unsettled him, so he tried to focus on the logistics of reaching Riven.

Dietz had no such reservations. He had long favored less civilized means to achieve his goals, both personally and professionally. He knew exactly where to find the sort of men who would remove obstacles for coin.

They set out as soon as morning light made the mountain road safe. The trail rising from the DragonPass cut narrowed quickly between two ridges before opening onto a stretch where one side hugged a sheer cliff dropping to jagged rocks below. Alaster kept his horse close to the mountainside, away from the drop. Their company spread out with horses and pack-mules as they traveled south. Alaster placed the mercenaries at the front, ready for the encounter Julleg had warned him about. Dietz rode near the head of the line to take command when the skirmish began.

That night, Dietz found a mountain glade where other travelers had camped. They pulled in for a much-needed rest. The hirelings built their own fire away from Alaster and Amets. Dietz and Lewis joined Alaster, as they often did, discussing their expectations for the Riven archive. Dietz and Lewis avoided the archives themselves, but they cared for the horses and repaired gear worn down by constant travel.

Alaster could hear the banter of the five hired men around their fire. Their talk was crude, their laughter rough. After Dietz and Lewis turned in, Alaster listened to the men debate what to expect in the coming conflict. He had told them the terms plainly, and they had agreed. But now they speculated about "fringe benefits" if the targeted party included women. Alaster felt sick. He once had a wife and daughter. He tried to dismiss their talk as crude campfire boasting, but he couldn't convince himself.

The laughter continued until rum dulled their senses and sleep overtook them. Alaster resolved to speak with Dietz in the morning about their comments.

At dawn, Dietz brushed off the concerns. "Just camp talk," he said. "Don't worry." Alaster tried to accept the explanation, but unease lingered.

The men prepared to leave, slower than Alaster hoped. Morning light filtered through the peaks longer than he liked before they finally mounted and took to the road. The trail narrowed again to a wagon's width, forcing them between a rising rock face and a sheer cliff. Alaster edged his horse as far left as possible. The others did the same. These men were lowlanders, unused to mountain paths. Only coin had drawn them into this hazardous terrain.

As they approached the pass, one of the mules caught the cliff's edge with its hoof. It slipped, braying in terror as it fought for footing. The man holding the halter had wrapped the lead around his hand earlier for a firmer grip. When the mule began to slide, he tried to release the halter—too late. The mule's weight yanked him from his horse.

He clawed for anything to stop his fall. His hand caught a branch of a small tree clinging to the cliffside. For a heartbeat, he hung there, struggling to free himself from the halter before the mule dragged him over.

The branch tore free.

Man and mule tumbled together into the rocks below.

Alaster leapt from his horse and ran to the cliff's edge, staring down at the broken bodies. The others joined him in stunned silence.

To his left, one of the hirelings exhaled sharply. "Damn, why didn't he let go?"

Shock rippled through the group. Alaster couldn't remember a time when his business dealings had resulted in someone's death.

Dietz eased up beside him. "Boss, I think there's an alpine glade up by the pass. We should stop for the day. What do ya' think?"

Alaster nodded, still staring at the cliff. "Make it so, Dietz."

Chapter Twenty-Three

In every conceivable manner, the family is a
link to our past, a bridge to our future.

—ALEX HALEY

Morning light revealed the aftermath of the storm. Most of the tents had held up well. Jack's tent had pulled two stakes free and collapsed on one side; the tent shared by Lily and Kendra sagged under the wind and rain but remained intact. Jack noticed the sagging canvas and went to check on them. Nathan had the same thought and arrived just after Jack.

Kendra crawled out and found two anxious faces waiting. "We're good, Jack. The wind made the tent slip a little and we had some water get in, but no harm."

Jack sighed in relief. "At least your tent didn't pull up its stakes. I need to make sure they're in firm ground next time."

Kendra's eyes widened when Jack described his tent collapsing. He showed her where the stakes had pulled free from the soaked earth. Together, they freed the tent, shook out the water, and spread it across high rocks to dry before continuing their journey.

Jack and Scott moved from tent to tent helping pack up. Kialin had no trouble with his wagon and pitched in with the rest of the group.

Two horses had pulled free from the high line, and Ronan drafted Casey to help round them up. Casey knew how to ride but had never lived outdoors for long stretches. Ronan hid a smile as he watched the tenderfoot grow more capable with each passing day. After the storm, Casey went straight to work cleaning up camp and helped Ronan return the horses to the line.

It was midmorning before everything was repacked and they could return to the ridge road. They passed a high-point marker left by some thoughtful traveler and began the descent toward DragonPass. The archive appeared as the road leveled and turned east. Kialin pulled his wagon into a small field used as a goat pasture by the monks.

He set the brake, hopped down, and unharnessed his team, leading them to the corral. The others followed suit, unsaddling their horses and letting them join Kialin's pair.

Kialin rang the bell at the main gate. A young postulant, clearly frustrated at being interrupted during chores, yanked the wooden door open while trying to repair a gear. "What do you want?" he snapped—then looked up and froze at the sight of Kialin's smirk. His face drained of color. "Oh, damn. I mean— welcome to DragonPass, Master Lyrien."

The boy clearly saw his future flashing before his eyes: mucking stalls forever or being dismissed from the order.

Kialin's smirk broke into laughter. "Calm down, son. Let's not make this larger than it is. You had no idea I was coming.

Stick your eyes back in their sockets and the head archivist will never know—unless you decide to confess."

The postulant stammered. "Yes, sir. I mean—no, sir. He shouldn't be bothered with something so insignificant."

Kialin grinned. "You will let me and my friends in, will you not?"

The boy nodded and stepped aside, leading the ten of them into the entryway and then to the guest rooms reserved for important visitors. Once they were settled, Kialin turned to him. "What is your name, boy?"

The postulant swallowed hard. "I'm Ezeen Agney, sir." He lowered his eyes. "I didn't realize it was you when I opened the door, Master Lyrien."

"You worry too much, Ezeen," Kialin said with a grin.

The next morning, Kialin explained to Jack that the secure files held the document he needed. "Jack, why don't you help Kendra with her research in the healer stacks." Jack agreed.

Kendra and Jack wound through the old archive to the level where the healer volumes were kept. They used the central table outside the stacks to examine the centuries-old material. Jack read potion recipes and set aside tomes when Kendra showed interest in a particular treatment or spell. While he searched for what she needed, she delved into older books and scrolls.

They worked together—yet separately—until nearly midday.

"Kendra, I'm getting hungry. Are you ready to take a break?"

"Uh-huh, we can..." She suddenly fell silent, eyes locked on the page. "Oh, gods be praised. I think I found it." She read faster. "I'm sure this is it. We need Kialin, right away." She looked up. "Get someone to bring him as fast as you can, Jack—please."

Kialin arrived in less than a quarter hour. "What have you found, Kendra?"

She handed him the yellowed book and pointed. "Right here. I think this is it."

Kialin scanned the paragraph, then read it again more carefully. "Oh, my." He looked at Kendra, then Jack, then back to Kendra. "This must be it. The reference to the Hope of Asher appeared only two paragraphs earlier. Nothing else until these last two sentences. There is a location mentioned in the next paragraph, but no explicit link between the location and the Hope."

His excitement grew. "Kendra, you've been chasing this relic for a while. Have you had a special feeling about it?"

Kendra thought back. "There was a rush when I first found a reference to it."

"Anything since then? Especially when the term 'Hope of Asher' appeared?"

Kendra nodded. "Every time, Kialin. Why?"

"How did it feel when you read the name of this place where the Hope may reside?"

Kendra smiled. "Like I just discovered a chest full of gold."

Kialin slammed his hand on the table. "I knew it! The relic has been calling you, Kendra. It wants you to find it. Let's see—where is the name of that place again?"

Without looking, Kendra said, "Linhallow."

Kialin and Jack both stared at her. She shrugged. "I thought the name sounded important, so I remembered it. I don't know where it is, though."

Kialin closed the book. "I know where to find Linhallow." He pushed the book to the center of the table. "I grew up less than a league from there. It felt like the end of the world."

❦

Alaster sent Lewis ahead to scout for the party Julleg had warned him about. Lewis had been gone for half a day when he rounded a turn in the mountain road at a canter. He pulled up in front of Alaster to report. "I found them. They are coming up the road only about two miles away. I counted nine in their party."

"Are you sure it is them?" Alaster wanted no mistakes in following Julleg's directions.

"It has to be them," Lewis said. "I saw the road from a curve above. There was nobody else on the road for as far as I could see."

"Very well, let's find a place to take them," Alaster ordered.

"Boss, that curve on the road has a nice little blind spot from the south," Lewis said. "I think we could surprise them there. We can stay hidden until we split them on the road and take them out in pieces."

Alaster looked toward the curve. "Show me."

Lewis led him a quarter mile south to the blind turn. Alaster agreed it was an ideal ambush point. "Good job, Lewis. This will do nicely." He rode back to hurry the others into position. Rocks and brush provided perfect cover.

Alaster and his men hid behind the brush, half of them readying bows for the first strike. The party appeared with a wagon just behind the lead horses. From his vantage point, Alaster saw another half-dozen riders following behind. He motioned for his men to hold until he signaled.

The wagon passed his perch. As the first trailing horsemen came into range, Alaster gave the signal.

The archers released their first volley. Three riders fell from their saddles. The man on the wagon turned at the commotion, and a second volley struck him down. Then the swordsmen rushed from cover, engaging the remaining riders while the archers prepared a final volley.

The so-called battle lasted less than two minutes. The final man dropped from his horse, critically wounded. On the ground, he looked up at Alaster and, with his last breath, asked, "Why?"

Alaster's hired men immediately began rummaging through the packs and wagon for valuables. Attacking an armed force usually meant better weapons, armor, or flasks of spirits. But this time, they found none of it.

"Hey, boss," one of the men called. "I think you need to see this."

Alaster walked to the wagon. He recognized it instantly—he had shipped wagons like this many times, full of goods for remote shops. "What the..." His triumph dissolved into confusion. "These are trade goods. This can't be the mercenaries we were supposed to eliminate."

Another voice called from nearby. "Same here, boss. The packs have trinkets, packaged clothing, and small trade goods. Looks like they're nothing more than merchants on the way to sell their goods."

A sinking feeling hollowed Alaster's chest. If these were merchants, where were the adventurers Julleg had ordered him to kill? He scanned the scene, left to right, dread rising.

No, no, no...

The words slipped out. "No, no, no. This can't be."

One of the men looked down from the wagon. "What should we do, boss?"

Alaster stared at the carnage, then at the cliff below. "Recover your arrows. Do not take anything from their packs or wagon. Throw the bodies off the cliff here. Take the wagon up the road about thirty paces with the driver in the seat and run it off the side. The vultures will take care of the rest."

The men obeyed quickly. They drove the horses forward and pushed the wagon over the cliff. The bodies followed. One of the hirelings, noticing Alaster's attention elsewhere, quietly pocketed a silver flask from a corpse. His lip twitched upward—pleased with his prize and with getting away with it.

After clearing the ambush site, Alaster and his team continued south toward Riven at a slow, deliberate pace. Alaster wanted them to appear as an unconnected group of travelers moving together for safety. By the time they reached Riven, the team had fractured back into its original parts: Alaster's small group seeking the relic, and a loose band of sell-swords already looking for their next employer.

Jack entered the kitchen to break his fast just as Kendra headed toward the healer documents for another day of research. Kialin followed her past Jack with a smile. "Sorry Jack, Kendra nabbed me first thing this morning. She has some difficult codex to translate." He glanced back into the kitchen. "Maybe Asta could help you with the scrolls you plan to study." He grinned and disappeared down the corridor.

Jack sat beside Asta. "Looks like you and I get to make sense of the scrolls in the restricted area. I hope Kialin made arrangements for us to work down there without him."

Asta swallowed a bite of pastry. "He said he did. He also told me you got into some of the Second Age histories and prophecies." She sipped her stout tea. "Those can be tricky, but I'm confident we can figure them out without disturbing any of the monks."

Jack shivered at the thought of involving the Manos monks. Kialin had warned him that the DragonPass archivists disliked relic-hunters. Discussing their research outside the vaults was unwise. Once Jack finished eating, he and Asta made their way to the restricted files and got to work.

Inside the vault, they gathered the scrolls from Kialin's list. The first few held little value. Jack found descriptions of relics he'd never heard of. Asta found only sparse references to the Heart—none within the last five centuries.

They worked through the morning until Jack stumbled on something that caught his eye. "Asta, my Second Age Manos is a little rusty. Could you take a look here?"

Asta laughed. "Since when could you read any Manos, Jack?"

He grinned. "I told you it was rusty—like a sword falling apart in my hands."

Asta walked around the table and leaned over his shoulder. "Which passage?"

Jack pointed to a word in the middle of the text. "Isn't this a word that means heart?"

Asta's eyes widened. She jumped to the beginning of the paragraph. "Yes, Jack, that word does mean heart. Good catch." She read quickly—then stopped. "Amazing. How is it that you can stumble on the right lines?"

"Lucky, I guess." Jack ducked, expecting a swat. "What does it say?"

Asta read carefully. "It's a little disjointed, but the meaning holds. First, it speaks of balance through unity. Unusual wording, even for Second Age prophecies. I remember one reference to balance and unity, but that was First Age—the days of solidarity among the gods. I hope there's more later in the scroll."

She unrolled the parchment. "Here—this line is clear on its own, but confusing in context. It speaks of two hearts beating as one, but the subject is the Heart of Sheol—singular."

Jack stared at the unfamiliar words. "Does it say where they hid the Heart?"

Asta shook her head. "Not here. It might be in other scrolls. This feels like a fragment—something copied because they didn't know where else to put it. Strange for the DragonPass monks."

She unrolled farther and stopped. "Hello. What have we here?"

Jack waited, tension rising. "Well, what is it, Asta?"

"Oh—sorry. This speaks of a Keeper, who from earlier texts we thought might be you. You remember those documents?"

Jack nodded. "I remember—if we interpreted them correctly. Why?"

Asta pointed. "Right here, it speaks of the Keeper, and in the same breath, someone closely connected to him called the Conservatrix."

Jack tilted his head. "What does that mean?"

"In the purest sense, Conservatrix implies partnership and shared responsibility with the Keeper. But it's feminine. In some First Age translations, it carried connotations of submission or servitude." She traced the words again. "Yes—the feminine form."

Jack tried to follow. "If I'm the Keeper, I'll have a female servant called a Conservatrix?"

"May have a servant. Or a partner—someone who shares the burden equally."

She rolled the scroll to the end—and gasped.

Jack's stomach tightened. "What is it? What did you find?"

Asta took a breath. "Jack, the Keeper's Conservatrix is, or becomes, the Keeper's wife so they can place or defend the Heart in its traditional place to balance the world." She looked up at him. "You must take a wife."

Kendra and Kialin joined Jack and Asta in the vault after Asta translated the prophecy that could affect Kendra. She confronted Asta at once. "Are you saying that I might be this Conservatrix you found in the scroll?"

Asta answered calmly. "That is one possible interpretation of the prophecy."

Kendra tried to make sense of it. "This role helps the Keeper in some way to restore Eldriko to its earlier state before. I do not know what that state was centuries ago."

"Millennia ago," Asta corrected softly.

Kendra drew a deep breath. "The Conservatrix is what? A slave? A partner? I'm a little confused."

Asta kept her tone steady. "The true role of the Conservatrix is confusing. The prophecy came in the Second Age, and words and meanings have evolved over the millennia. Some might translate the word as a servant, while other scholars might interpret it as a partner to the Keeper."

Kendra turned away, her thoughts racing. *How would I know if it means me?*

Asta opened the scroll but kept it angled away. "I found a rune in the text—a marker to let the possible Conservatrix know she might be selected. Then it falls to the candidate to decide if she is willing to serve within the restrictions, and the choice of the Keeper to accept the candidate."

Kendra shook her head. "Servant... partner. How can I make an informed decision?"

Asta met her eyes. "Are you saying you would consider the chance to accept the role?"

Kendra looked first at Jack, then back to Asta. "I would be willing to serve, if I meet the requirements, and if the role is not that of a servant."

Jack cleared his throat. "I don't know how much my feelings about this might have on any of this, but..."

Asta cut in gently. "Jack, as the Keeper, your thoughts are as important as any of the candidates'. Tell me what is on your mind."

Jack took a breath. "I would not feel comfortable taking this Conservatrix if it meant that she is a slave or servant or whatever—anything other than an equal partner."

Asta smiled. "The requirements in the scroll suggest that the ambiguity of the role could be defined by the Keeper. The prophet intended the Keeper to have someone who would help him with his duties to the Heart. If he needed a servant, the rune would seek a servant's mindset; if he needed an equal partner, the rune would find an equal."

Kendra looked at Jack. "What would you require of me, should I agree?"

Jack hesitated long enough for Kendra's worry to rise. Then he spoke. "If I am the Keeper, and if I need a Conservatrix, I must choose an equal partner. That decision is even more important since the prophecy demands that my Conservatrix also be my wife." He paused. "Kendra, would you take the test of the rune, knowing that if you pass, you could be both Conservatrix and wife to me as the Keeper of the Heart?"

Kendra's mind raced. She turned to Asta. "Show me the rune."

Asta glanced at Jack, then laid the scroll on the table with the rune exposed. "Kendra, open your thoughts to the rune. Reach out and touch it."

Kendra steadied herself. She cleared her thoughts as best she could and touched the rune. A faint vibration pulsed through the parchment, followed by a rising warmth. Her mind filled with memories of the Heart—visions of a dark cavern where the Heart glowed softly, waiting.

At the same moment, Jack gasped. He felt the Heart reaching for him—but not only him. It touched both him and Kendra together. He saw the same cavern, the same glow, the same connection forming through her.

Kendra slowly opened her eyes and searched for Jack. When their eyes met, the rune spoke through them both.

"It is you, my Beloved."

❧

The cool spring mist kept Kendra close to the archives of DragonPass. Even so, she found comfort in a small copse of elm trees that sheltered her from the damp weather in the wide mountain pass. Morning light broke through the dense clouds, offering hope of a drier midday. She walked beneath the graceful canopy of the elms.

Kendra suddenly felt Taimi's presence beneath the branches. Without looking toward her, she spoke. "It's been a while, Taimi. I assume you have some news for me."

Taimi stepped from the low-hanging limbs. "You are learning to recognize signs of my presence. I'm impressed." She paused. "How do you feel your studies of the healing arts are progressing?"

"I think I am learning at every archive I visit." Kendra smiled, proud of her progress.

Taimi considered her answer. "Today, were you able to locate the subset of volumes regarding the healing spells collected by the Healing Guild of the Third Age?"

Kendra's brow creased. "I did not find a section of the archives dealing with healing spells at DragonPass similar to the Blackhaven stacks."

Taimi's expression didn't change. "Could that be the result of your focusing on prophecies from the Second Age? Prophecies that you believed would help you find a lost relic?"

Kendra felt the color drain from her face. "I'm sorry. Jack and Asta needed my help in their research." She turned toward the archive entrance. "I'll return to the vault and find those spells before supper."

Taimi raised a hand, stopping her. "No need. You stumbled onto a fortunate hole in the archival system, but let's not tell the Manos about it." She watched confusion and surprise flood Kendra's face. "It happens that the Manos records about the Conservatrix and the relic called the Hope of Asher have close links to our spells of healing."

"What? How is that possible?" Kendra's confusion masked her relief that she had unintentionally completed part of her task.

Taimi waved her to silence. "It is not important. But I will say that the Manos' inaccurate filing system led to the scrolls related to the Conservatrix and the healing spells being shelved together. Once we discovered this error, we began to suspect it was a function of fate. We now believe that the healing spells and the role of Conservatrix are more linked than we previously understood."

Kendra's mouth fell open. Questions flooded her mind, but only one escaped—and it was embarrassingly self-focused. "Then I did something right in helping Asta and Jack?"

Taimi nodded slowly. "It appears so, Kendra. Remember this, however—such happy mistakes are few in the annals of the gods. Do be careful in the future. Time is fleeting."

Chapter Twenty-Four

You must submit to supreme suffering in order
to discover the completion of joy.

—John Calvin

They had been riding through low rolling hills for half a fortnight. From the tops of the higher ridges, Kendra occasionally glimpsed the thick fog hugging the cold northern seawater. Kialin had told her before they left DragonPass that the journey to Linhallow would take a fortnight and a half. He had found a reference naming Linhallow as the possible resting place of the Hope of Asher.

Kendra had spent the last fortnight thinking about the prophecy that suggested she would inherit the Hope. The Conservatrix prophecy added even more choices, more weight. She hoped Linhallow would hold answers the DragonPass scroll had not.

"There it is. My old homestead." Kialin pointed to a two-story wooden house surrounded by freshly planted fields. "My brother took over the farm after Pa died. This is the first time I've been back since that day."

"How did your father die, Kialin?" Kendra asked softly.

Kialin kept his eyes on the farm. "A strange day, it was. Spring, unusually warm. High clouds at first, then wind, then heavy clouds below the high ones. Rain. Late in the day, lightning bouncing between the clouds. Then we saw it—the funnel coming from the southwest." He paused, steadying himself. "Pa ran to help Galorn get the team-horses to shelter. Lightning struck a tree fifteen paces away. The team bolted, ran Pa down, trampled him." He rode in silence for a moment. "He died in the field while Galorn rounded up the team. Ma and I did what we could, but we knew time would claim him."

Kendra looked at him gently. "Are you going to stop and visit your brother?"

Kialin reined his team to the right, away from the Lyrien farm. "Not today, Kendra. We have a more important stop to make."

Kendra sighed. "Kialin, it's your family who—"

"...will still be there after we take care of business with Glyn Couley. Kendra, we got behind in this race by more than a fortnight coming across Asher to Linhallow, and I need to know if that was time wasted." His tone was harsher than she had ever heard.

Kendra tried to speak with him after that, but he withdrew into his thoughts, letting the horses guide the way. He finally reined in at the next farm.

"Hello, the house." His voice boomed like a drill sergeant.

A young man stepped onto the porch. "How may I help you, sir?"

Kialin lowered his voice. "I am looking for Glyn Couley. Does he still own this property?"

"What is your business with Glyn?" the young man snapped.

"Okay, you two—behave yourselves." A striking woman with auburn hair and a hint of gray stepped out. "Kialin Lyrien! When did you come back to town? What has it been, now? Not a day less than ninety years, I bet." Her sternness melted as she embraced him with a hug that nearly crushed him.

"Mother, do you know this...?"

"Watch it, pup." Kialin kept an arm around her. "I've known her since before you were born." Recognition dawned. "Dara? Did he call you mother?"

Dara laughed. "He did, you old buzzard. Where did you run off to? You missed his entire childhood. He's an adolescent of almost eighty years now."

"Time slips away when one is busy." Kialin looked around. "Where is Glyn? I have a need to ask some tough questions."

Dara turned to her son. "K, go find your father. Tell him we have a special visitor but say nothing more. Now go!"

Kialin and Dara sat on the porch reminiscing until Glyn rounded the corner.

"Well, well, what have we here? What made you come home, Kialin?"

"Hello, Glyn. It's been a long time. I wish it were a casual visit, but it isn't." Kialin noticed Glyn tense as he glanced at the companions. "No need for that. Asta has a letter from Teyr that will explain everything. First, I need to know if it is still safe."

Glyn's eyes flicked over the group, lingering on Kyneos. "I—um, yes, Kialin, it is safe." He said nothing more with strangers present.

"Asta, bring Teyr's letter, if you would."

Asta handed him the parchment. Kialin passed it to Glyn. "This will answer any questions Teyr wanted you to have answers for."

Glyn read it, then handed it to Dara.

Dara sighed dramatically. "The time finally came." She returned the letter. "Does that mean we'll be free of this task when you leave? I don't know what I'll do after all these years. Pretending to be a farmer got into my bones." She looked toward the village. "I don't think I could even live inside Linhallow after more than a hundred years out here."

Kialin understood she wasn't really asking. "Dara, I expect you and Glyn may have the opportunity to do whatever you want after today." He turned to Glyn. "Where is it? The need is great, and time is slipping."

"How much time do we have?" Glyn asked.

"I'm not sure. It could be years; it could be months. Prophecies are exact in some ways and imprecise in others. I'm treating this as an immediate need."

Glyn nodded. "This knowledge is not known. Who must be present?"

Kialin looked at Kendra, then Jack. "Jack and Kendra cannot stay behind."

"All right. You and those two follow me." Glyn started around the house. His son moved to follow, but Glyn stopped him. "K, stay with your mother. This is not your concern."

Glyn led Jack, Kendra, and Kialin behind the barn to a small hidden entrance to a corn crib. Boxes concealed a narrow door. He moved them aside, unlocked the door, and led them down a tight stairway beneath the barn. He lit an oil lamp and guided them to a second door—thick, braced oak, bolted and locked.

Inside was a single sturdy table with a chest built into it.

"Glyn, is this some kind of prison?" Kialin asked. He had seen nothing this secure outside the restricted vault at DragonPass.

Glyn began unlocking the chest. "I was told to secure this item, guard it, protect it, and reveal it only to the bearer of a letter from the Madam Chief herself. You met those requirements. So here we are."

He lifted the lid.

Kendra gasped.

When Kendra gasped, Jack leaned around her to see inside the chest. An intricate gem setting held a bright blue stone, glowing with a soft, cool light. Before he could speak, he heard Kendra's voice—dreamy, distant, awestruck.

"Oh, it is me."

Her eyes never left the relic.

Glyn smiled. "Yes, I believe you are the one, miss." The glow faded to a low shimmer. "Did you hear it calling?"

Still entranced, Kendra nodded. "I heard it in my head back in DragonPass. I thought I had lost my mind. The voice was so calming and alluring, I just had to follow its pull. The closer we got to Linhallow, the stronger the pull felt."

"The Hope knew its legacy and its partner before you were born," Glyn said. "You may take it now, Miss Kendra. I would keep it well hidden, although I understand if anyone other than the Hope's chosen partner was to touch it, they would get a nasty surprise." He chuckled.

Jack saw her hesitation. When she finally reached for the relic, he heard her exhale one soft word.

"Ohhh."

Her fingers closed around the Hope of Asher, and she drew it to her chest in a gentle, instinctive embrace.

Kialin watched with reverence. He had studied relics his entire life, but this was the first he had ever seen. The bonding surpassed anything he had imagined—simple, profound, and unmistakably alive.

"Miss Kendra, are you ready to return to the house? Dara and I can tell you what we know of the gem." Glyn closed the chest, leaving it unlocked, and led them back through the underground passage.

As they approached the farmhouse, Dara waited on the porch with a smile. "I have homemade mead." She poured mugs for everyone, and they settled on the wrap-around porch to talk about the journey from DragonPass.

Dara looked at Kendra. "I know this is a momentous step for you. Do you have any questions?"

Jack and Kialin exchanged a glance. Kialin turned to Glyn. "Would you show Jack and I around your homestead? It looks like there is more to it than meets the eye." Glyn nodded and led them away, leaving the women to speak privately.

Kendra considered her first question. "How long have you and Glyn been the guardians of this relic?"

Dara thought. "I think we replaced the previous guardians almost a century ago."

"Did you have any questions when you took this assignment?"

Dara laughed. "Oh, yes, dear. Did you know the scrolls about the relics are somewhat vague?"

Kendra laughed with her. "Somewhat? When I first read them, I thought I was filling a role under Jack. I want my own place in this worldwide drama."

"What term does the scroll use for you, dear?"

"Conservatrix," Kendra said. "All anyone could tell me was that the word had different meanings."

Dara nodded. "You did not know what they expected of you, did you?"

Kendra shook her head. "I'm still not completely sure. You have lived a life under similar conditions. How did it work for you?"

Dara grinned. "I had the same worries, but I quickly learned that Glyn and I served as equals. Eventually, we followed the local conventions and married in the village temple. I don't think it made any difference between the two of us, but it made the villagers more comfortable. After we married, they accepted us into the community."

Kendra nodded slowly. "The scroll suggested the marriage option."

Dara studied her. "Kendra, how do you feel about Jack?"

The question startled her. She had only met him when he arrived in Asher from another world. "We get along well, and we even talked about the possibility of taking things further. Why?"

"I learned that the gods take a person's feelings into account when writing the prophecies. It might be hard to believe, but they may have recognized that you and Jack could find such feelings. The gods included the possibility of marriage in the prophecy simply because you both would discover an attraction." Dara offered more mead.

"Then I am not forced to marry?"

"Of course not, dear. The suggestion only found its way into the prophecy when the gods foresaw the possibility of you both benefiting from the union." Dara watched her closely. "Does that ease your mind, Kendra?"

Relief washed across Kendra's face. "Yes. My parents were forced into marriage by local custom. I feared I faced the same, first in their home, and then when they sent me to my uncle's farm." She smiled. "Honestly, when I met Jack, it was like a chart to freedom to my own choices."

Dara cleared her throat. "Kendra, you need to know that the term Conservatrix has a meaning closer to partner than to servant. Asta told me she explained that, but I wanted you to hear it from me as well. The term is fluid enough that if you wished for a servant's role, you would have it. The choice will be yours completely."

Kendra looked thoughtful. "What if Jack wants me in a servant's role and I do not desire that?"

Dara sipped her mead. "If you do not want a servant's role, then the gods will have prepared Jack for your decision. Follow your heart and the gods will have already smoothed your trail."

❦

Clouds hung low over the hills surrounding Linhallow as Jack led his party onto the coast road toward Mistdale. Glyn's and Dara's warmth had only grown after Kendra accepted the Hope of Asher. Both guardians seemed lighter, as if a century-long burden had finally slipped from their shoulders. Dara smiled with the relief of someone who could finally imagine an ordinary life.

As the Union pulled away from the small farm, smiles and tears mingled freely—though Kyneos' expression remained unreadable to both Manos and Eratha. Within an hour, the road curved west enough for the sea to appear, gray and restless beneath the cliffs, before bending south along the shoreline.

Jack dropped from the lead and circled back along the right side of the caravan, then crossed to the left. He eased his horse beside Kendra's and rode quietly for a few moments. When she glanced at him, he smiled. "That was quite an adventure back there."

Kendra chuckled. "I knew the relic called to me, but when I looked into that chest, it overwhelmed me."

He studied her, as though he could see the shift inside her. "How does it feel now?"

She smiled faintly. "The intensity has eased, but I can feel a weight I didn't expect. Dara told me that in time I wouldn't even notice it." She paused. "I hope that day comes soon."

Jack scanned the hills ahead. "Are you sorry you accepted the title of Conservatrix?"

Kendra sighed. "It's complicated. Such responsibility... such weight. Yet the feeling of knowing I can heal others with the relic is empowering." She rode in silence for a moment. Jack let her think. "It isn't just the healing, though. I can see things I never saw before."

Jack thought of Loki's sight. "See things? Like what?"

"It's hard to explain. I see auras around certain people. I just can't figure out what it means." She lowered her voice. "Look up there. What do you see?"

Jack looked toward Scott riding point. "Just Scott doing what he always does—protecting our lead."

"I see a light blue glow around him. Not his horse. Just him. I started seeing it a couple of days after the Hope selected me."

Jack turned sharply. "The Hope of Asher selected you?"

Kendra nodded. "That's the only way I can describe it. It felt like waiting in line at a barn dance, hoping someone would choose me. When it did, I felt giddy—like my first dance."

Jack smiled at the image. Then another thought struck him. "Where is the relic now?"

Kendra pulled it out briefly before tucking it back beneath her shirt. "I put it on the first night. I can't bring myself to take it off. It feels comforting... protective."

Jack nodded. "Before you took the relic, you had concerns about the Conservatrix prophecy." He hesitated. "Do you still have them?"

Kendra shook her head. "Not really. Asta and Dara explained it in a way that eased most of my worry." She chose her next words carefully. "There are still questions about how the Conservatrix role will affect you and me."

Jack felt the same. The prophecy's wording had unsettled him—not the idea of partnership, but the implication of something deeper. His mind had drawn a line from Emily on Earth to this self-sacrificing woman beside him.

"Kendra, I don't want the Conservatrix to have any negative impact on what we've been given." His voice carried the weight of his conviction. "That isn't what's worrying you, is it?"

She stared past Scott and shook her head. "The prophecy spoke of something deeper than what we already have. It laid out a lifelong partnership... but it also suggested more."

Jack felt the direction of her thoughts. "Does that scare you, Kendra?"

"In a way, it does." She looked away. "The idea of marriage doesn't scare me. What scares me is a marriage dictated by a family member or an ancient relic. The fear would be the same."

Jack nodded slowly. "I understand. I was married before. It didn't work out. She left me. I don't want to face that pain again." He gathered himself. "That doesn't mean I would never marry again. But I want both of us on the same journey. Emily and I never were—I just didn't know it."

Kendra drew a deep breath. "Jack, do you think the relic is controlling me?"

"Kialin explained it. He said it has a personality, and it may try to influence you, but it will never control you."

She exhaled in relief. "Good. I can feel its influence, but it's never overpowering." She hesitated. "The relic wants us to marry."

Jack looked at her quickly, anxiety flickering. "I—"

Kendra chuckled softly. "Jack, I'm not trying to trap you with the relic. You needed to know it's whispering thoughts of marriage to me."

Jack steadied himself. "Kendra, I told you Emily and I were never on the same journey. You and I have been on a parallel one for months. I count on you in many ways. I told you my feelings were growing." He glanced at her—she rode close, unshaken. "It's one thing for the relic to want us to marry. What do you want?"

Kendra had known the question would come, but it still startled her. "I know I will marry. My family made that clear. I would like some say in it, though." She paused. "Jack, we've worked well together for some time. My feelings grew for you even before I learned of the relic or the Conservatrix. Without either, I had foreseen the possibility of you asking me to marry you. Is that what you're doing, Jack?"

Jack rode in silence for a few seconds that felt like hours. Then he stopped circling the question.

"Kendra Hess, would you marry me? I mean—assuming you wouldn't marry me just to stop the relic from pushing." He grinned.

Kendra's thoughts raced. She asked the relic silently: *Is this your doing, or do I have agency?*

A voice deep within her mind and soul answered: *Only you can make that decision.*

"Yes, Jack, I will marry you." She smiled. "The Hope of Asher approves of my choice."

Jack whooped loudly, and Kendra laughed.

Chapter Twenty-Five

There is no remedy for love than to love more.

—Henry David Thoreau

Asta nudged her horse forward until she caught up with Scott at the front of the line. Behind them, Jack had been talking with Kendra—right up until he whooped, spun his horse, and galloped toward Kialin's wagon. Asta watched him race off just as she reached Scott.

"What do you think that is about?"

Scott laughed, shaking his head. "If I had to guess, I'd say she just agreed to marry our fearless leader. It's all he's talked about for the last three days."

Asta stared toward Kialin's wagon, mouth open, then looked back at Scott. "I know that crazy prophecy suggested they could marry, but that seems quick."

Scott grinned. "The prophecy might've nudged him this morning, but that boy has been falling for her for months. I saw it when I first met you on the Weir ranch."

"How could you know all the way back then? You had just met him." Confusion creased Asta's brow.

Scott studied her for a moment. "You forgot I knew Jack before he got here. We spent three years together in the worst conditions you can imagine. I knew him when he was married before. That boy was smitten when I first met you." He shrugged. "He just didn't know he was hooked yet."

Asta frowned. "Hooked?"

"You know—like a fish on a line? She might not have cast the line, but she held the rod and reel. Jack was in her creel already, even on that day." Scott's grin widened. "I'm happy for them both."

Asta thought about it—about the way Jack and Kendra had always moved around each other, even before anyone named it. Scott was right. The connection had been there long before Linhallow.

"I am too," she said softly. "The way Mother talked, I couldn't imagine Jack finding happiness this quickly."

Scott eased his horse a little closer. "Have you thought about us spending more time together?"

Asta smiled and shook her head. "Are you always this bad, Scott? You tease like we'll follow Jack's and Kendra's example."

Scott glanced over his shoulder at the newly engaged pair before turning back to her. "We've had fun together, and I don't want that to end. But have you thought about us wanting more?"

Asta laughed, eyes bright. "Is it you with the fishing rod now, Scott?"

Scott laughed too. "You could say I've mounted the reel and threaded the line." His expression softened. "We get along well. Seeing them like this makes me wonder if we can have what they have."

Asta tilted her head. "Are you asking me to marry you, Scott?"

"Who has the fishing rod and reel now, Asta Rhann?" Scott grinned. "I'm asking you to consider our long-term future together."

Asta narrowed her eyes playfully. "Just together, or a relationship with several end options?"

Scott's face grew serious. "I want to be with you, Asta. If that means just spending time together, I'm fine with that. If it means more—including the possibility of marriage—I'm in for that too."

"Scott, I..." Asta began, but he continued.

"I've lived an adventurous life—the military, range riding, and now this journey with people who feel like family. And I found an intriguing woman who loves travel and the outdoors as much as I do. Yes, I'd like to spend as much of my life with you as you can stand."

Asta's expression softened. "You are the first man who shared my interests that I did not scare off somehow." She looked up into his eyes. "I want to spend time with you." Then her gaze dropped. "Scott, you must understand something. We are different races. Not skin tones—races. You are human and I am Manos. If we stay together, and you live a full century, I will still outlive you by more than a hundred years. You will age while I will not."

"What are you saying, Asta?" Scott's confusion was plain.

"If you can live with those differences, then I can as well." Her voice softened. "If we both want a bond of marriage at some time, that suits me too."

⁊

Jack walked the perimeter of the camp. They had stopped a little early, knowing they had only a short ride left before reaching Mistdale just after midday. As he finished his survey of the grounds, Kyneos approached. His quiet, padded footsteps startled Jack.

"Damn, those pads let you sneak up on me every time." Jack exhaled, easing the tension from his shoulders. "How are you tonight, Kyneos?" He had grown increasingly comfortable around the Kethan, though those silent steps still caught him off guard.

"Good evening, Jack. Is everything well with the camp?" Kyneos had learned that traveling with a group differed greatly from traveling alone, and Jack's attention to detail impressed him.

Jack shifted his path to walk beside him. "Right as rain. They all know how to set a secure camp, even this close to Mistdale."

Kyneos nodded. "They do set up an adequate boundary. You should be proud of their commitment to you as leader."

Jack winced. "I know they think of me as their leader, but after my tour of duty ended, I hoped never to be responsible for the lives of others again."

Kyneos glanced at him. "What we hope for, and the responsibility God places on us, are often incongruent, do you not find it so?"

Jack chuckled. "It does seem that God sometimes has a twisted sense of humor. I mean, just look at the giraffe. When God designed that creature, He had to be playing a joke on Adam and Eve." He found it interesting that only Kyneos spoke of God in the singular.

"Jack, you are from Earth, are you not?" Kyneos asked carefully.

"Until I died, I was." Jack wondered where this was going.

"Did you follow The Way?"

Jack thought for a moment. "Oh—you mean the Church? Yeah. My family always attended the Congregational Church in town."

Kyneos' expression—as much as Jack could read one on a wolf's face—grew thoughtful. "How do you deal with the gods of these people? I am not judging them. I have simply been trying to find my own path as a minority faith in this world."

Jack hadn't thought much about Earth's religion since arriving here. "I guess I don't make a big deal out of it. I don't understand their gods, but I think God has some kind of dominion over Eldriko as well as Earth." He paused. "Scott told me you were part of the Church on Earth before coming here."

Kyneos nodded. "My people were, back in the Roman age. I was born on Eldriko to Kethan parents and raised in their faith of Earth."

"How long have your kind been on Eldriko?"

"We have been here since the genocide of the fourth century. Since my people came from a small region, they all arrived here together at the time of their death." Kyneos spoke calmly, as though reciting history long internalized.

"Here, in Asher?" Jack asked.

"Not in Asher. We found ourselves on a southern chain of islands that offered isolation. You can understand why we sought security there." He looked toward the darkening horizon. "This has been a nice retreat after..."

"After what?"

Kyneos sighed. "Jack, we Kethan were persecuted for centuries on Earth. We found safety on those islands for many generations—until smugglers discovered us. They attacked in force one evening. Of the four hundred Kethan living there, only those from my island escaped. We fled to Westorn. About a century ago, some of us crossed to the northwestern plains of Asher." A shadow crossed his expression. "Mine has been a solitary life in Asher. I have not seen another Kethan for more than eighty years."

He looked west toward the sea. "Your people are the first to accept me in more than half a century. Thank you, Jack."

Jack reached up and laid a hand on Kyneos' shoulder. "We are your family as long as you want us, my friend." Then he remembered the question that had started this path. "Kyneos, how do you handle the polytheism of Eldriko?"

"We found it hard to justify. The last time I met another Kethan, she told me a village of our people settled on an island off Westorn and kept their ancient faith free from heresies. She said the elders still debate the idea of these people worshiping many gods but remain free of their influence." He studied Jack. "You, however, live alongside such beliefs. Do they tempt you?"

Jack thought. "Honestly, it doesn't come up. Scott follows his beliefs—faithfully. The Manos have their own practices, but they keep them private." He paused. "I'm not sure the Fairmen have any religion at all."

"What is the ceremony I hear Kialin speak of? Are you submitting yourself to a pagan priest for it?" Kyneos' concern was clear.

"I'm not sure I fully understand it. There are prophecies that include me in Eldriko's restoration. They must officially declare me as the fulfillment of that prophecy. As for a pagan priest—I think he's called an abbot. In their society, he's the ultimate civil authority. He'll also solemnize the marriage of Kendra and me."

Kyneos smiled. "I heard you were marrying Kendra. You two seem to fit well together."

Jack's smile faded. "I love her, Kyneos, I do. But back on Earth, marriage and I didn't work well. I came home from the military to an empty house and a note saying she couldn't take it anymore. How do I know that won't happen again?"

Kyneos regarded him with deep understanding. "Jack, that is a risk we all take when we give our love to someone. We hope—and fear—that our chosen mate will return the love we freely give. Often they do; sometimes they do not have the ability to love." He patted Jack's back. "Keep your trust in God to show you the correct path and give all your love to Kendra. Take care of each other, and God will handle the rest."

Loki followed Jack's caravan as it pulled up outside Mistdale. She watched him begin laying out the encampment around Kialin's wagon. Hunger gnawed at her belly, and the soft yips of her pups reminded her of their need as well. The journey had been long since their weaning. After spotting Jack's camp, Loki found a nearby ravine with a small cave—safe enough for her pups to wait while she hunted near her human.

She left them playing in the ravine and slipped into the early dawn light. Skirting the Manos city, she moved through the edge of the woods pressed against the slow-moving river. Ahead, she saw a woman walking away from the city toward a field of fragrant plants growing above the riverbank. The woman clipped herbs and placed them in a shallow basket.

A man approached her with a hard, determined stride. "Teyr! I would have a word with you."

The woman straightened, facing him.

"What is it now, Jaren? Can I not have a moment's peace to restock my kitchen herbs?"

The man scowled, stopping several paces away. "You know what I want. I saw that ragtag group of Offlanders camped outside our gate again. I do not care that the Arch-Monk has joined them. They have no business with respectable Manos." His jaw clenched as he waited for her answer.

Teyr held her ground. "Kialin left a message for me with the gate guards last night when they pulled in. I will meet with Jack and Asta later this morning."

Jaren's face reddened. "The council has not—"

Teyr cut him off. "...given you authority to conduct negotiations with Offlanders." Her tone shifted—unmistakably the Madam Chief of Mistdale.

He swallowed his anger, trying to regain control. "Madam Chief, I respectfully protest this break with protocol."

Loki eased closer, hugging the brush. She smelled a faint trace of Jack on the woman—and the sharp, rising ire of the man. She crept nearer.

Teyr calmly picked a few more stalks and placed them in her basket. "Jaren, the council voted last night to allow me to continue communication with Jack Marshall. We have a shared interest in what he has to say."

Jaren exploded. "That is most irregular. I was not informed of such a vote."

"We sent a runner to your townhouse. She searched for you at your regular pub with no success," Teyr said evenly. "She even went to the home of Laeree Starn looking for you. That is your current mistress, is it not?"

Jaren's rage broke loose. "Why I should just—" He strode toward her, fists clenched, face red.

Loki burst from the brush, canines bared, snarling. She planted herself between them, hackles raised, fangs gleaming. Jaren froze mid-stride. He had come unarmed. He backed away three steps from the coyote guarding the Madam Chief. Shock silenced him. He glanced at Teyr, then back at Loki.

"This is not over, Teyr. I will force another vote in council before I allow you to bring those Offlanders back into our hallowed chambers."

He retreated, keeping distance between himself and the silent, watchful coyote. Once far enough, he turned and hurried toward the gate, disappearing behind the city walls.

Loki watched until he vanished. Then she relaxed, turned toward Teyr, and sat back on her haunches.

Teyr crouched before her, voice soft. "You are that coyote that follows Jack, I think. He calls you Loki, does he not?"

Loki lowered her head, studying her. Then she rose, trotted toward the woods on the city-side of the river, and with one last glance over her shoulder, slipped into the brush.

Chapter Twenty-Six

Loss is part of life.
If you don't have loss, you don't grow.

—Dominick Cruz

Being back in a town after the emotional events on the mountain road brought Alaster a measure of comfort. The driving force behind his pursuit of the Heart came from Amets' discovery of the relic's resurrective power. Yet he still struggled to understand how he had come to actively hunt a competitor. That had never been his way as a merchant, and he had always succeeded without such tactics.

His spiritual search had become a passion—one that pushed him to follow the urgings of a stranger with a powerful, unsettling presence named Julleg. Whenever Julleg appeared, Alaster felt a certainty of conviction that bordered on absolute. But that certainty faded with time, leaving him uneasy. In the week since the mountain encounter, he had begun to doubt the wisdom of following Julleg's directions. As he walked the darkening streets of Riven, he even wondered whether he had passed the point of needing Julleg's guidance at all.

Suddenly, a familiar voice boomed from an alley to his right. "It took you long enough to get here."

Julleg stepped from the shadows, a faint reddish aura lighting the air behind him.

Alaster's heart hammered. His breath caught. Every doubt he had felt moments earlier vanished under Julleg's presence. Certainty flooded him—certainty that only Julleg could help him find the relic that would resurrect his daughter.

Julleg seemed larger than he had in DragonPass, his presence heavier, more oppressive. Alaster fought the instinct to step back. "I only arrived at midday."

Julleg glared, dismissing the excuse. "What were you thinking? I gave you a simple task. All you had to do was kill the adventurer you crossed in the mountains."

Alaster's mouth fell open. "We took care of them. Their bodies are at the bottom of a steep cliff in the mountains."

"FOOL! You murdered a band of merchants, not the adventurers I sent you to kill." Julleg's anger intensified. "You killed the wrong band. Jack Marshall is still a threat to my plans."

Alaster tried to explain. "But they were the only people we met on the road to the south. I did just what you wanted. I killed the band coming north."

Julleg stared at him with contempt. "Did they look like adventurers to you? Didn't you notice the wagons and packs? You are a merchant. Those packs should have been familiar. Or are you that stupid?" He didn't wait for a response. "You can still redeem yourself. Jack Marshall is on his way to Mistdale before continuing his search for the Heart. Get there as quickly as you can and put an end to his quest."

Alaster blinked, trying to process the order. "You want me to kill this Jack Marshall in the city of Mistdale?"

Julleg shook his head. "You stupid fool, not inside the city. Jack has a habit of walking in the woods to calm his thoughts. It is a custom he started as a young man before coming to Eldriko. Find him when he is alone and bring this quest of his to an end."

Julleg turned and strode away, his form dissolving into a pale fog. Alaster stared at the spot where he vanished. All his earlier doubts evaporated. He had to reach Mistdale as fast as possible.

He hurried to the pub beside the inn where he had left Amets half an hour earlier. Bursting into the main room, he spotted Amets at a table in the back. As he approached, he began issuing orders.

"Let's get packed. We leave first thing in the morning. I want fresh horses for this journey, so get Lewis to take care of that tonight—whatever the cost."

§❧

Kendra brought Jack a mug of sweet-smelling liquid. He sipped it, savoring the warm, spicy sweetness. Jack glanced at her. "What is this?" She looked worried as she answered. "You don't like it? I can get you something else."

Jack quickly eased her concern. "Oh, no. It's very good. It's like a tea I used to drink in my former life. It was called chai."

Kendra smiled at the name. "Chai—I like that." But something weighed on her mind as she sat making small talk.

"Okay, Kendra, out with it. What's on your mind?" Jack smiled, hoping to reassure her.

Kendra studied him for a long moment. "Jack, you said you were married before, in your former life, but that it didn't work out." She hesitated. "What happened? What made your marriage fail?"

Jack thought for a moment while she watched his expression. "I think there were too many differences between our expectations of life in general, and our ability to communicate—or our lack of that ability."

Kendra frowned. "What differences in your expectations?"

Jack took a deep breath. "Emily loved city life. She grew up with concerts, plays, parties every week. My upbringing was milking cows, collecting eggs, planting, harvesting—and hunting and fishing when I had time. Emily hated all of that."

Kendra looked confused. "Why did you marry each other if you wanted different lives?"

Jack chuckled at her directness. "We were in love—or thought we were. Maybe it was just lust. I don't know anymore." He paused, and she let him gather his thoughts. "I think the real strain came when I joined the army. I left her alone on the farm— a life she hated—and went off to serve. Neither of us imagined I'd come home wounded. When I finally got back, she was gone."

Kendra's voice was flat. "That is heartless. She abandoned you."

Jack nodded. "She did. She left a note, but no forwarding address. I heard later she met an accountant in the city and moved in with him before I was even wounded."

Kendra shook her head. "I could never abandon you like that."

Jack looked out the window. "I never expected to marry again." He looked back at her. "I probably shouldn't have married a city woman." He shrugged. "I can't change the past, but what about us?"

Kendra understood his meaning. "I'm a farming girl. Cities don't appeal to me. Well—except the archives. Those are intriguing." She smiled.

Jack grinned. "It's no surprise to anyone, my dear Kendra, that you love the archives. If that's your only attraction to the city, I think we'll be good."

Kendra chuckled softly. "That's good to know, Jack. You seem to find some pleasure in the archives as well."

Jack had to admit it. The histories gave him a way to understand Eldriko. It was the one thing cities offered that both he and Kendra appreciated. "When all this is over, what do you want to do, Kendra?"

"I've been giving that a lot of thought." Her voice carried a tentative weight. "We've had such a following that it feels like our journey is with family. I want to consider each of them—and anyone else who might join us. We have ten individuals in our caravan, though a few of us have become closer."

"We are developing into a community, aren't we?" Jack had seen the progression but hadn't followed it to her conclusion.

"Jack, if we all stay together, who would accept us?" His confusion showed. "Think about it. Have we passed any village that would accept who we all are? What about Kyneos? Where in southern Asher could he live safely? People still fear and hate Offlanders—and your kind have been here for more than two centuries."

Jack realized she understood her people far better than he did. "Where could we settle, if not in one of the communities of Asher?"

Kendra clearly had an answer but hesitated. Jack nudged her. "Come on, Kendra. You obviously have ideas you're reluctant to share. Just tell me."

Kendra took a breath. "I spoke with Asta about that weeks ago. I thought about the other islands on Eldriko, but I don't know enough about them. And everyone in the Union has roots in Asher—even Kyneos." She paused. "Asta had an intriguing idea. We'd need to discuss it with Teyr, but Asta doesn't think we'd face obstacles."

Jack held his hands out. "What is this idea? You can tell me."

"All right." Kendra continued. "Asta told me that near Linhallow lies a land unsettled, but close enough to Mistdale that the council has debated annexing it for decades. They fear undesirables might squat there and cause problems." She watched Jack's reaction. "A vast land joined to Asher by a mountainous isthmus north of Linhallow—virtually unsettled, with vast resources. Asta thinks Teyr could convince the council to recognize a community of settlers—if we can gather enough people—as a commonwealth with the Manos. A land with our ideals, our beliefs, a place where our citizens are free of orthodox biases. Do you think that could work for us?"

Jack considered it—a community of their own, not Offlanders alone, not Manos alone, not Eratha or Kethan alone, but a blend of all who shared their values. "Let's talk with Asta about this idea. That could be just the place for us to call home."

The Master of Arms ushered Jack and Asta into the office of the Madam Chief of the Council of Mistdale after a short wait. Teyr continued writing in her journal as they stood before her desk. When the door closed behind the Master of Arms, she finally looked up and set her pen aside.

Teyr rose and came around the desk to embrace Asta with a gentle kiss. "I am relieved you returned safely, my Eydis." She smiled with the warmth of a mother. Then she turned to Jack and embraced him as well. "I hope my man Delon proved useful."

Jack smiled. "Yes, ma'am—useful and timely as well."

The three of them settled into the sitting area. They caught up on everything that had happened in the months since Jack and Asta left Mistdale with the others dedicated to helping him.

"You left with six of you and returned with ten," Teyr remarked. "You are picking up strays, it seems."

Jack tried not to laugh but failed. "We did seem to find unattached companions with similar ideas along the way, yes ma'am." He took a slow breath. "That is actually why I requested this audience."

Teyr's eyebrow arched. "Really? I am intrigued. How do I come into play with these strays of yours?"

Asta shifted in her seat. "Mother, please hear him out. His idea could solve a problem for you and himself with the stroke of your pen."

Teyr nodded and gestured to Jack. "Please, enlighten me, dear Jack." Her tone suggested formality, but her smile assured him of her interest.

Jack cleared his throat and began explaining the problem: Offlanders struggling to find a place in established communities, Kyneos surviving only through stealth, Eratha with no prospects as second or third sons. Teyr asked pointed questions about the makeup of his group—questions that revealed she already knew far more than Jack expected.

Teyr grinned at his surprise. "My dear boy, I have eyes and ears across the land. Little happens without my knowledge. Now, tell me how you want me to help you."

Jack smiled, conceding the point. "Teyr, Asta told me the council had an ongoing concern about some wild territory north of here. She called it Winwiven. I think I can help you and the council with that issue."

Teyr sat up straighter, leaning forward. "Tell me about your solution for my problem."

Jack's expression didn't change. "Give Winwiven to us."

The suggestion blindsided her. It had been decades since anyone had surprised her so completely. "What do you mean— give Winwiven to you?"

Jack shrugged. "Just that. Let us set up a community there. Let us recruit immigrants from other regions who share our beliefs about community. In return for the land, we will establish our government as a free commonwealth with the Manos. We will trade with Mistdale and any Manos town or city as part of the agreement."

The idea intrigued her. "How can you govern a territory so vast?"

"Initially, we can't," Jack admitted. "But in time, we can bring in enough people from Asher and other islands to create a self-sustaining society."

Teyr considered him. "If we grant you that land, how would you secure the people of Asher from another island placing mercenaries in your midst and launching an attack?"

Jack kept his voice steady. "Madam Chief, the isthmus between Asher and Winwiven is a rugged mountain range with a narrow, twisting trail, is it not?"

Teyr smiled. "You have done your research, Jack—just as I would expect the son of Jassinn Elenya to do. That trail is narrow. In some places, no more than six abreast. At the southern trailhead, I believe we estimated no more than eight men at arms could pass together."

Jack smiled. "I believe that estimate was reported as seven men at arms and eight unarmed tradesmen."

Teyr nodded, impressed. "Yes, I believe you are correct. When would you start recruiting immigrants for Winwiven, should the council approve?"

Jack was ready. "Personally, I have an earlier responsibility to the council and the Madam Chief that delays my direct involvement. But we could begin settling the territory within a month or two under the administration of my hand-picked representative and an overseer approved by the council."

Teyr asked the question she already knew the answer to. "Do you have anyone in mind for both positions?"

"I do, Madam Chief. As my representative, I name Nathan Martin and Lily Thompson. As the Manos overseer, I can think of no better selection than Delon Oakel, the Madam Chief's own secretary."

Teyr asked, "Why Nathan Martin and Lily Thompson?"

"I selected Nathan because he proved his ability to lead during our journey. I added Lily for a personal reason—they are to marry. My representative would not be effective if his wife did not join him."

Teyr smiled at him.

"Jack, I will bring this to the council this afternoon. Hearing your request and your reasoning, I expect passage." She couldn't have been prouder of her husband's Earthly son.

Chapter Twenty-Seven

*The greatness of a community is most
accurately measured by the compassionate
actions of its members.*

—Coretta Scott King

Alaster arrived in Mistdale but saw no sign of a traveling band encamped outside the walls. He had never visited the Manos capital before and found it charming—a classic city whose wards were laid out with enviable precision. Many towns across Asher admired Mistdale's organization and the preservation of its historic Old City along the harbor.

He found a waterfront pub favored by those who surrendered easily to gossip. Within two days, he overheard an inebriated craftsman excitedly reveal that Teyr's adventurers had returned after an extended sojourn. The man claimed the group had left numbering six and returned months later with ten—including a creature previously known only in myth. That was enough for Alaster. He decided to walk the city walls and discreetly observe the camp.

From the rampart, he saw a mixture of Asher's peoples: Eratha, Manos, Offlanders, and the wolf-like creature that walked as a man. As he watched, a guard approached.

"Excuse me, what is going on out there?" Alaster asked, playing the stranger.

The guard paused, glancing toward the field beside the river. "That is Madam Chief's stepson back from his adventures. She is meeting with him as we speak." He started to turn away, then added, "Rumor is the council will honor him with a banquet at week's end. A big deal for citizens more important than me." He resumed his rounds.

As he walked away, Alaster called, "What's his name?"

Without turning, the guard replied, "Sir Jack Marshall."

Alaster's head snapped toward him. Had he heard correctly? Jack Marshall? He needed to see the man's face. Over the next few days, he lingered near the river gate, pretending to admire the gardens along the walls. Finally, he heard someone in the camp call Jack's name. A young man with a commanding presence turned to answer.

Alaster stared in disbelief. He had seen that man before—at the Red Griffin Inn in Alderg. Perhaps in Blackhaven as well, though the memory was hazy.

He began watching Jack's every move. Jack had few regular habits, but one stood out: each evening he walked along the river near the woods. As Alaster observed, a plan began to form—a dreadful, final plan.

The next afternoon, he prepared. He had his sword sharpened by the local smith. He purchased leather armor from the armorer, unconcerned by the cost. A merchant of his standing could afford it. He spent the morning shadow-fencing behind the livery, adjusting to the altered balance the armor imposed. He wanted the muscle-memory ready for the evening.

Alaster donned the leather armor beneath a tunic, belted on his blade, and walked to the river gate. He followed the river to the woods and found cover near a cow path running parallel to the water. He sat on a fallen log hidden by brush and waited.

As evening light retreated and the guards prepared for shift change, Jack walked to the river and turned up the familiar trail. Alaster dipped his head just enough to watch him approach.

He waited until Jack was close—but struck a pace too early. Jack turned toward the rustling sound of Alaster rushing from cover with his blade drawn. Jack stepped carefully toward the river, sliding Targonith effortlessly from its scabbard, settling into a standard defensive posture.

Without a word, Alaster pressed the attack. Jack retreated a few steps, parrying the thrusts. Then, turning Alaster's blade aside, Jack seized the initiative. Alaster parried and retreated in turn. He misjudged Jack's advance and fell off-balance. Turning left in his next attack, he scored the first hit—an off-arm slash that cut just past Jack's leather guards.

໑໖

Jack ignored the pain of the minor wound as he countered Alaster's attack, slashing beneath Alaster's guard and cutting into his side, tearing through the new leather armor.

Alaster flinched, breath catching, but resumed his attack. Jack moved lighter now, adjusting to the rhythm of the fight. Two quick slashes glanced off Alaster's leather shirt. Alaster's counterstrike caught Jack's shoulder, drawing blood again.

Jack shrugged off the hit and pressed forward, landing a deep thrust into Alaster's shoulder. The blade struck bone, sending a jolt of pain through Alaster's left side. He parried Jack's slower follow-up and shuffled left, trying to escape Jack's nimble blade. He flicked his sword outward, catching Jack's neck with a shallow cut that bled freely but didn't slow him.

The nick surprised Jack, and he retreated a step. Alaster used the moment to catch his breath. The fight was wearing on both of them. Jack's footwork slowed, though his bladework remained sharp. Alaster showed the strain of fatigue and blood loss.

Their next exchange landed blows on both sides. Alaster's blade thrust into Jack's side, missing vital organs but sending a wave of pain through him. Jack's blade—Targonith—struck deeper, catching the outer lobe of Alaster's liver.

Alaster inhaled sharply as the sword pierced him. When Jack withdrew the blade, blood poured freely. Alaster's arms dropped to his sides. Jack recognized the wound instantly—the kind of fatal injury he had seen too many times on Earth. He stepped back as Alaster staggered, his sword slipping from his hand.

Alaster looked at Jack. "How?" His legs gave way, and he collapsed at the river's edge. His blood mingled with the tannin-stained water.

Jack scanned the area for other threats. Finding none, he knelt beside the man he now recognized as Alaster Kempe. Kyneos arrived at a run. Jack shouted, "Quick, fetch Kendra. Tell her to bring her medical bag."

Kyneos sprinted toward Kialin's wagon, calling for her. Kendra and Kialin rushed to Jack's side. Kendra examined Jack's wounds first—non-lethal—then turned to the stranger with the mortal wound. She looked at Jack and shook her head.

Alaster weakly motioned Jack closer. In a whisper barely worthy of the name, he said, "Not me. Julleg. Julleg made me..." His breath hitched as more blood escaped. "Made me do it. Did it for my Donia—my daughter." He met Jack's eyes. "Forgive me; forgive my family, please."

A soft sigh escaped him as his spirit passed on. Jack closed Alaster's eyes with a gentle hand. Kendra, not realizing he had died, continued working.

Jack touched her shoulder. "Kendra..." She kept trying. "Kendra, he's gone. He's not here anymore."

She pushed his hand away. "I can save him—I can. Let me..." Then she looked again—really looked—and saw only a body, a shell still leaking blood with no purpose left.

Kendra bowed her head, trying to process the death of a man she had fought to save, despite his attempt to kill the man she would marry in a few days. Then she remembered Jack's wounds and turned to him.

"They aren't too bad, my love." Jack tried to reassure her.

Kendra shot him a cold look. "You let me decide that sir. Have you suddenly become a healer, too?"

Jack lay back and let her work. He smiled as she carefully removed his shirt to check for other wounds. "Hey there, that can wait until we are married, you know."

Kendra gave him a look that made him wonder if she might add a few wounds of her own. "Keep that up and you might be on your own after the wedding." She shook her head, trying to hide a smile. "Men!"

Jack spent the next several days resting in Teyr's cottage, allowing his wounds to begin healing. Kendra stayed close during those first days, finding every excuse to change a dressing, refresh the topical herbs, or make him drink some bitter tincture. Jack suspected she enjoyed every moment of tending to him.

By the third day after the fight with Alaster, Jack began to feel more like himself. The wound in his side still ached, but it had begun to knit. Kendra kept a close eye on the forming scar, though her worry eased a little each day.

A couple of days later, Kendra brought Jalianna Emeria, the Master Healer of Mistdale, to confirm her assessment. Jalianna probed Jack's wounds, asked her questions, and finally agreed with Kendra's evaluation. She spoke with Kendra in low tones Jack couldn't make out. Kendra nodded at something her mentor said before Jalianna departed.

After she left, Kendra settled into the chair beside Jack's bed. "Master Jalianna thinks you are well enough to attend the ceremony now. The Abbot is ready whenever you are. How about the day after the morrow?"

Jack had spoken with Teyr about the ceremony, but Alaster's attack had driven all thoughts of it from his mind. Now he remembered: the ritual that would solemnize both his and Kendra's roles as co-Keepers of the Heart of Sheol—and their marriage under Manos law. He looked into Kendra's inquiring eyes, smiled, and nodded. "I think I'll be up for it by then. Didn't Teyr say there is supposed to be a feast after the ceremony?"

Kendra grinned. "She did say something about lots of food, drink, and revelry. Jack, I think you need to take it easy at the festival after the ceremony. I already made sure a comfortable chair would be placed on the platform. Our only duties include being visible, partaking of food and drink, and polite interaction with our guests." Her expression shifted. "Jack, promise me you won't overdo it at the festival."

Jack saw the flicker of worry. "I'll be good, my dear." Then a mischievous smile crept in. "What type drinks are they providing?"

Kendra lightly slapped his uninjured arm. "Mead, for you. I may have some rum."

Jack chuckled. "Party pooper." Their smiles matched, warm and easy.

𝔰❧

The following days, leading up to the ceremony kept Jack in a whirl. Kendra stayed close, watching him with the vigilance of a healer and the tenderness of a soon-to-be wife. Teyr allowed her full authority in caring for him. Teyr's "cottage" would never have earned that name on Earth; Jack would have called it a comfortable townhouse with three suites. She placed him in the first-floor suite, complete with a sitting area, where he could heal and meet with the Abbot to prepare for the ceremony.

The traditional state marriage ceremony alone could last more than two hours. Jack stoically agreed, but both Kendra and Teyr protested that he wasn't healed enough to stand that long. The Abbot reluctantly set tradition aside and allowed a tall pub chair to be placed for Jack—on the condition that its humble origins be hidden beneath regal coverings.

Late in the day before the ceremony, Scott arrived with a garment bag. Jack eyed him skeptically as Scott peeled it open.

"What is that?"

Scott grinned. "Your nuptial robe."

"My what?" Jack's eyes widened.

Scott held up both hands. "Hey, I'm just the delivery man. Don't kill the messenger."

The indigo robe was embroidered with intricate Manos patterns symbolizing unity, protection, and balance. Subtle motifs nodded to the Manos reverence for nature. But one symbol caught Jack's eye—the ichthys. Its muted embroidery matched the Manos style, but its placement beneath the throat was unmistakably intentional.

Scott noticed his focus. "Kyneos insisted that a symbol of your Earthly faith have a place in this ceremony."

Jack lifted the robe. "Let's see how it fits." It settled on him like a tailored garment, though heavier than he expected. "I hope it won't be too hot wherever the ceremony takes place."

The next day passed slowly as Jack waited for the evening ceremony. The worst part was Kendra's absence that afternoon. Scott tried to distract him, with little success. Finally, a monk arrived to lead Jack to the pavilion by the seashore.

The structure rose from rough-hewn timbers supporting a vaulted plaster dome. Artistic Manos symbols adorned the beams. Movable yew panels with padded silk screens allowed the walls to retract, letting the sea breeze and evening light into the space. The front of the pavilion faced north, its floor marked with Manos myths and legends. A woven wool carpet ran from the southern entry to a majestic oaken archway carved with exquisite craftsmanship.

Jack and Scott were led to a small room behind the archway to await Kendra. Monks lit beeswax candles and sandalwood incense. Ringed candle holders rose halfway to the dome, casting a soft glow across the white plaster ceiling. Musicians tuned their instruments in the left front corner, then began playing haunting music in a minor key. In the right front corner, a small choir of monks chanted low, melodic lines that filled the pavilion.

The Abbot emerged from behind the archway, dressed in a saffron robe embroidered with muted gray celestial symbols.

The music softened as Kendra entered. Jack and Scott moved into place beside the tall chair prepared for him. Kendra reached her mark on the floor. The Abbot waited for silence before beginning.

"We come before you to present to you the product of a prophecy fulfilled..."

He spoke of relics, of caretakers, of the Manos' long stewardship of history. He spoke of Offlanders—the curiosity they inspired, the fear they provoked—and of the trust Jack had earned. He nodded to Kialin, standing with Kendra on the west side of the pavilion.

The liturgy continued, long enough for some guests to nod off. When a councilman's head drooped, the Abbot raised his voice theatrically, jolting the man awake to the laughter of those nearby.

"My children, I must inform you that we have discovered our Keeper of the Heart... In this age, the prophecy revealed the need of co-Keepers... Jack Marshall and Kendra Hess."

He turned to them. "Do you understand the expectations and duties of the Keepers of the Heart?" They affirmed. The guests cheered—most of them. A few murmured disapprovals but dared not voice it.

The Abbot beamed. "It is my pleasure to also present Kendra and Jack as more than co-Keepers. In my office this morning, they solemnized their intention to live as wife and husband under the customs of the Manos. They signed the Volume of Intention of Unity with the required witnesses. Will the witnesses come forward?"

Teyr rose from the front row and stepped behind Jack. Kialin, already beside Kendra, cleared his throat. The Abbot nodded. "Of course, Arch-Monk Lyrien."

He turned back to the guests. "Does anyone here have sound and compelling reason to deny these two...?"

Silence fell. Even a sigh felt dangerous. After the traditional five breaths, the Abbot's grin returned.

"With no objections recorded, Kendra Hess, you may take your husband to the festival to greet your benefactors."

Kendra took Jack's hand and led him from the pavilion to the village green, where the celebration would last long into the night—with eating, drinking, and dancing.

Music filled the center of Mistdale, celebrating the wedding of Kendra and Jack. Citizens poured into the streets, cheerful and unrestrained. Even Jaren Gwath made a respectful appearance at what had become a city-wide party, though he kept a careful distance from Teyr after their confrontation outside the walls.

Jack and Kendra stood with Teyr and Asta in a family line, thanking guests for their attendance and support. The entire city turned out for what quickly became an unofficial holiday. Teyr beamed with pride as the often-stoic community erupted into a spontaneous, inclusive festival. The post-wedding celebration lasted until dawn, and few noticed when the newlyweds slipped away. The merriment spilled into a week-long celebration of love and acceptance, with Manos, Eratha, Fairmen, and Offlanders mingling freely and forming new friendships.

After several hours, Jack and Kendra slipped away from the festival-turned-community-gathering and followed the path toward the council guest cottage. Teyr had offered it as a wedding retreat for her stepson and his new bride.

Jack reached out and gently took Kendra's hand. The path through the council garden offered a soft, fragrant transition from the boisterous celebration to the quiet intimacy of their retreat. Kendra looked at him with the same love she had felt growing since their earliest days on the road.

Jack finally broke the silence. "After what happened to me before, I wasn't sure I could ever trust enough to marry another time."

Kendra softly chuckled. "I knew you would come around with time." She grinned and squeezed his hand.

Jack laughed. "Thank you for your patience, my love."

They found the door of the guest cottage slightly ajar. Jack pushed it open and led Kendra into the regally appointed sitting area. A dining table stood at the far end with two chairs, an oak sideboard, and a decanter placed neatly at its center. Jack checked it out of curiosity and found it filled with chilled water scented with oranges. A closed door led from the dining area; when Jack opened it, he discovered a bedchamber with a large canopied bed and curtains gathered at the foot.

Kendra sank onto an overstuffed bench while Jack explored their wedding apartment. "This is beautiful, Jack." Her voice carried both awe and exhaustion.

Jack sat beside her. "The last week has been a whirlwind." He looked at her with quiet admiration. "Are you happy, Kendra? So much happened in such a short amount of time."

Kendra met his eyes. "My father sent me to Hadon to find a suitable mate. All I saw in that sleepy village were more of the farm boys I grew up with. And then I met you. Dressed in that dreadful green and brown—what did you call it?"

Jack grinned. "My camouflage."

"Camouflage, yes." Kendra laughed. "Such a strange name for unusual clothing. But there was a sense about you. Vulnerable, yet sure of yourself." She paused. "I knew right away that I needed to get to know you."

Jack smiled as he shared his own memory. "I found this redheaded beauty offering to help me when I wasn't even sure where I was—or if I was even alive." He gently took her hand again. "In some ways, I don't think I was alive anymore. You helped me find a life—a purpose in those first days in your world. Some might say Teyr gave me purpose, but they'd be mistaken.

You gave me that purpose. At first, just to see your smile each morning or hear your voice."

He noticed her blush. "Or to see a blush like that. Each day, your presence drew me into your world—not Eldriko, but Kendra's world." He paused, thinking of Earth. "The thought of us together scared me for a long time. I mean, after what happened with Emily."

A flicker of jealousy and anger crossed Kendra's heart, but she steadied herself. "I am not that woman. The gods fated me to meet you and for us to be together. Love is an abstract word where the gods are concerned, but we are meant for each other. Love is just a bonus for me."

"I thought I knew love in my first marriage, but now I see she may not have loved me at all; I only thought I loved her. It didn't feel anything like what I feel today." Jack looked deeply into his eyes. "I don't know if I believed in destiny before, but I know meeting you was meant to be."

Kendra took a breath. "Jack, when are you going to make me a proper wife?" She leaned in and kissed him deeply.

When the kiss broke, Jack teased her. "You should see the bed in the next room." A grin crossed his face. "It is huge with curtains all around it."

Kendra glanced toward the door. "Really?" She looked up at him. "Show me!"

Jack stood and pulled her to her feet. Then he swept her into his arms and carried her into the bedchamber. He set her gently on the plush bed and smiled down at her.

Kendra leaned back. "Make me your wife, Jack."

The morning light roused Jack from the events of the previous night, though he realized only a few hours had passed. Kendra lay nestled in the circle of his arms, her breath warm against his chest. The soft glow of dawn framed her face, and Jack couldn't help but smile at the sight.

She stirred, eyelids fluttering open, and a slow smile spread across her lips. "Good morning, husband."

Jack tightened his embrace, drawing her closer. "Good morning, wife."

For a long moment, neither of them moved. The world outside the cottage could wait—the festival, the council, the responsibilities that would soon reclaim their attention. Here, in the quiet warmth of the guest chamber, there was only the steady rhythm of her breathing and the peace he had never thought he would feel again.

Whatever the day held for them, it could come later.

❧

Jack joined Kialin in his long-abandoned office in the Mistdale archive headquarters to discuss their plans. He paused over the notes outlining Kialin's proposed route to the islands. "Kialin, I have a question for you."

Kialin kept his eyes on the map spread before him and grunted, "Uh-huh."

"Why didn't you say anything about that tradition?" Jack set his notes aside.

Kialin still studied the map, though a chuckle escaped him. "And what tradition might that be?"

"You know full well what tradition." Jack tried to keep the irritation out of his voice. "That business of keeping newlywed couples imprisoned for two weeks. I thought Teyr was joking— but she wasn't. I love Kendra, but I'm a social person. How could you do that to me?"

Kialin finally gave up and laughed outright. "Oh, Jack, I am sorry. Every Manos couple for the last five hundred years felt exactly as you do."

Jack pressed on. "What is the logic behind it?"

Kialin set the map down. "The Elders believed that if a couple could survive a fortnight alone together, they could weather any marital storm. It worked for me."

Jack turned sharply. "You are married?" He had never suspected Kialin had a wife.

"Was married, Jack. I lost her a century ago." Kialin's gaze drifted to the window overlooking the gardens surrounding the cottage Jack had enjoyed for the past two weeks.

Jack hesitated, unsure whether to ask more.

"She contracted an ailment the healers could not identify," Kialin continued quietly. "They tried every herb and incantation, but nothing lasted. She would rally, then fall again. One day a rural seer stopped me in the market and told me she had a vision—that a practitioner of the dark arts had targeted my wife with an uncurable illness." He exhaled slowly. "That night, she slipped away into the arms of Sheol."

Jack couldn't imagine the weight of that loss. Kialin returned to the table, refocusing on the maps and the islands Jack would soon explore.

"Who are you taking with you when you set sail?" Kialin asked.

Jack mentally reviewed his list. "Kendra, of course. Asta, Scott, Casey, Kyneos, and you. The others are joining Nathan as the core group to set up the Winwiven colony."

Kialin shook his head. "You know Teyr does not call Winwiven a colony. She intends it to be an independent commonwealth allied with the Manos."

Jack waved him off. "She says that, but—"

"Jack," Kialin interrupted gently, "you know Teyr well enough to know she stands by her convictions." He paused. "There is something else about Winwiven you have a right to know. I am joining Nathan—to establish an archive in the mountains of the northeast. I want to find land north of Linhallow."

Jack stared at him. "You are leaving me?"

A light rap sounded at the door. Without looking away from Jack, Kialin called, "Come!"

A female Manos archivist entered. "You sent for me, Master Lyrien?"

"Come in, come in," Kialin said warmly. "Have a seat." He welcomed his former intern with genuine affection. "I assume you have restored order to our Mistdale archive."

She sat beside Jack, subtly sliding her chair a little farther from him. "I have, Master Lyrien," she answered carefully, offering no judgment of the previous archivist.

Kialin nodded with a pensive expression. "I should never have assigned him to the Mistdale files. His skills are better suited to restoring the Noset archives."

The archivist's eyes brightened. "We really are going to return Noset to a functional archive? Being part of that restoration would be an honor."

Kialin ignored her enthusiasm for the moment and turned back to Jack. "Jack, I am going to Winwiven, but I would not leave you alone on your quest. You need someone with the skills to understand the scrolls." He motioned to the woman. "Jack, meet my replacement, Catheira Tessill. We call her Kat."

In unison, Jack and Catheira blurted, "What?"

Catheira spoke first. "Master, you want me to leave my studies at the archive?"

Jack tried to speak over her. "I need someone I can trust to know what I need on this journey. Someone who knows the blade."

Kialin raised both hands. "Now, now. Let me explain."

They fell silent.

"Jack, you are correct—you need a scholar in the ancient arts, and Catheira is the best I have. I trained her myself. As for her skill with a blade, trust me, she knows what is needed." Kialin saw Jack's skepticism. "If you doubt me, ask Asta."

Jack's eyes widened. If Asta vouched for her, she was more than capable.

Kialin turned to the archivist. "Catheira—"

She interrupted firmly but respectfully. "Call me Kat."

Kialin nodded. "Yes, of course. Forgive me, Kat. You are an excellent academician, and I have no doubt you will oversee any archive I assign to you. But I have greater aspirations for you than you have for yourself. Within the next hundred years, I must relinquish oversight of all the archives. I will be two hundred seventy-five by then. I would like to settle into managing an archival masterpiece—one I plan to build in Winwiven. I need you prepared to take my place."

Kat's mouth fell open. "Me? Take your place, Master?"

Kialin smiled. "You are ready as an archivist, but not yet in dealing with the wilds of Eldriko. Traveling with Jack and the Union will prepare you."

Kat processed this, then nodded. "Kialin, I accept your challenge. May the gods grant me the wisdom to succeed."

Kialin looked at Jack. "Agreed, my friend?"

Jack nodded. "I trust your decision, Kialin."

Kat left to prepare for her departure, and Kialin launched into his plans for the grand archive he envisioned in Winwiven. Jack soon drifted into his own thoughts—expectations for the journey ahead, and the realization that he would be without the voice of wisdom he had come to rely upon.

He felt another weight as well. Throughout Asher, he had traveled with nine companions he trusted with his life. Leaving

Asher, he would have five trusted companions and a rookie archivist in lands unknown to him and only partly known to the others.

Jack had come to rely on Kialin's knowledge. Now the Union looked to him for leadership—and they gave everything they had to help him reach his goal.

God, how Jack had come to hate being responsible for the lives of those so willing to give them.

&

Waking in Sheol

—The Sheol Prophecies: Book One—

Beyond Sheol's Prophecies
—The Maker's Journey—

M. Alden Phillips

He began in retail sales before moving into a support role in medical research—where questions often mattered more than answers. That curiosity led him to study history, earning two degrees before devoting himself to counseling, where he spent his career listening to stories shaped by pain, hope, and longing.

After retiring, he turned to photographic art and fiction, crafting images and tales that echo the mythic and the deeply human. His visual work, steeped in mood and atmosphere, informs the emotional texture of his writing. Waking in Sheol opens a world where magic lingers in forgotten corners, and emotions speak louder than spells.

‡

Drawing from a lifetime of study and empathy, Phillips writes with quiet intensity—exploring love, fear, and redemption. His stories are both escape and return: a way to step beyond the known while honoring what's real. He writes with the quiet conviction that stories can heal.

‡

For correspondence: Alden@mAldenPhillips.com